Hunter Steele was born in Edinburgh in 1949. He was educated at Daniel Stewart's College, and at the Universities of Edinburgh, London and Cambridge. He is based in Scotland, and from 1986 to 1987 he was Creative Writing Fellow at the Universities of Glasgow and Strathclyde. He has contributed to *Mind*, the *British Journal of Aesthetics* and *Penthouse*, and his other published novels are *McCandy*, *The Wishdoctor's Song* and *Chasing the Gilded Shadow*. In progress is a monstrous saga of intrigue, copulation and death in 16th-century France.

HUNTER STEELE

Lord Hamlet's Castle

PALADIN
GRAFTON BOOKS

A Division of the Collins Publishing Group

LONDON GLASGOW
TORONTO SYDNEY AUCKLAND

Paladin
Grafton Books
A Division of the Collins Publishing Group
8 Grafton Street, London W1X 3LA

Published in Paladin Books 1988

First published in Great Britain by
André Deutsch Ltd 1987

ISBN 0-586-08694-3

Printed and bound in Great Britain by
Collins, Glasgow

Set in Ehrhardt

Again for Boo
And for Kristian and Martin
And Liam too

This book began some years ago, when I was teaching English. One of my students, a young actress named Monika, had been cast as Ophelia in a European film of *Hamlet*. Following my lecture on *Macbeth*, prior to a school excursion to Stratford, Monika asked if I could deepen her understanding of her Ophelia part. I did my best, but the project foundered financially, and the film has yet to be made.

Why persist with my interpretation?

Because the bones of the story, the subterranean struts and motivational frets, in all their lustful viciousness, their erectile sensuality, have never been completely bared before.

Here they are.

H.S., Provence, 1986.

CONTENTS

Be absolute for death: either death or life
Shall thereby be the sweeter. Reason thus with life:
If I do lose thee, I do lose a thing
That none but fools would keep; a breath thou art,
Servile to all the skyey influences
That dost this habitation where thou keep'st
Hourly afflict. Merely, thou art death's fool,
For him thou labour'st by thy flight to shun,
And yet runn'st toward him still.

The Duke, *Measure for Measure*

The old man, stricken in years, totters about or rests, in a corner, now only a shadow, a ghost, of his former self. What still remains there for death to destroy? One day a slumber is his last, and his dreams are ——. They are the dreams that Hamlet asks about in the famous monologue. I believe that we dream them just now.

Arthur Schopenhauer

Out, out, brief candle!
Life's but a walking shadow, a poor player,
That struts and frets his hour upon the stage,
And then is heard no more. It is a tale
Told by an idiot, full of sound and fury,
Signifying nothing.

Macbeth

Angie, ain't it good to be alive?

Mick Jagger

1
CLIFF-HANGERS

It is Denmark in the xteenth century. The Castle of Elsinore is situated above the town of Aarhus, on the east coast of Jutland, Denmark's mainland. It nestles behind a chalk cliff, which protects it from cannon-fire from the sea.

(Some locate the Castle on the island of Zealand, to the east. They insist that since the *town* of Elsinore is on Zealand the *Castle* must be there too. Like arguing that because someone is in Denmark Street he must be in Denmark. In any case, the castle at Elsinore is called the Castle of Kronborg.)

September. Old Hamlet has been dead for three weeks. Three weeks of suspicion and fear. Dire omens everywhere. The harvest failed. Litters of piglets stillborn. Uncles suddenly dead, without remembering favourite nephews in their wills.

And Young Hamlet has been summoned from Wittenberg, to attend his father's funeral.

Confusion here is caused by the three different funeral services. The first took place the day after Old Hamlet's death. Hamlet was thus not present. In the meantime Old Hamlet's body has been shipped to Roskilde on the island of Zealand. The cathedral at Roskilde is the traditional burial place of Danish monarchs. The two remaining services take place simultaneously – one at Roskilde, the other back at the Castle. Because of rumoured Danger from the north the court has remained at Aarhus. Thus, a rather peculiar situation prevents Hamlet from paying last respects to his father 'in person'.

Not that much love was lost between them. Hamlet's grief is more dutiful than deep. At the same time, the Prince despises Claudius, his uncle, Old Hamlet's half-brother. Hamlet knows that Claudius has been manoeuvring both for the throne (Hamlet's birthright) and for Gertrude (Hamlet's mother). Hamlet's birthday is December 24th. This year is his thirtieth. According to a law introduced by Hamlet I (Hamlet's great-grandfather) no heir-apparent may succeed until his thirtieth birthday. Hamlet knows this. And he knows Claudius knows it. So?

The cynical Prince suspects foul play from the outset.

The action begins on the cliff above the Castle. It is not mountainous, but steep, stark, and forbidding. Crawling with cracks and honeycombed with endless interconnecting caves.

Francisco, a soldier, is coming to the end of his guard duty. It is night, and extremely cold. Colder far than the moderate climate of Denmark today.

Bernardo, an officer in the Castle security force, comes to relieve Francisco.

'Who's there?' he shouts. He can see a silhouetted figure, but a fog has blown in from the sea and he wants to be sure the figure is Francisco. Also to give Francisco ample warning. Morale is low in the ranks, paranoia rife, and Bernardo has no wish to exit prematurely on a reflex lunge of Francisco's sword.

'*You* answer *me*,' Francisco shouts back. 'Stand and show yourself.'

'Long live the King,' cries Bernardo, moving closer through the swirling mist.

'Bernardo?'

'The same.' Bernardo claps Francisco affectionately on the shoulder.

A gust of wind blows fragments of fog in a crazy dance.

Some flustered nocturnal bird of prey shrieks eerily.

Francisco sighs with inward relief.

'You are very prompt,' he observes.

Bernardo qualifies:

'It's after twelve. Off you go to bed, Francisco.'

'I won't say no. It is bitter cold, and I am sick at heart.' Since Old Hamlet's death a number of Francisco's fellow soldiers have disappeared without trace in mysterious circumstances. He is anxious.

'Quiet watch?' asks Bernardo.

'Not a mouse has stirred.'

'Well, goodnight.' Then Bernardo remembers something important:

'If you meet Horatio and Marcellus,' he requests, 'bid them haste.' Bernardo is made of sterner stuff than Francisco, but he has a special reason for not wanting to be left alone.

'I think I hear them,' Francisco exclaims. 'WHO GOES?'

After a clatter of confident boots and a jangle of swords Horatio and Marcellus emerge from the miasmic night. Horatio answers Francisco's challenge:

'FRIENDS!'

'And liegemen to the Dane,' adds Marcellus, for this is the official password.

'Well,' coughs Francisco, recognizing Horatio and Marcellus, 'goodnight, all.'

'Farewell, honest soldier,' cries Marcellus. 'But who has relieved you?'

'Bernardo,' answers Francisco, departing. 'Goodnight.'

'Hello there! Bernardo!' shouts Marcellus, as Francisco disappears into the thicker puddles of mist that lap around the erectile projections of the Castle's turrets.

But Bernardo is already patrolling the clifftop, and is only dimly visible.

'What?' he calls back harshly. 'Is Horatio there?'

'A piece of him,' shouts Horatio, attempting levity.

Horatio is Hamlet's friend and fellow philosophy student at Wittenberg. Though intelligent in an orderly, brown-eyed, scholarly way, he is basically a cheerful, generous, but simple-minded soul.

Little sense of humour.

Tonight, however, Horatio feels it his duty to reassure Marcellus and Bernardo. They have dragged him out to witness the appalling Apparition which, they claim, was hovering round the clifftop on the previous two nights.

'Welcome, Horatio. Welcome, Marcellus.' Earnest relief warms Bernardo's voice.

'What!' exclaims Horatio. 'Has this thing appeared again tonight?' He hangs a gentle sneer on 'thing'.

'I have seen nothing,' mutters Bernardo grimly. A jagged scar across his furrowed military brow pulses angrily.

Marcellus tries to save the situation:

'Horatio says it's all our fantasy,' he laments. 'He refuses to believe in this dreadful sight, which we have now seen twice. But I have persuaded him to share our watch tonight. So, if the Apparition walks again, he can confirm what we have seen. And speak to it!'

'Tush!' scoffs Horatio. 'It won't appear.'

'Well,' responds Bernardo, 'sit down awhile, and let us convince you.'

'As you will.' Horatio sits resignedly on a mist-wet boulder.

'Last night,' begins Bernardo, voice trembling, 'when that star shone where it is burning *even now*,' he points dramatically up into the fog, 'Marcellus and myself, just as the bell struck one . . .'

But Marcellus sees the Apparition loom again, further along the cliff.

'Peace!' Marcellus hisses. 'Be silent! Look, where it comes again.'

'Just like the King that's dead,' warbles Bernardo.

'You are a scholar; speak to it, Horatio,' begs Marcellus, supposing that all scholars speak Latin and hence can exercise devils.

'Does it not *look* like the King?' asks Bernardo. Actually the resemblance between the shadowy Apparition and deceased Old Hamlet is hardly proven, but Bernardo is now supremely suggestible. Butter would melt instantly on his imagination.

'Very like him,' admits Horatio, his humour and scepticism curdled. 'It harrows me with wonder.'

'It wishes to be spoken to,' interprets Bernardo, as the Apparition glides closer, gesturing. It seems clad in heavy armour, gleaming dully in the fog. The visor is up but the face beneath is a black bearded blur. Certainly the figure is *like* Old Hamlet, but perhaps a shade taller? Heavier? Glowing with a dim, yellow, other-worldly luminosity? As it moves with a slow, light-yet-heavy, menacing step.

'Question it, Horatio,' implores Marcellus.

Horatio takes a brave step towards the hovering spectre. Scraps of shredded mist beetle his determined eyebrows, like cobwebs washed from ancient rafters.

'What *are* you?' he challenges. 'By heaven, I charge you, *speak*!'

The Apparition rotates. Slinks metallically away, back into its haven of ghoulish grey gloom.

'It is offended,' suggests Marcellus.

'See!' concurs Bernardo. 'It stalks away.'

'Stay!' Horatio rages. 'Speak, speak! I charge you, *speak*!'

The iron-clad Apparition disappears without a murmur.

So chilling was its presence, however, that Horatio and company make no move to pursue it.

'It is gone,' Marcellus marvels fearfully, 'and will not answer.'

'Well now, Horatio!' goads Bernardo. 'You tremble and look pale. Is it not more than fantasy: this thing?'

'Before my God,' testifies Horatio, 'never could I have believed it, without the testimony of my eyes.'

'Is it not like the *King*?' insists Marcellus.

'As you to yourself,' the scholar concedes. 'Such was the armour that slew Old Fortinbras. Such his warlike frown when once he felled the Poles upon the ice. It is most strange.'

So are Horatio's comments, since he could hardly have been present at those belligerent encounters. Nevertheless, Marcellus reinforces Horatio's change of mind:

'Thus twice before we saw this thing. Exactly at this hour.'

Horatio shivers. Stares myopically into the scudding wet fog.

'I know not what to think,' he admits. 'But I'm sure it foretells evil.'

Three hours pass.

The fog recedes. The atmosphere grows less deathly chill and ominous. Marcellus, Bernardo and Horatio, squat in a manly huddle, discuss the state of the nation.

'Why', asks Marcellus, 'so strict a watch throughout our land? The people made to labour day and night to service war? Such heavy production of brass cannon? Unprecedented importation of foreign implements of war? So many young lads conscripted into shipwrights? Who can enlighten me?'

'Perhaps I can,' volunteers Horatio. 'Our last King, whose image has appeared this night, once slew Old Fortinbras of Norway. By his death, Fortinbras, whose jealousy provoked the combat, forfeited to Hamlet great estates.

'Now, since Old Hamlet's death, Young Fortinbras has been busy in Norway, sweeping together armies of reckless undisciplined outlaws. His purpose, as our noble Council sees it, is to recover by coercion the lands his father lost. And this, I take it, is the motive behind our preparations, the secret watch we are set to keep, the bustle, unease and distrust, that riddle our nation.'

Bernardo assents:

'And well it agrees that the portentous figure we saw this night appears so like the King that caused these wars.'

Another hour swirls by.

The sea fog pours in again, thicker than ever, like a recurrent cancer neurosis. Somewhere above it an electric storm brews. Thunder blasts and shakes the cliff to the roots of its deepest burrows. A bolt of lightning darts through the syrupy obscurity and strikes Horatio's sword, which is propped against a nearby rock. A dribble of black bubbling moltenness is all that remains of the weapon. The manly huddle is badly shaken. Horatio resolves to restore courage and calm.

'This is but a speck to trouble the mind's eye,' he says shakily, convincing himself, if not Marcellus and Bernardo. He draws breath to continue, but loses it in a strangled gasp as he sees the Apparition once more, lurking on the fringe of visibility.

'Behold!' he croaks. 'There! It comes again.'

The Apparition *is* approaching, metallically wooden, terrifying yet never clearly discernible.

'Stay, illusion,' Horatio orders. 'If you have a voice, or can make any sound, speak to me. If you have foreknowledge of your country's fate, I beg you, SPEAK!'

But he makes no physical move towards the fearful object.

Now crows an eldritch cock. The strange sound is both near and distant. An aural illusion of the fog? In any case, as the curious cock crows, the Apparition rotates once more and stages a lumbering retreat.

'Stop it, Marcellus,' cries Horatio, as the figure fades from their straining view.

'Shall I strike it?' inquires Marcellus, moving forward reluctantly.

16

'If it will not stand,' Horatio advises.

But the Apparition vanishes altogether.

Horatio and Bernardo rush after it.

'It is here,' calls Bernardo, seeming in the fog.

'It is *here*,' yells Horatio, ten paces distant, hallucinating phantoms.

'It is gone,' Marcellus corrects them. 'We do wrong to insult its majesty with our show of violence. For it is, like the air, invulnerable.'

'It was about to speak when the cock crowed,' says Bernardo, though there was no good evidence of this.

'And then it started like a Guilty Thing, upon a Fearful Summons,' Horatio continues. Then launches into a ramble which proves that his philosophical studies have been largely a waste of time. As he discourses, the fog slowly dissipates.

The first icy tinges of dawn appear on the horizon.

'Yes,' he concludes, 'the cock is trumpet to the morning. Whose lofty shrill awakes the god of day. And does not his warning send the wandering spirit, whether it move in sea or fire, earth or air, scurrying to its daylight confinement? As we have seen tonight?' Horatio pauses.

Marcellus parades his own superstition:

'Some say,' he ventures, 'that on Christmas Eve the cock sings all night long. And then no spirit dares abroad. No witch has power to charm; the nights are wholesome; so hallowed is that time.'

'So I have heard,' responds Horatio. He slaps his mitted hands together, to revive his flagging circulation.

The sunlight increases its frosty strength, gobbling up nocturnal fantasies and fears.

'But look!' Horatio exclaims. 'See how the morning, in a cloak of russet gold, walks over the dew of yon eastern hill. Like a friendly messenger, and our relief.'

In fact the highest hill in Denmark, Himmelbjerg (the Sky Mountain) is a mere 530 feet above sea level. Moreover, it is situated to the northwest of Aarhus. Horatio is probably staring across the bay to Grenna, where the only high hills are created by his own short sight. Still, his russet-gold exaggeration is a fair excuse to quit the present scene:

'Let us break our watch,' he proposes, 'and impart to Young Hamlet what we have seen tonight. I feel this spirit, dumb to us, will speak to him. Do you agree?'

Yes.

Then they clank away towards the Castle. Yawning, shivering, stretching. Cold, damp, sodden with stiffening aches, Bernardo feels a nagging rheumatic throb in his right foot, which once was crushed in battle by a charging enemy warhorse.

And a sudden-soaring bird of prey circles lazily above the crenellated nipples of the Castle's phallic turrets, the shallow schizoid sunlight glinting greenly in its greedy gimlet eyes.

2
ROUND ONE

In the Great Council Chamber in the Castle. Those present include:

Claudius, newly crowned King of Denmark, and uncle to Hamlet;

Gertrude, Queen of Denmark, mother to Hamlet, and newly wife to Claudius;

The State Councillors of Denmark, grey and witless;

Polonius, Chief Secretary of State, director of the secret police, and second-most powerful man in the land;

Laertes, son to Polonius, and a pain;

Voltimand and Cornelius, Denmark's tandem ambassadors to Norway;

Various attendants, plumy courtiers, sycophants, lackeys;

And the rangy chameleon hypostar, Hamlet himself.

Late afternoon. Horatio, Marcellus and Bernardo have been sleeping, but the rest of the court has had a busy day. Early in the morning there was a meeting of the dread Inner Council, in the Secret Chamber, presided over by Claudius and Polonius.

At this meeting, Claudius persuaded the Council to allow him to marry Gertrude, his dead brother's wife, and to crown him King of Denmark. His principal argument? That the nation needs a strong ruler, skilled in politics and experienced in war, to consolidate national unity against the current threat from Norway:

Young Fortinbras.

Claudius was assisted by Voltimand and Cornelius, whose testimony swayed the reluctant Council. Having just returned from Norway, Voltimand and Cornelius were ideally placed to recount the aggressive movements of Young Fortinbras.

In fact, the story told by Voltimand and Cornelius was scripted by Claudius. But the Council did not know this.

Immediately after the secret meeting of the Inner Council, the entire court turned out to attend a service in memory of Old Hamlet. This was held at noon, while Old Hamlet's actual remains were laid to rest in the Mausoleum of Roskilde Cathedral, many miles across the icy water to the east. Then the court adjourned to dress more festively for the royal wedding and coronation. These ceremonies took place jointly, beginning at three o'clock in Aarhus Cathedral.

Both were attended by Hamlet, who refused to change the sombre clothes he had worn to the funeral service. The colourful splendour of the occasion was thus qualified by the dark blemish and constant scowl of his brooding presence.

Like a little black spot on a big pink lung.

Following the cathedral ceremonies, Claudius and Gertrude rode back to the Castle in their gold-bossed marriage carriage, snaking triumphally through the fresh snow that had fallen during their wedding service. As Hamlet trotted blackly behind them on his giant snorting Woden, a flurry of ravens flew by, blinding the stallion and causing him to buck, rear, and disrupt the stately pomp of the march.

Once back at the Castle, the court disbanded for a further hour before reconvening, now, in the Great Council Chamber.

The assembly stands.

Claudius and Gertrude make their first royal entry together.

The assembly sits.

Hamlet has remained seated. Like a rebellious black vulture. The court has been marshalled, on benches, in an orderly cluster round the raised regal thrones. But Hamlet squats on the floor, to one side.

He is whittling with a long-bladed dagger at a chunk of wood from a cypress tree. This must be significant, since cypress trees do not grow in Denmark. The Prince gives off vibrations like a wounded wolf at a fancy-dress ball. His behaviour consterns the court marshals, but none dare interfere with him. Now and then he whets his dagger on the soft belly of the snakeskin belt lying on the tiled floor beside him.

Polonius calls for silence:

Claudius is about to speak.

This is Claudius' first address, as King, to the full Great Council. He knows his prowess as orator, but still feels on probation. Sensing an opportunity to consolidate his power over Hamlet, Claudius descends slowly from his throne. Strides majestically in front of the assembly. Like a barrister before a jury.

Loose flowing robes emphasize the width of Claudius' meaty shoulders and minimize the bilious bulge of his belly. His colours are brilliant golds and greens, and startling crimsons. His robes and crown are extravagantly studded and flecked with shimmering jewels.

Gertrude, sitting demurely behind him, is similarly bedecked, her gorgeous gown cut low round the ripe pinkness of her magnificent chest.

Claudius clears his throat.

'The death of Hamlet, our dear brother,' he rumbles, 'is still green. Our heart in grief, our Kingdom contracts in one long brow of woe.' Neatly he slips into the Royal *Our*. His voice appears deep and easy. The voice of a born leader, so the gullible think. But not Hamlet, who knows Claudius has several drinks inside him.

'Yet,' the new King continues, 'nature must be tempered by discretion. We must be candid; think of our own interests. For these reasons, we have, with as it were, a defeated joy, taken to wife our former sister, now our Queen. This your wisdoms have approved. For which, our thanks.' He waves expansive largesse around the hall.

An appreciative buzz responds.

But Claudius has to raise his voice, above the subversive scrapes of Hamlet's carving. He takes a deep breath, affecting avuncular unconcern. As King, he can't afford an open confrontation with the Prince. Not yet.

'Now', he booms, 'to Young Fortinbras. He pesters us with messages. Demands the surrender of lands lost by his father, in full legality, to our most valiant brother. Does he suppose us weak?

Think our state disjointed, following our brother's death? In any case, we have written to Norway, uncle of Young Fortinbras.' Claudius withdraws from his voluminous robes an imposing scroll.

'The old man,' he declaims, 'impotent and bed-ridden, is scarcely aware of his nephew's purpose. We advise him of it, and demand that it be thwarted. And we hereby dispatch you, good Cornelius, and you, Voltimand, to bear this greeting to Norway.'

Voltimand and Cornelius bow obsequiously. Their practised ambassadorial eyes blink inscrutably, like dirty pebbles in the heads of snowmen.

'In that and all things we will show our duty,' Cornelius replies.

'We doubt it not,' breezes Claudius. 'Heartily farewell.' He gestures their dismissal.

The ambassadors exit with a purposeful step.

Claudius gazes after them for a pregnant moment.

The courtiers sheepishly follow his gaze.

Hamlet continues whittling.

Claudius thinks of the very different orders he gave Voltimand and Cornelius in private. Wonders if he can trust them. Banishing such diplomatic reflections, he projects a grand smile:

'And now, Laertes,' he beams, 'you had some request? But what could you ask that we would not give? Denmark is more indebted to your father than is the hungry mouth to the hand. So speak, Laertes. What is your request?' All in oily unclish tones. Oozing benevolence. Claudius, ostensibly speaking to Laertes, is cementing his relationship with Polonius.

Polonius has been instrumental in securing the crown for Claudius. Now, Claudius is seen to be grateful, in a charade of mutual admiration.

Hamlet sneers to the eyes of the carving he gouges.

Laertes leaps to his feet with unnecessary vigour. Steps forward. Bows tersely.

'My lord,' he brays, 'though I came willingly to Denmark, to show my duty in your coronation, I now beg leave to return to France. It is there, I confess, that all my wishes bend.' He smiles submissively with his thick-lipped mouth. His coarse-textured yellow complexion crinkles obediently. But no light shines in his ego-rigid eyes.

He doesn't explain *why* he yearns to return to France, for his reasons would not bear scrutiny. Claudius and Polonius know this, so they don't press him. Laertes is a wastrel and a womanizer, a bully and a boor. So it is convenient that he should dissipate himself in decadent France, far from Denmark's public eye. Also, Laertes' songs are less unpopular in France. Consequently, he feels, France is more deserving of his presence.

'Your father's consent?' inquires Claudius rhetorically. 'What does Polonius say?' Claudius wheels like a painted seagull and leers false affection at Polonius, who rises, creaking, from his front-row seat.

He is old and gnarled, a skinny man with a little good-living pot-belly tucked away. Firelight flickers reflections on his ancient pate. Untold unwashedness lurks suspected beneath his wispy whiskers.

'My lord,' he sighs with a semblance of paternal resignation, 'his laboursome petition has wrung my unwilling consent.'

'Then, Laertes,' Claudius pronounces, 'your time is your own. Spend it where you please.' He gestures.

Polonius and Laertes retire to their seats.

Claudius now winds up to tackle the trickiest item on his agenda: Hamlet.

One problem is that Claudius is only nine years older than Hamlet. This is due to his being Old Hamlet's half-brother, born of a younger mother. Old Hamlet was over sixty when he died, but Claudius is only thirty-eight. Consequently, despite his receding hairline and spreading midriff, he is uneasy about how to harden the authority of his new position.

'And now, my cousin Hamlet, and my son . . .' Claudius tries to exude confident majesty. He succeeds in fooling everyone except Hamlet, who cuts him short by mimicking darkly to his maturing figurine:

'A little more than kin, and less than kind!' Here is a pun on 'kined'. Does it imply that Claudius was mothered by a cow?

Claudius isn't sure, and this rattles him.

'Why such cloudy eyes?' he asks limply, cold sweat welling in the matted rugs of his armpits.

'Not so, my lord,' snaps Hamlet. Throwing back his tall, strong frame, he pretends to shade his eyes. 'They are too much in the *sun*,' he puns, complaining of a surfeit of *fathers*.

Claudius' toiling face is saved by Gertrude, who steps in with a motherly homily.

She descends gracefully from her throne.

All eyes except Hamlet's fasten eagerly upon her.

Everyone watches Gertrude when she moves, and often when she doesn't, and she knows it. She is an amazing figure of a woman, not least because of her age. She is forty-three, only fourteen years older than Hamlet. Such small age gaps between mothers and first children were common in olden Scandinavia, especially among royalty. The Regent Queen Margaret, Valdemar's daughter, was married to King Haakon of Norway, in 1363, at the age of barely ten. Gertrude was married to Old Hamlet when she was thirteen, to consolidate an alliance with Sweden, her homeland, and she had Hamlet the following year.

Immature motherhood seems only to have improved her physical charms. Her sophisticated statuesque beauty is particularly provocative just because it soon must wither. Here lies Gertrude's overwhelming attraction for Claudius. To him she is like a vintage wine that must be breached before deterioration sets in. Moreover, she is his brother's vintage wine, therefore forbidden liquor, and doubly delicious.

For as long as he can remember, Claudius had been bowing to the power of his hated and, in latter years, despised elder brother. And secretly burning for his brother's beauteous Queen. This condition was aggravated for Claudius by memories of the time when he and Gertrude (the new child-queen) used to play together during the day, then Claudius would be doomed to bed and Gertrude whisked away to hostess a martial banquet before being rogered through the night by leonine Old Hamlet.

Now? Old Hamlet is dead, and Gertrude belongs to Claudius.

'Come, Hamlet,' she urges, in a muted husky voice. 'Put away your mourning clothes. Shed this black and gloomy mood.' As she speaks, Gertrude glides sedately towards her fractious son, who is squatting near one of the huge log fires which warm the great hall.

The eyes of the court roll as the curvaceous Queen moves, like the eyes of a slavering hound following a forbidden rump steak to the frying pan.

Lurid shadows dance from the log-fire flames.

24

'Regard King Claudius as a *friend*,' Gertrude cajoles, smiling down at her glowering son. 'Let not your gaze downcast for ever,' she implores, her bosom maternal with emotion. 'You will not find your noble father in the dust. It is common knowledge that all must die, passing through nature to eternity.'

'Yes, madam,' nods Hamlet to his sculpting, formally polite before the court. 'It *is* common.'

The sarcasm is lost on his mother.

'You accept this,' she ponders, 'and yet it seems heavily upon you. Why so?'

Hamlet leaps lithely to his feet. He is angry now, but not so angry as he pretends. His carving he hurls into the adjacent blazing fire. It crudely depicts a copulating couple. Two crowns are fleetingly discernible on the lewdly naked figures, before the flames distort, dissolve and consume them.

'*Seems*, madam?' snarls Hamlet at Gertrude, who recoils in hurt dismay. 'I know not "seems". *My* mourning clothes are not alone, good mother.'

A raking accusation. 'Unfelt heavy sighs? Rivers of tears from scarlet eyes? These things well might *seem*, and be portrayed by actors on the stage. But I, madam, have within me the *reality* of mourning woe.'

This condemns Gertrude. Suggests the grief she expressed at Old Hamlet's passing was a sham. Hamlet is thus somewhat unfair to Gertrude, who still felt *some* affection for the old King when he died. But she is sufficiently sensitive, and sensible, to abandon her exchange with Hamlet and retire in a wounded fluster to the lofty refuge of her throne.

Now although it is true that Hamlet disapproves of the *rapidity* of Gertrude's remarriage, what really riles him is that Gertrude married *Claudius*, whom he detests: as the incarnation of those qualities he does his best to suppress in himself:

Lust, jealousy, malice, greed for power, and . . .

What particularly disgusted Hamlet today was Claudius' bulging eagerness to get Gertrude into bed during the hour between the return from the cathedral and the present Great Council meeting. Hamlet also knows that Gertrude responded passionately to Claudius' importunate bulging, after only a moment's reserve.

Hence his current verbal attack on her.

However, Hamlet is the only third person who knows this carnal interlude took place, so the point of his onslaught is lost on the court. It is also largely wasted on Claudius and Gertrude, since neither knows that Hamlet knows of their fornical pantings.

So the court sympathies vacillate away from the gloomy Prince, in favour of his mortified mother.

Hamlet, sensing the change of corporate mood, retires to his patch in a huddle of eloquent silence.

Claudius drives home the advantage which Gertrude's discomfiture has won him, with a paternalistic sermon. This is spoken at Hamlet, but Claudius is playing to the court. He is too shrewd to hope that Hamlet will be taken in.

As Claudius drones, the courtiers nod and smile approvingly.

Polonius, on the foremost bench, maintains a beam of politic benevolence. Further back, his daughter, Ophelia, looks radiant but rather bored. She wants Hamlet to stay in Denmark, but she is also confident that he won't be allowed to leave. Glinting calculation therefore slumbers in her Baltic-blue eyes.

In the shadowy depths of the hall, a muted flicker illumines Osric's baby-plump cheeks. A compound of rich landed playboy and double-secret agent, Osric is just back from Norway. His public purpose was to inspect the vast forest estates he owns in that country. But his deep-structure mission was to execute various clandestine transactions for Claudius.

Almost in darkness, behind all the courtiers, loom the marble-esque protective phantoms of the new Castle guard:

Claudius' personal Switzers.

Such men, trained Swiss mercenaries, are an insurance policy against native Danish treachery. Among these stalwart soldiers, but not *of* them, stands the astounding brawny hulk of Claudio, Gertrude's personal bodyguard, who came with her from Sweden so many years ago.

Finally, in a shrouded doorway at the back, Horatio, Marcellus and Bernardo look on, pale, gaunt and grave.

'It is commendable, Hamlet,' raps Claudius, 'to mourn your father so. But your father lost a father! And that father lost his! Each survivor is obliged, by his filial duty, to mourn for some reasonable time. But to persevere in obsequious sorrow is impious. Unmanly grief . . .'

Like a great majestic snake with a resonant voice, Claudius mesmerizes an audience composed mostly of sycophantic rabbits.

'We pray you,' he sermonizes, 'rid yourself of this useless sorrow. And think of *us* as Father. For, let the world take note, *you* are our heir. And we do love you, as a father loves his son.'

This is convincing stuff, at least to the courtiers:

If Gertrude bore Old Hamlet no children after Hamlet, is she likely to bear Claudius a new heir now, at the age of forty-three?

Yet Claudius has lurid alternative thoughts on the succession. Despite his present lust for Gertrude, he knows her days of glamour are numbered. And the prospect of a fresh young buxom queen, with a thriving brood of bawling heirs, is no stranger to his seedy deliberations.

'As for your desire to return to school in Wittenberg,' he advises Hamlet, 'it is much against our wishes. And we beseech you remain here: principal courtier of our great court.'

The philistine referring to Hamlet's philosophical researches as 'school' is a jibe which Claudius is right in thinking only Hamlet will notice. What Claudius really wants, at this stage, is to monitor Hamlet's activities. Already he has had nightmares about vast armies forming at Wittenberg, under Hamlet's generalship. The Prince has done his national service, both in the privateering Danish navy and in the more conventional army. Though he detests the regimentation of miltary life, he is a capable soldier and leader when need be.

Gertrude shares Claudius' desire that Hamlet should stay in Denmark, but her motives are very different. She dotes on him, her only child, and sets great store by his opinions. At such difficult times as these, she depends on him for comfort and advice.

'Let not your mother pray in vain, Hamlet,' she pleads, rising impulsively from her throne. 'I beg you, stay with us. Do not go to Wittenberg.' She clasps her hands below her chin, squeezing her mammoth breasts together and deepening her vertiginous cleavage.

'I shall obey you as best I can, madam,' replies Hamlet in a faraway voice. He shakes his shoulder-length brown hair irritably, and gazes disdainfully into the fire.

The court heaves a sigh of relief that no more trouble will be immediately forthcoming from the Prince.

Claudius is delighted with the outcome of this encounter. When not conspiring, he is a notorious toper and glutton. Already his thoughts are turning like pigs on spits to the coming celebration feast. Also, he can hardly wait to get Gertrude back into bed. Beneath his robes his swinish puce pizzle distends in anticipation. Having got what he wants, he brings the meeting to an abrupt triumphant close.

'That is a loving fair reply, Hamlet,' he concedes magnanimously. 'Be as ourself in Denmark. Do whatever we would do. Madam, come.' He extends his Kingly arm for Gertrude to take. 'Hamlet's agreement has set my heart smiling. Tonight each health that Denmark drinks shall be echoed to the heavens by the great cannon on the battlements. Come away.'

Claudius here rubs clever salt in Hamlet's wounds, knowing how the Prince dislikes ritual revelry. He and Gertrude sweep through the great arched doorway at the east end of the chamber, initiating a general exit.

Bodies rise and stretch.

Buzzing gossip breaks and swells.

Only Hamlet sits motionless, staring morosely into flames of crackling amber.

3
FIRST ENTRY

The Prince maintains his posture for several minutes.

During this time his restless thoughts retrace happier days. He recalls the gay and reckless company of the Copenhagen players. Recollects his carefree buccaneering days on the pirate ships of the Danish navy, which sailed from Lemvig, on the west coast, to prey like greedy terriers on treasure-laden galleons from New Spain.

Still reminiscing, Hamlet rises. Buckles his belt and replaces his dagger. As if in a trance he shuffles across to a different fireplace – behind the elevated thrones so recently vacated by Claudius and Gertrude.

Then a transformation.

Hamlet glances furtively about him. Residual snoopers? No. Quick as a striking cobra he darts into the fireplace. Sidles sweating round the back of the enormous hearth, and disappears.

The body of the Castle was built in the fourteenth century, at the direction of Valdemar, father of the child-queen Margaret. However, extensive alterations and fortifications were commissioned by Hamlet I, Hamlet's great-grandfather. This wily old monarch was a skin-deep Platonist, subscribing to the ideal of the Philosopher-King, at least when it suited him. He it was who initiated the traditions governing the Danish succession. The law forbidding any heir to be crowned before age thirty is just one example. Likewise the tradition that future kings should study philosophy at Wittenberg, after completing their first degrees at Copenhagen. Both these fads followed the old King's shallow admiration for Plato, a fellow fascist.

The main motive behind the modifications made by Hamlet I was his desire to improve the Castle's protection against cannon-fire from the sea. At that time, the power and effectiveness of naval artillery were improving daily. To combat this, Hamlet I had the sea-facing walls strengthened by several layers of reinforced brick and the sea-facing roofs covered by a heavy thickness of (hopefully) cannonball-proof copper. These changes were effected by the famous Dutch architects, Hans and Lourens Steenwinckel, assisted by an imported shipload of Dutch artisans. And all their work was supervised by Hamlet I in person.

At the same time, craving Platonic security and permanence, the old King completely transformed the structure of the inner Castle, creating an intricate labyrinth of secret passages and stairways enabling him to move in total stealth all round the building. The entrances to these clandestine pathways were concealed behind enormous sandstone fireplaces. While the Castle was remodelled, strict security was enforced and the court banished to Copenhagen. When the work was complete, the only people who knew about the peeping-Tom warren were the Dutch craftsmen who built it and Hamlet I himself. Since the ship transporting the Dutch workers back to the Netherlands was 'lost at sea', with no survivors, the King was left in sole possession of his sprawling secret maze.

Endless tabs were thereby daily and nocturnally kept on errant courtiers, political insurgents, unclad ladies-in-waiting, and numerous others. Evidence of the success of this device? That Hamlet I was the first Danish king to make the succession hereditary for more than one generation. Helped by the tradition, which he also began, whereby each heir received the secrets of the Castle's architecture only in his thirtieth year. This esoteric rite was continued by Hamlet II, and by his son, Hamlet III (this Hamlet's father).

The latter, Old Hamlet, imparted the royal snooping secrets to Young Hamlet two months before his death. At this sombre session Old Hamlet revealed to Hamlet many things of solemn moment. That he feared for his health. That his days on earth were probably numbered. That Hamlet must reconcile his love of leisure and meditation with the busy life a monarch inevitably leads. That he desired Hamlet to bear in mind the pending need for a new queen and heir.

Hamlet received these paternal platitudes with polite respect.

His father he considered cold and humourless as the smile that never reached his eyes. Also, for years Hamlet had been dreading life enmeshed in politics, intrigue and conspiracy. That was the last intimate exchange between Hamlet and his father, and since the old man died the son has had a bad filial-failure conscience.

But why is the Prince so angry *now*?

Because of Claudius' victory in Round One. Also the fastness of his mother's new carnal bond. Aggravated by recognition, deep down, that his resentment is partly selfish and irrational. Selfish? Premised on his loathing of Claudius. Irrational? Since he really would like his mother to be *happy*.

Claudius is Gertrude's final fling, despite her still-blooming attractions. If she hadn't married Claudius, he would not be King, and the throne would have passed to Hamlet on his thirtieth birthday. Gertrude then could never remarry. She would be terminally cloistered as Dowager Queen. Her relationship to the court would be completely different. She would lose all her treasured power, and pass beyond the sexual pale.

Gertrude has always enjoyed being serviced by a man with the power of death over other men. Natural perversity? But also a hangover from her teenage nights of being pounded moaning into the mattress by Old Hamlet in his humourless meaty prime. She loved to feel as putty in the calloused battle-scarred hands of a grizzly King. Yet she also relished her authority over notables, especially women, twice her age. This power ambivalence has never left her.

Hamlet perceives these traits in his mother, and so is doubly furious with himself. He resents Gertrude's recent behaviour because her present interests conflict with his own. As he begins his furtive journey back to his bedchamber he detours to see if Claudius and Gertrude are enloined yet again. The total stealth of his mission is facilitated by a system of chinks in the brickwork, which allows just enough light into the extramural maze, from the adjacent chambers and corridors, to permit constant monitoring of all activity within the inner Castle.

The Prince's prowl takes him up a narrow winding stairway and round three sides of a square. This esoteric network, since his last return from Wittenberg, has furnished him with almost magical powers of unobserved observation, which multiplies loss of whatever confidence in his motive purity. Of late he has even abused his spyhole system to scrutinize Ophelia as she undresses and takes her bath.

At present, Hamlet steps over a decomposing rat as he nears the primal couch. He puts his eye to a vantage chink and espies Claudius and Gertrude, stark missionary naked.

Gertrude has always been highly sexed, and Old Hamlet had not been much help to her, in this area, for some years. Claudius, though not her ideal bedfellow, can at least get it up. And for the moment, he is uncompromisingly keen to put it in.

And move it about.

Hamlet's peeping nose wrinkles as his mother's moans and staccato gasps merge into a high-pitched wail. Underscored by a low animal grunting, like a farting bassoon, from Claudius.

Hamlet eyes with revulsion the sag in Claudius' plunging buttocks, and the dangle-berried cleft of colourless hair between them. Grotesque shadows are cast by roaring fires on either side of the fleshy cavortings. On the floor, beside the luxurious four-poster bed, Hamlet sees the jewelled silver goblet out of which Claudius loves to drink hot spiced fortified wine. The goblet has been knocked over in the heat of lust. Red liquor like maidenhead blood stains the floor.

Suddenly the Kingly coitus interrupts.

A bellow of rage and pain.

Claudius jack-knifes into a half-sit, clutching his cramped right thigh. As he twists, his waggling organ ejaculates. Sperm spurt bubbles over his pubic hair, the bed's finely tapestried golden coverlet, and Gertrude's dimpled knee.

Hamlet eyeballs aghast the red inflamed frustrated lips of the very organ that coughed him into the world thirty years ago. His impulse is anguish, but swordsman reflexes abort his cry. Nevertheless, around his short pointed beard, his complexion turns the pallor of shock as he leaves the royal couple to their marital mopping.

Now? He *should* return to his chamber, to prepare for coming confrontations with Claudius. But . . . what he really *wants* is to follow his private catwalk round to Polonius' house and spy on

Ophelia. It will, in any case, advantage him to find out what Polonius is up to. Won't it?

And then there are Ophelia's breasts.

Polonius is sitting at his desk of cluttered scrolls. One of his umpteen agents stands beside him, intent. Polonius hisses sibilant instructions in his greasy ear. Hamlet screws up his eyes. Bends his ear to the brickwork. Can't quite make out what is being said. This is part of his tragedy. He can often *see* something cooking, without being able to *hear* exactly what. Since Hamlet I, so many aspiring conspirators have met sticky ends that soiled consciences now almost literally believe that walls have ears. Consequently, illicit transactions hatch safer in ear-kissing whispers.

Hamlet abandons Polonius.

He paces on towards Ophelia's chamber. Pauses for a glance at Laertes. The latter is packing for Paris. Hamlet notes with contempt the piles of fancy clothes from which Laertes seduces loose serving wenches and other sundry ladies. He sees Laertes flick lovingly through a sheaf of his latest songs.

Every young man of substance in Hamlet's generation is an aspirant troubadour. Laertes, in Hamlet's opinion, is the most insipid of all. Lyrics limp; tunes trite; sentiments sickly soppy. If Laertes were not so pathologically heterosexual and stupidly fearless, he could easily be thought a pansy.

Hamlet sneers coldly. Moves on.

Ophelia is in her pre-banquet bath. She loves her body but is prevented, by Polonius' glowering vigilance, from spreading it about. And what splendid biology it is. Breasts full, firm, high, jutting; altogether wonderful. Everything a normal man could hope for, though less mountainously smothering than Gertrude's. And whereas Gertrude's nipples are wide and dark, where Hamlet once sucked, Ophelia's tips are a neat petite pink, where Hamlet has never sucked yet.

Ophelia is not a Good Girl. She has the persona of a well-bred maiden. Intelligent and cultured, for a woman of this age. These qualities form part of her attraction for Hamlet. But the diligent student of human nature can't ignore her greed, ambition, and callousness.

He peeps.

Ophelia dreamily soaps her chest.

Reclining in a huge wooden bath like a flat-bottomed clinker rowing boat. Every night she has this balneal extravagance filled by staggering lackeys from Polonius' kitchens. Polonius indulges such idiosyncrasies in his daughter, hoping to keep her out of mischief.

Like packing Laertes off to France.

When Hamlet first came to spy on Ophelia he had difficulty finding a suitable chink in her brickwork. This was because of the mass of tapestries adorning her walls. Weaving is one of her accomplishments. Her chamber is bright with copies, in cloth, ranging from the mutually masturbating wrestlers of a Michelangelo to the frenzied Big Fish Eating Little Ones of a Brueghel. Hamlet admires Ophelia's powers of emulation, but frowns upon her lack of originality. It never occurs to him that her detailed imitations keep her sane during the lonely captivity enforced by Polonius, since he caught her astride a pageboy two years back.

Now Hamlet watches.

She rises from her bath. Towels off by the fire. Shadows lick her sumptuous body. She pads across the chamber to a full-length mirror on the wall opposite the fire. Unpins and lets fall her gorgeous gold mane. She has an arousingly Scandinavian combination of pure blonde hair and jet-black pubes – rich and thick, like cream, yet dark and glossy, like glorious sin.

Admiring her reflection, Ophelia combs out her dimple-tickling fleece. Her left hand creeps down. She touches herself. Slowly. Gently. Then she begins to engorge and secrete. Her movements become violent and abandoned, savage and destructive. She drops her comb. Her right forearm moves across her breasts. Massages them in a short sawing cuddle. Gasps of anticipation escape her clenched teeth.

In his sepulchral chill behind the wall, Hamlet is taken aback. Shame and revulsion well up from his convoluted morals. He considers stealing away and leaving Ophelia to masturbate in privacy. But what if the tables turned? If it were *her* behind the wall, spying on *his* hand-relief?

Despite the cold, the Prince has become urgently excited within his hose. He takes out his stiffness and pumps in time to Ophelia's heavy touching. Her gasps swell to a muted crescendo. Her whole body convulses in miraculous orgonal discharge.

As Hamlet spurts silently against the outside of her chamber wall.

Ophelia is now temporarily content. She has only one dimension of shame to deal with, and she has had plenty of practice. She returns to her bath, then starts to dress for the banquet.

Outside, in the deepening chill, Hamlet wrestles with dark remorse. Orgasm over, he feels emptiness without catharsis. Isolation without consolation. He tucks himself away, disgustedly. Begins the long, winding, cheerless trek back to his chamber.

And ponders his relationship with Ophelia.

Since his return from Wittenberg she has gone out of her way, albeit subtly, to solicit his attentions, with particular enthusiasm for his songs. This is a vulnerable area. He knows Ophelia's appreciation is motivated, but he still feels flattered by her encomiastic interest. And yet . . .

Such thoughts dart tauntingly across the revolving stage of the Prince's consciousness, as he burrows round the Castle secrecy. Reluctantly he concludes that Ophelia's recent ministrations owe more to his potential as King than to his mastery of minstrelsy. Ophelia knows Hamlet has been interested in her, sexually, for years. Hamlet knows she knows it. And she knows Hamlet knows she knows it. But he, abhorring marital twines, has always taken his sexual satisfactions elsewhere. In flirtations with faraway serving girls, or long months of monkish abstinence.

When Old Hamlet died, Ophelia calculated that Hamlet would be forced to think of *heirs*. Hence of a *wife*. So Ophelia put herself forward. And what could be more understandable? Although still a beauty, she is getting on in years, for an unmarried girl in Denmark at this time.

She is twenty-seven. Two years younger than Hamlet.

Why hasn't she married?

Because Polonius has always hoped she might bag Hamlet. That way, Polonius would be tenured by blood; grandfather to kings of Denmark.

Why, then, did Polonius not work to secure the succession for Hamlet, rather than wicked uncle Claudius? Ophelia has been asking this for days, leaving tempers in the Polonius family unpleasantly frayed.

Polonius' motives are complex, but shrewd. He knows Hamlet despises him. Consequently, Polonius decided, it would be dangerous to crown Hamlet *before* his own position had been cemented by Hamlet's marriage to Ophelia. After all, might not *King* Hamlet take his marriage prospects elsewhere? Leaving both Polonius and Ophelia out in the cold? Literally!

Such considerations resolved Polonius to support Claudius; plus the possibility that Gertrude might suddenly contract a terminal illness, or suffer a fatal riding accident, or otherwise exit swiftly. Then? Claudius would need a bright new queen, all bursting with the eggs of heirs.

Ophelia, perhaps?

This last contingency has occupied Ophelia herself, since she realized that Claudius must be King. Not that she has neglected Hamlet, but she likes to keep her options open. Again, what if Hamlet should rid himself of Claudius? He would still require heirs, hence a queen.

Suspicions of these sordidities torment Hamlet as he nears his room. Suddenly, through the carnal performance in Ophelia's chamber, a lonely memory bubbles up like a mermaid's sigh from the sunken galleon of his childhood.

He and Ophelia and Laertes as infants were very close. Taught together; bathed together; until a certain age they even slept together. Old Hamlet believed in having young children raised in company, he too being a skin-deep Platonist. In one scene of joyful innocence, from Hamlet's ninth year, the three children are splashing about, being bathed by a robustly youthful Gertrude. Old Caesar the wolfhound, their constant companion in those days, tries to jump in with them. The bath tilts, water swills over the floor. Screams of mock terror and childish delight ensue, with smiling admonitions from Gertrude to Caesar.

The following year Old Hamlet decided that the young Prince must begin his adult education. Hamlet was separated from his childhood chums. To return never again to the same intimate innocence.

Old Caesar, he recollects with a wistful sigh, passed away painfully three years later.

Before he enters his chamber, by a concealed entrance behind the fireplace, Hamlet checks through a spyhole that no one is snooping. Nobody is, but . . . a wave of nausea breaks over him as he sniffs another dead rat. It is not the deadness of these rats that is inexplicable, but rather how they got here. The maze is supposed to be completely sealed, except when a secret entrance admits its kingly visitor. So . . . cursing softly, Hamlet noses out the present offender.

He secures the decomposing rodent by the tip of its tail, wincing at its cold scaly feel, and carries it through the fireplace to his bedchamber. The room is almost dark. Some thin sneaking daylight remains outside the shuttered single window. It is freezing, for the fire has not been lit. This is to save the Prince from roasting when he leaves his spy network. As he carries the putrid corpse to the window a cluster of fattening grey maggots sprays out of the rat's belly and scatters on the floor.

Hamlet stamps on the maggots. Unbolts the shutters. Hurls the offensive rat out of the window. The north-west sky still trails a few wisps of dingy crimson. But darkness gallops up from the east. It is freezing hard. From far below his lofty pinnacle comes a hivish buzz of banquet preparations.

Eight o'clock.

Hamlet bolts the shutters. Lights a candle. Paces round his room, deep in thought. Presently he realizes with a shock how numbly cold he is. He lights the fire.

The kindling splutters.

The Prince shrugs into the coarse hairy pile of the brown bearskin coat he received of a boisterous boyar, during a mushroom-gathering expedition to Russia with the notorious Professor Faust. Squeezing the matted bearskin into the seat at his little walnut writing desk, he opens his diary. Sets out ink and quill. Writes quickly, as in an important exam:

If only this too solid flesh would melt, thaw, resolve into dew! Or if the Almighty had not forbidden us self-slaughter!
God! How weary, stale, flat, and unprofitable this world. A plague on it!

This unweeded garden, which grows to seed; possessed by rogues and monsters.

That it should come to this! A King who was compared to this, an angel to a devil; a Greek god to a satyr. A King so loving to my mother . . . now dead.

Heaven and earth! Must I remember? How she hung on him, as if her appetite grew by what it fed on. And yet, within one month, she married. How frail a woman is! One month?

God! Any beast of the field mourns longer. And yet, she married. With my father's brother? As like my father as I to Hercules!

Within a month, before the salt of most unrighteous tears had left her red-rubbed eyes, she married. Oh! With such wicked speed, to incestuous sheets. It is not good. Nor can it come to good. But break, my heart, for I must hold my tongue!

Thus Hamlet uses his diary as a tactical weapon. He knows that he is spied on constantly. And he is sure the paymaster is Claudius. Since his diary is an obvious target for snoopers, why not use it to feed the enemy false information? Food for paranoia?

How better to force hostile hands?

For instance, anyone in the Castle with a sprinkling of wit would wonder at Hamlet's appeals to the 'Almighty'. Here, indeed, is the germ of the Prince's madness strategy. And fuel for a rift between Claudius and Gertrude:

Hamlet deplores his mother's wanton behaviour. Hints that it has driven him near suicide. Yet anyone less enamoured of Hamlet, such as Claudius, might wonder whether 'this too too solid flesh' refers to Hamlet. Or to Hamlet's *enemy*?

Perhaps *Claudius*?

Thus seeding the suspicion that Hamlet is toying with toppling Claudius?

This interpretation, of course, could only be adopted by someone sharing Claudius' interests. Such as Claudius. Thus, a wedge might drive between Claudius and Gertrude over how to deal with Hamlet.

Henceforth the Prince will use his diary as an ink-blot, to be interpreted by whichever illicit onlooker looks on. This is confirmed by the style he adopts; for example, the profusion of juvenile exclamation marks.

Hamlet's last sentence says 'break my heart, for I must hold my tongue!' Why? Because he hears martial footsteps clanking along the corridor towards his room. On one level, discretion obliges him to stop writing. But no snooper (coming later) will realize that he stopped writing simply because he heard footsteps approaching.

Won't the snooper rather think Hamlet is suffering his heart to break, *literally*, because he fears to express his feelings?

A schoolboy pun on 'break, my heart', but might it not be very effective?

If the snooper, or his master, were tumorous with paranoia about the nature and intensity of Hamlet's unexpressed feelings.

4
INTIMATIONS

The martial footsteps halt outside Hamlet's door. The Prince leaps up from his desk. Shrugs out of his bearskin, lest it hamper self-defence. Crosses to the window. Draws back the shutters. Strikes a dreamy pose, gazing into the freezing darkness outside.

Rat-a-tat.

Yes?

The door opens.

Clanking footsteps carry Horatio, Marcellus and Bernardo into the room. Horatio leads. He is clad, as ever, in drab brown mufti. Tribulation simmers in his muddy eyes. He coughs gently.

Hamlet continues staring out of his window, projecting a conical white exhalation of frozen breath into the gloom without. Far below:

Plates bang. Cutlery tinkles. A fallen dish breaks. Orders are shouted. Other sounds suggest carousing in the kitchens.

Horatio shuffles.

'Hail to your lordship,' he ventures stiffly, never able to forget Hamlet's royal blood.

'I am glad to see you well.' Hamlet replies distantly, without turning his head. He has not recognized Horatio's voice. Now he faces his visitors, and:

'Horatio!' he exclaims. Rushes forward. Embraces Horatio. Clasps his hand. He is really surprised, and pleased.

'The same, my lord,' Horatio replies. 'Your poor servant ever.'

'My *friend*, Horatio. And what brings you here from Wittenberg? Ah, Marcellus?'

'My lord . . .' Marcellus bows politely.

But Hamlet cuts him short:

'Glad to see you,' the Prince raps curtly. 'Good evening, sir,' he adds, to Bernardo. 'But tell me, Horatio, what brings you from Wittenberg?'

Horatio gets Hamlet's unsplintered attention. The Prince is like a man who bumps into his longlost best friend in the lobby of a Transylvanian inn.

Marcellus and Bernardo exchange a diplomatic glance. They stand back patiently in their soldierly brasses and leathers.

'A truant disposition brings me here, my lord,' Horatio replies, uncomfortably.

'You are no truant,' retorts the Prince. 'But tell me: why have you come? We'll teach you to drink deeply, before you go.' Hamlet squeezes his friend's arm affectionately. But his warm welcome is developing an undertone of insistent curiosity.

'My lord, I came to see your father's funeral.'

'I pray you, do not mock me, old friend. I think you came to see my mother's wedding.' Hamlet's sarcasm is not shafted at Horatio.

'Indeed, my lord,' admits Horatio, 'the wedding followed hard on the funeral's heels.'

'Thrift, Horatio!' Hamlet mocks, waving his arms like a ham actor. 'The funeral baked meats plundered for the marriage tables! I would rather meet my dearest enemy in heaven than see my mother marry thus.' He raises his bent right hand to his brow. Gazes round the cobwebs in the corners of the ceiling. 'My father!' he exclaims. 'I think I see my father.'

The Prince is merely letting off steam, trying to jerk himself into a more sociable frame of mind.

Horatio finds his royal companion's exclamation extremely alarming.

'Oh!' he gasps. 'Where, my lord?' He squints fearfully into the chamber's darker crannies. Terrible urgency in his voice.

Hamlet doesn't notice:

'In my mind's eye,' he replies flippantly.

'I saw him once,' stalls Horatio. 'He was a goodly King.'

'He was a man, for all his faults,' reflects Hamlet. 'I shall not look upon his like again.' He falls silent.

Horatio tries to muster his flagging courage.

Marcellus and Bernardo shuffle their heavily booted feet.

Horatio takes the plunge:

'My lord,' he quavers, 'I think I saw him last night.'

'Saw whom?'

'My lord, the King. Your father.'

'The King. My father!' howls Hamlet, incredulously. Has Horatio joined with the enemy? Come to torment him?

The fragile camaraderie disperses like a cloud of frightened starlings.

Horatio quails before Hamlet's savage scowl, and begs:

'I pray you, listen until we unfold this marvel to you.'

Hamlet sniffs suspiciously. But Horatio is high in his esteem. He respects the pious earnestness in his friend's voice. 'For God's sake, then, let me hear,' he commands.

So Horatio embarks on his hoary tale:

'Two nights', he recounts, 'had these gentlemen, Marcellus and Bernardo, been thus encountered. On their watch, in the dead of night, a figure like your father appeared before them. Fully armed, from head to toe. Thrice each night he marched solemnly by them, close enough to touch them with his sword.

'They, almost jellied with their quaking, stood dumbly. These happenings, in fearful secrecy, they did impart to me. The following night I kept watch with them. Indeed the Apparition did appear, just as described. I knew your father, my lord. My own two hands are no more similar than this Apparition to him.' Horatio splays his unremarkable hands before his face.

Hamlet sees instantly that Horatio is carried away by his apocalyptic tidings. He compares Horatio's claim that the Apparition and Old Hamlet seemed similar as twin hands with 'I saw him once', which Horatio muttered a few moments earlier.

In fact, Horatio's acquaintance with Old Hamlet was minimal. His present avowals prove only that his beliefs are barely less ductile than those of Marcellus and Bernardo. So Hamlet's scepticism mounts, but guardedly:

'Where was this?'

'Upon the cliff above the Castle, my lord, where we watched.'

'Did you not speak to it?'

'My lord, I did. But it made no reply. And yet once, I thought, it lifted up its head as if to speak. But then the morning cock crew loud. And at that sound it shrank hastily away, and vanished from our sight.'

When Horatio was recounting his story, he referred to the Apparition as 'he'. Now, following Hamlet, he reverts to 'it'.

'Very strange,' Hamlet muses, stroking his beard.

'Upon my life, my lord,' Horatio gambles rashly, 'it is true.'

'Indeed,' Hamlet reassures him. 'But it troubles me.' He turns to Marcellus and Bernardo:

'You watch tonight?'

'We do, my lord.'

'This thing was armed, you say?'

'Indeed, my lord.' Marcellus replies.

'Top to toe?'

'Head to foot, my lord.'

'Then did you not see his face?'

'Oh yes, my lord! He wore his visor up.'

'Oh! And was he frowning?'

'His countenance suggested sorrow, rather than anger,' Horatio speculates.

'Pale, or red?'

'Very pale, my lord.'

'And did he fix his eyes upon you?'

'Most constantly.' Horatio's memory of the encounter is already in tatters. In truth the Apparition stared *past* them, rather than *at* them.

Hamlet is satisfied that here is no reliable information. As he switches between 'it' and 'he' in his questions, the others guilelessly follow his lead in their answers.

'I wish I had been there,' he comments with feeling.

'My lord,' Horatio exclaims, 'it would have amazed you greatly.'

'No doubt. Did it stay long?'

Horatio reflects. Gently rubs a thinning patch of brown on the crown of his good-hearted pate. 'While one might count to a hundred,' he estimates.

'Longer, longer.' Marcellus and Bernardo protest together.

'Not when I saw it,' Horatio insists.

'His beard was grizzled, was it not?' Hamlet resumes.

'As in his life, like sable streaked with silver.'

But Horatio only saw Old Hamlet *once*! This nags Hamlet like premonite indigestion. Disturbed by his visitors' story, he has little faith in their interpretation.

'I will watch with you tonight,' he declares. 'Perhaps it will walk again.'

'I warrant it will.'

But on what *evidence*, Horatio? Echoes of 'it' and 'he'? The Prince pronounces sternly:

'If it appears as my noble father's person, I'll speak to it. Even though hell itself howl me down. I pray you all,' he instructs, 'keep secret your encounter. And whatever comes to pass tonight, keep secret also. I will not forget the duty and the love that you have shown. So, fare you well. I'll visit you upon the cliff, near midnight.'

Horatio, Marcellus and Bernardo bow.

'Our duty to your honour,' they chant.

'I thank you kindly. Farewell.'

The visitors clatter away.

Hamlet paces round his room like a scalded wolf in a tiny cage. He has suspected all along that *some* nastiness attended his father's passing.

Now this!

As Philosopher-Prince he is uncommitted to ghosts. Yet he lives in superstitious times. Can he deny a residual childish dread of the supernatural? The Apparition was, apparently, *armed from head to foot*! Yet . . . ghosts normally wear harmless white burial shrouds! Why then should the ghost of his father parade in armour?

Hamlet pokes the fire. Throws on more logs. Tongues of lecherous flame leap up. The Prince half-focuses on the fire's roasting heart. Plunges into a whirling mushroom recurrence. Cannon-membered demons and toad-breathing harlots leer, wink and beckon. He shakes his head furiously. Reminds himself that Faust is wrong. That the ghouls which torment him have no objective reality. Mere dramatic disturbances of his own mind.

Then doubts:

Could Faust be right after all? Might this paternal Apparition be *really* a devil from hell, to seduce him into soul-forfeiting mischief?

The images fade.

Hamlet wonders:

Whatever the *true* explanation of the Apparition on the cliff, might he not *hint*, in his doublethink diary, that he is being suborned by the ambassadors of darkness? To cross-ferment his 'madness'?

The grey flecks in his pale blue eyes glow redly, like shards of smouldering charcoal, as he scratches into his diary the following postscript:

My father's spirit (in arms!)? All is not well. I doubt foul play! I wish the night were here. Till then sit still, oh my troubled soul. Have patience. Foul deeds needs rise, in time, to light.

Hamlet blots what he has written. Decides to take another anonymous prowl round the Castle, before the banquet. Crosses to the roasting recess behind his fireplace. Gingerly re-enters his Fallopian passageways, and heads back towards the royal bed-chamber.

The Apparition's questionable appearance, he feels, justifies his surveillance activities. If foul play killed Old Hamlet, then who but Young Hamlet should sniff it out?

5
LAERTES LEAVES

A comfortable public room in Polonius' house. As warm and cheerful as the Castle can get. Yet Ophelia, in her skimpy banquet gown, is hugging the fireplace. The decor is peccably bourgeois. China eider-ducks fly in garish squadrons round the walls.

Laertes is bidding Ophelia farewell. He is dressed in (for him) sensible travelling leathers. By contrast, Ophelia's sparse white dress might suit a modest maiden on an ancient Greek vase. This garment was chosen with cunning. Ophelia knows that Gertrude, as Queen, could never appear in such a creation. Also that no other court lady has the body to carry it off. Thus:

Ophelia fancies outstaging Gertrude and simultaneously captivating Hamlet.

Laertes claps a gauntlet flourish of penultimentality.

'My luggage is aboard,' he announces. 'I must say farewell. And sister, *do* write to me.'

'You doubt that?' There is a lilt of mockery to Ophelia's query, but Laertes ignores it. She knows that, though Laertes has evinced no sexual interest in her for years, he is jealous of the attention she has recently lavished on Hamlet and his songs.

'As for Hamlet, and his attentions,' Laertes drones, 'think them freaks of passion. Trifling toys in his blood. The perfumed indulgence of a minute.'

'No more?' Ophelia taunts.

'Think it not. Perhaps he does love you now, and perhaps his love is pure. But he cannot carve for himself, as ordinary men might do. On his choice depends the safety of the state. Therefore he must yield to the voice of that body, whereof he is the head. If he *says* he loves you, believe it no further than his honourable *deeds*.'

Ophelia greets this dirge with a parody of sisterly reticence. She reflects with sour amusement that Hamlet has never vouchsafed her the remotest protestation of love. Her only comfort is her cynical superiority, which Laertes' paranoid jealousy arouses.

Unbeknown to them, this sentiment is shared by Hamlet, through Polonius' drawing-room wall. Having journeyed round to the royal bedchamber, the snooping Prince found the royal couple merely preening for the banquet. After that, Hamlet gave Polonius a look, but the old man was sitting scribbling on his own, probably signing death warrants. So now Hamlet spies live on Polonius' drawing-room. He missed the first exchanges between Ophelia and Laertes, but he is quick to catch on.

And he stifles a snort of disgust, as Laertes' empty rhetoric gives way to native nastiness:

He wraps his arm round his sister's back. Gives her right breast a suggestive squeeze. The delicate rotundities of Ophelia's nipples are just visible through her filmy garment. She indulges her body in an ambiguous shiver. Disentangles from Laertes' slimy grasp.

Laertes, seeing his sister unmoved by his platitudes, reverts to innuendo:

'Think carefully,' he sneers, 'what loss your *honour* may sustain! If eagerly you creed his songs; lose your heart; open your *chaste treasure*, to his *unmastered importunity*.

'Fear it, Ophelia. Desire is danger. Keep clear of it. Fastidious maidens mask their naked beauty from the moon! For virtue suffers calumny. Nature's infants fall oft to the canker-worm, before their buds mature. Be wary, then. Best fear him. In the liquid morning dew of youth, contagious folly is most dangerous.'

This last slice of pompous tripe, served steaming on its platter of tarnished sarcasm, induces an Ophelia chortle. Laertes, one year her junior, is twenty-six. *Youth?*

(Ophelia was the first child of Polonius' second marriage, the first having been childless. Resentful of lost time, Polonius quickly set his second wife to breeding. The year after she produced Laertes she died in agony, trying to give birth to twins. Save the Mother and Lose the Child? Or? Polonius, eager for more male heirs, lost the mother. As it happened, the twins, identical sickly girls, only survived a month, despite the best wet-nursing. Polonius' catholic handling of this unhappy episode caused friction between him and Old Hamlet, an ardent Lutheran. Ambition then decided Polonius to abandon the matrimonial life and consolidate his career.)

'I will remember this good lesson,' Ophelia vows, 'and keep it, as watchman to my heart.' She screws up her eyes and holds her hands fetchingly to her bosom, in a send-up of Laertes' solicitous unction.

Behind the brickwork, Hamlet chews his cold-numbed lips. His money is on Ophelia.

'But do not, dear brother,' she counsels, 'as unreverend vicars do, show *me* the steep and thorny way to heaven, while *you*, a puffed and reckless libertine, waltz gaily along the primrose path of dalliance.' As she delivers this thrust, her eyes rove round Laertes' unlovely person, and she recalls, in déjà-vu detail, her own sexual initiation at the loins of this sibling body, now so stockily repugnant.

One day, just fourteen and thirteen, they were following a hunting expedition in the forests of Silkeborg – the Lake District of Denmark. This foray had been organized on Polonius' country estate by his head gamekeeper, for the entertainment of important guests. Polonius did not take part himself, not being sporty, but the children were allowed to tag behind the main party, at a respectful distance.

This they did, until a bounding stag was sighted, deep in the dark heart of the woodland. Then the hunt and the hounds took off in pursuit, to a strident discord of shouts, bays, bugle blasts and hunting-horn hoots. Laertes and Ophelia were left standing. Their elderly ponies could never keep pace with the fiery steeds in front.

What to do?

The youngsters tracked the bugles as best they could. But the chase went on and on. The sounds grew ever more distant. An hour later the dark sky was thick with snow. The first flakes fell. The frenzied yelping dogs were barely audible. The children could still see, in the mangled carpet of the previous day's snowfall, the trail the huntsmen had blazed. But how long could this cue survive? They judged, from the fast blackening sky, that heavier snow was on the way, so they elected to backtrack to familiar territory, before all landmarks were obliterated.

Alas. As they trotted, slower and slower, the snow fell even more heavily. Soon a freak blizzard was upon them. As if some heavenly butcher were cramming clouds through an infinite meatgrinder and strewing the resultant snowy mince all over the world.

Visibility neared zero. Laertes and Ophelia became hopelessly lost. Their ponies refused to carry them any further. The children were forced to dismount and tug the unwilling animals along behind them. Consequently, their feet and legs became as cold, wet and miserable as their heads and shoulders had been for some time. Their riding clothes, designed for cold-dry weather, afforded scant protection against the penetrating damp of armpit-melted snow.

After what seemed an age making no headway, Ophelia burst into tears. She had never been so miserably cold, and she was thoroughly frightened. Laertes, newly pubescent, refused to acknowledge fear. He put his arm around his sister's shoulders, and encouraged her to keep going until they found some shelter.

Just when he too was verging on despair, they found themselves suddenly out of the interminable tall pines and on the shore of a large inland lake. So obscured was their vision, indeed, that they almost stumbled into the water. Even once they realized what lay before them, they found the sight of the billowing snow landing on the water unnervingly sinister. Falling faster than it could melt, the snow formed a shifting flaky layer on the surface of the water, like the rippling white coat of some enormous unknown animal.

If, now, they kept edging round the shore, might not the lost waifs unearth some habitation? Sure enough, after battling along the narrow white fringe between forest and lake for forty battered minutes, they caught a brown speckled glimpse of some wooden structure set back in the trees. This they then made for in a surge of relief, hope, and agonized apprehension. The fresh snow was climbing over their knees, and walking had become an impossible nightmare.

One half of the snug woodman's hut was a shelter for livestock. There they stabled their grateful ponies. The other half was a one-room haven of peace and potential warmth (or 'bothy', as they said in olden Scotland). In this they found a rough-straw mattress, several blankets, a fire ready laid, and a plentiful supply of logs.

Laertes rubbed down and fed the ponies while Ophelia lit the fire. Only then, as the logs blazed, and their sodden clothes steamed, did the ramific implications of their situation begin to rankle.

Come now, dear sister, urged Laertes. We must take off our clothes and dry them, or we shall die of pneumonia.

Yes, Laertes, I suppose so, she replied hesitantly. You turn your face to the fire, and I will hand you my clothes and lie down under this blanket. Then I will turn my face to the wall, and you can hang up all our clothes to dry, before lying down under that other blanket.

As you say, Ophelia.

Laertes stared fixedly into the flowering fire.

Ophelia peeled her lithe young charms out of their squelchy drapery. She towelled off with the least saturated of her clothes, handed them to Laertes, and burrowed her quick pink shivers beneath the coarse cotton blankets on the rough straw mattress.

Laertes stripped himself, wrung out all the clothes, and hung them on an old hairy twine-line in front of the fire. As the fire gained in heat, huge clouds of steam rose from the sodden clothing, like puffs of smoke, to dampen the low wooden ceiling of the hut. Laertes slipped under the blankets, beside his sister, on the outside of the tattered bed.

Are you asleep, dear sister?

No, Laertes, but I am terribly cold; all the heat from the fire is being eaten by our wet clothes.

Yes, he agreed, it is deathly cold.

Then came a pregnant pause, filled only by spitting and crackling from the fire and a steady steamy hiss from the drying garments.

Laertes lightly touched his sister's shoulder.

Then do you not think, dear Ophelia, he murmured, that we should lie *together*, thus *combining* the warmth of our blankets and bodies?

Yes, Laertes, she answered in a faint voice; that seems to be what the situation demands.

So together they snuggled, to share their body heat. Ophelia, at

Hamlet, unseen, slopes off to humour his mother by dressing for the banquet. Festivities begin in twenty minutes. Meanwhile, Laertes fidgets violently, kicking heels and sucking teeth. Anxious not to miss his tide.

'Neither a borrower nor a lender be,' Polonius gushes. 'For loans often lose both themselves and friends, and borrowing dulls the edge of thrift. Above all: *be true to your own self.* Then it will follow, as night follows day, that you cannot be false to any man. Farewell. And let my blessing season these few precepts in your memory.' He hugs his son once more.

Laertes submits tensely. Over his father's shoulder he scowls at Ophelia, who is enjoying herself.

'Most humbly I take my leave, my lord.' Laertes is tight with constricted anger.

'The time invites you.' Polonius now intones dismissal. 'Go. Your servants await you.'

Laertes bows.

'Farewell, Ophelia,' he concludes, 'and remember well what I have said.'

Ophelia feigns winsome naivety.

'It is locked away in my memory,' she swears. 'And yourself shall keep the key.'

'Farewell then.' Laertes exits hastily, before any more prattling precepts bubble from the rancid stewpot of his father's brain. To clinch the safety of his departure, he has thrown Polonius a juicy sprat:

'What is it, Ophelia, that he said to you?' Polonius rises like a mackerel to sewage.

Ophelia casts her long lashes down.

'My lord, it was something concerning Lord Hamlet,' slithers out of her dutifully, as if neither Laertes nor promises existed.

'Indeed?' Polonius reflects. 'I am told that, of late, he has given private time to you. And that you have been most free in giving him audience. If this is true, as my sources assure me, then you do not understand your position as befits both my daughter and your own honour. Now, what has passed between you? Tell me the *truth.*'

'My lord, he has made me tenders of affection.'

'Pooh! You speak like a green girl, untested in such perilous circumstances.' Polonius harks to the day he caught her astride the pageboy. 'And do you *believe* his tenders?'

'I do not know, my lord, what I should think.'

'Indeed! Then I'll teach you. Think yourself a baby, to take these devious tenders seriously. Put a higher price on your favours, or you'll render me a fool.'

'My lord, he importunes me with love in an *honourable* fashion.'

'Fashion you may call it! Go on.'

'He supports his speech, my lord, with holy vows.'

Polonius scoffs: 'Snares to catch pheasants! When the blood burns, the soul is prodigal in lending vows to the tongue. These flashes, my dear daughter, give more light than heat. You must not mistake them for fire.'

Polonius deceives himself into righteous paternal anger. His present plans for Ophelia do not include Hamlet.

'As for Lord Hamlet,' he rams, 'remember that, compared with you, he is young. And walks with a longer tether.' Alluding to the never-farness of the old-maids' shelf. 'In short, Ophelia, do not believe his vows. They are not what they seem. Their colourful dress is merely to beguile you. Hence do I *forbid* you, to bandy even *words* with him. Mark me carefully. Now, come away.'

'I shall obey, my lord.' She sniffs softly, as if close to tears.

Polonius departs for the banquet, like a resplendent elder swan.

Ophelia follows after, like a beautiful cygnet in a questioning cold fury:

Why is Polonius so adamant that she must avoid Hamlet?

Has her father some sinister pact with Claudius?

Should she maintain pursuit of Hamlet?

Or aim at good King Claudius?

Or *both*?

6
BRINKMANSHIP

Again on the murky precipitous clifftop which towers like a gigantic fissure-ridden protective garden wall between the Castle and the sea.

Marcellus and Bernardo patrol.

Swirling icy grey horribleness prevails.

Hamlet and Horatio have slipped away from the riotous banquet below, to join Marcellus and Bernardo in their watch. Hamlet's bearskin sits like a cloak on his wide shoulders. Under his belt, beside his sabre, he has tucked his diary.

Horatio and Bernardo carry long slowburning torches, which radiate a few indistinct yards into the gloom. The dirty-yellow torchlight throws grotesque phantoms all around the four men, and ghoulifies their features.

'Very cold,' observes Hamlet, flapping his arms across his chest.

'Pretty nippy,' chatters Horatio.

'What hour?' inquires the Prince.

'Still before twelve,' opines Horatio.

'No, it has struck,' Marcellus corrects him.

'I did not hear it.' Horatio tries to sound unconcerned. 'Then soon the spirit may walk.' He is interrupted by a flourish of trumpets, maniacal yells, and a volley of cannon-fire, resounding up from the Castle. 'What does this mean, my lord?'

'The King stays up tonight to revel and carouse,' explains Hamlet. 'And as he drains his Rhenish down, the kettledrum and trumpet proclaim his prowess as a drinker.'

(In the banquet hall, Claudius triumphantly reels about, propelling a flustered Gertrude in a flatfooted nuptial waltz. Osric looks on, blandly imperturbable, his chubby cheeks a bilious hue. Ophelia sits alone, smiling tightly as she nurses her bruised aspirations.

Despite her devastating attire and coiffure, Hamlet has fled the banquet. *Why?* Wildly drunken dance musicians play wildly drunken dance music, and the courtiers sound like an orchestrated pigs' dinner.)

On the cold clammy cliff, Horatio inquires:

'Is it a custom?' Re the King's drinking habits.

'Yes.' Hamlet stamps his feet, to speed his circulation. 'A custom of heavy-headed toping that ruins our reputation abroad, where they call us drunken swine.'

Yet Hamlet is quite a boozer himself, when the mood takes him. This canny hypocrisy drives him now to more serious comments on dissipation and the sad immutability of character:

'Indeed,' he says, still apropos Danish inebriation, 'it detracts from all our achievements; which, at their height, are beyond compare. In such cases, a single defect, whether innate or the produce of ill-fortune, corrupts a man's entire being; no matter how infinite his virtues. Thus an evil dram breaks down the battlements of reason, extinguishes all that is noble, and brings one to disgrace.'

There is the fatalism that delays Hamlet's action against Claudius. Philosophically, the Prince cannot *blame* Gertrude, Ophelia, even Claudius. For who should throw the first stone? Yet ... his emotional heritage is bound to outrage.

Hamlet prowls fretfully round the puddle of torchlight thrown by Horatio and Bernardo.

Suddenly:

'Look, my lord,' cried Horatio. 'It comes.'

Hamlet whirls about, scowling suspiciously.

On the rim of their vision, scarcely grazed by the weak yellow torchlight, the Apparition lurks luminous. Tall, like the old King, yet lumpishly undefined.

Hamlet draws from the possible responses he brewed earlier, while eating.

'Angels and ministers of grace defend us,' he cries majestically. 'Are you a spirit from heaven or a goblin from hell? Are your intentions wicked or charitable? You come in such a questionable shape that I will speak to you. I'll call you Hamlet, King, father, royal Dane. Oh, *answer* me!'

As Hamlet addresses the Apparition, he moves forward a few paces.

The Apparition retires correspondingly, its armour glistening grey in the fabulous fog.

Hamlet notes with aggressive interest that the Apparition has its visor down.

'Let me not burst in ignorance,' the Prince exclaims. 'But tell me why your consecrated bones have burst forth thus, from the ponderous marble sepulchre wherein we saw you buried.'

Here Hamlet is testing the putative ghost. Angling for a fishy response to the proposition that he, Young Hamlet, was present at his father's interment.

But the hovering Apparition keeps mum, beating its slow retreat in time to Hamlet's slow advance.

'What does this mean, old corpse?' Hamlet changing tone. 'Why, in full armour once more, do you return to horrify the night? While we poor mortals tremble! Wherefore? What should we do?' But Hamlet neither looks nor sounds like a man trembling. He looks furiously suspicious.

As if to shake the Prince's confidence, the Apparition beckons.

A menacing gesture.

Far away below the angry high-tide waves smash roaring against the rocks.

The Apparition edges closer to the high stark brow of the cliff.

Horatio's snub nostrils twitch with apprehension.

'It beckons you go with it,' he warns Hamlet. 'As if to impart to you alone.'

The Apparition continues back and gestures to Hamlet, slowly, heavily, like a noiseless mechanized waxwork.

'It waves you to a more isolated place,' remarks Marcellus, struck with awe. 'But do not go.'

'By no means,' echoes Horatio.

'If it will not speak, I'll follow it.'

'Do not, my lord.'

'Why? What should I fear? I do not price my life above a pin. And my *soul*! What can it do to that? Immortal as itself! It waves me forth again. I'll follow.' In full awareness of the treacherous crevices which honeycomb the crumbling cliff.

Horatio, seeing Hamlet undeterred by possible *physical* damage or death, tries to sway the Prince with the prospect of *insanity*:

'What if it tempt you, my lord,' he urges, 'to the dreadful summit? There to assume some other horrid form? Which might dethrone your reason into *madness*! Think of it. The very place pumps desperation into every brain that looks so many fathoms to the sea and hears it roar beneath. Think of it, my lord.'

Hamlet is not impressed.

'It waves me still,' he comments. 'Go on. I'll follow you.' He shoos the others back towards the Castle.

'You shall not go, my lord.' Marcellus grabs Hamlet's arm.

'Hold off!'

'Be ruled. You shall not go.' Horatio seizes Hamlet's other arm.

The Apparition's tireless clockwork-like retreat continues.

'My fate cries out,' cries Hamlet.

The Apparition beckons patiently.

'Still I am called for. Unhand me, gentlemen.' The Prince breaks away from Marcellus and Horatio with practised ease.

Bernardo moves forward as if to bar his way.

Hamlet is running out of patience. He draws and brandishes his sabre.

'By heaven!' he blasphemes.'I'll ghost him that hinders me.' He takes Bernardo's torch with his left hand. With his naked blade he prods his loyal companions Castlewards. 'Away, I say!' he orders. 'Go on. I'll follow.' He backs watchfully towards the Apparition, which backs cautiously into invisibility.

Hamlet disappears from view.

Horatio, Marcellus and Bernardo argue. Whether to obey the Prince or follow after him, in case of some dreadful development?

Meanwhile . . .

The Apparition dimly silhouettes against the double darkness of the emptiness beyond the cliff and out to sea. Thunderous crashing waves blast the cliffbase below.

'Where would you lead me?' shouts Hamlet. 'Speak. I'll go no further.'

'Mark me,' the Apparition booms in a throaty bass, distorted through its visor.

'I will.'

'The hour has almost come, when I to sulphurous and torment-ing flames must render myself up.'

'Alas! Poor ghost.' Is there irony here, in the Prince's flinty voice?

The Apparition appears not to notice.

'Do not pity me,' it commands. 'But listen carefully to what I shall unfold.'

'Speak,' Hamlet enthuses. 'I am bound to hear.' He puns on 'bound', to test the Apparition for wit.

Its reply?

Humourlessly consistent with Old Hamlet:

'So will you be bound to *revenge*, when I have spoken.'

'*What?*'

'I am your father's spirit,' the Apparition rumbles hypnotically, 'doomed, for a certain time, to walk the night. And during the day confined to fast in fires till the foul crimes done in my mortal life are purged away. If I were not forbidden to reveal the secrets of my prison-house, I could unfold a tale whose lightest word would harrow up your soul, freeze your young blood, and set your every hair to stand like quills upon the fretful porcupine. But such revelation cannot be made, to ears of flesh and blood.'

Thus the Apparition projects the air of one who *knows*.

Hamlet stays deadpan. His brain is whirling.

'Listen, oh *listen!*' the Apparition implores. 'If ever you did love your father . . .'

'Oh, God!'

'Revenge his most unnatural *murder*.'

'Murder?'

'Murder most foul! None more strange, foul, and unnatural.'

'Tell me quickly,' Hamlet urges. 'That I may swoop to my revenge.' He has decided to play along with the Apparition, learn what he can, and appear successfully duped. Time for detailed investigations later.

'It is given out that, while I was sleeping in my orchard, a serpent stung me. In this way, all Denmark is abused by false report. For know this, oh noble youth, the serpent that did sting your father's life now wears his *crown*.'

'Oh, my prophetic soul! My uncle?'

'That same incestuous and adulterous beast. His traitorous gifts and witchcraft wit won to his shameful lust the will of my most seeming Queen. Oh, wicked wit and gifts, that so seduce! Oh, Hamlet, what a tragedy! When I loved her so dearly! That she should stoop beneath a wretch whose parts were poor compared with mine!'

The Apparition's ranting hardens Hamlet's suspicion that here is a phoney:

Why the armour?

The visor down?

And isn't it a shade too tall for Old Hamlet? Or is this a trick of the fog? Then again:

If the Apparition *is* bogus, what of its skulking accomplices?

Elsewhere in the fog:

'Let's follow,' Marcellus agitates. 'It is not right to obey him in this.'

'Oh, what will come of it?' wails Horatio.

'Something is rotten in the state of Denmark,' Marcellus generalizes.

'Heaven will direct the outcome,' Horatio hopes.

'No,' Marcellus decides at last. 'Let's follow him.' He strides into the gloom where Hamlet vanished.

Horatio scurries after him, fearfully glum.

Bernardo, lightless since Hamlet borrowed his torch, brings up a miserable rear. Terrified of being left alone.

While the Apparition harangues:

'Thus *lust*', it cries, re Gertrude, 'will weary of a heavenly bed, and prey on garbage. But wait,' it gestures dramatically. 'I scent the morning air, and must be brief. On the day of my death, I was sleeping in my orchard; as was my custom in the afternoon. Upon my sleeping privacy your uncle steals! With cursed hebona in a vial. Into the porches of my ears he pours this leprous distilment. Swift as quicksilver it curdles up my thin and wholesome blood, and all my smooth body erupts in a loathsome crust!'

The Apparition is declaiming more eloquently, in its casing of steel, than was ever Old Hamlet's style. Then *who* . . .

'Thus, while sleeping, was I dispatched of crown. Of Queen. Life itself. And all by my brother's hand. Cut off in the blossom of my sins. Disappointed; unblessed; unanointed. All my imperfections unforgiven.'

Hamlet freezes. Here is *proof* of Apparition fraud! Old Hamlet, pining for *Catholic* rites? Never! But Hamlet coolly follows the maxim: Always give spurious apparitions enough rope to hang themselves.

'Oh, horrible!' the suspect raves on. '*Most* horrible! Do not tolerate it. Nor let Royal Denmark's bed creak loud with damnèd incest.

'But! Do not taint your mind or contrive revenges on your mother. Leave her to heaven, and the thorns in her own bosom.' The Apparition pauses, as in sorrow, and for breath.

Then come haunting unseen owl hoots, faint through the driving din of the ocean on the rocks:

Whoo, whoo, calls. *Whoo, whoo!*

This seems to startle the Apparition.

'Fare you well,' it croaks hastily. 'The glow-worm's fire begins to pale, and shows the morning near.'

Glow-worms? On misty clifftops?

What can the Apparition mean?

Perhaps in a panic to . . .

'Adieu, adieu! Hamlet, remember me.'

Lips of sodden fog purse greedily around the Apparition's precipitous departure.

This leaves Hamlet alone with his guttering torch. Racing suspicions mobilize his madness strategy. First stage? A frantic performance lest the Apparition's corporal lieutenants be lurking close by:

'All you hosts of heaven!' the Prince declaims. 'Oh, earth! What else? Shall I include hell? Oh, God! Hold up, oh my heart. Hold out! And you, my sinews, bear me up! Remember you? Indeed, poor ghost. As long as memory holds in this distracted skull.' He feverishly tousles his fog-drenched hair. 'Remember you? My memory slate I'll wipe away, and your commandment alone shall fill the volume of my brain.' He lurches forward, as if to hurl himself from the clifftop, and hysterically howls:

'Yes, by heaven! Oh, most pernicious woman! Oh, villain. Smiling damned *villain*! My diary. Where is my diary? To record that one may smile, and smile, *and* be a villain. At least in Denmark.' He feigns frenzied scribbling. Then:

'So, uncle,' he concludes, 'there you are.' And to the vanished Apparition:

'Now to my promise. You said, "Adieu, adieu! Remember me." I have writ it down, and swear to keep it.'

Clattering; stumbling.

Winded oaths herald his companions.

The Prince snaps shut his diary. Tucks it away.

'My lord!' calls Horatio.

Hamlet does not answer. Watching the flickering orange halo of Horatio's torch, he marvels at the sequence:

Owl hoots; Apparition exits; companions arrive.

'Lord Hamlet!' shouts Marcellus.

'Heaven secure him!' wails Horatio. He fears that Hamlet must have fallen to his death.

'So be it!' Marcellus is ready to abandon the search.

'Hello! HELLO, MY LORD!' shrieks Horatio, in an agonized last try.

Hamlet now hails the vague bulks of their bodies in the dark hanging hoar. Breezily:

'Hello, boy! Come, bird. Come.' As if comforting a fallen fledgeling.

Horatio and Marcellus burst anxiously upon the scene.

Bernardo follows.

'How is it, my noble lord?' inquires Bernardo.

'What news, my lord?' echoes Horatio.

'Wonderful!'

'Do tell us, my lord.'

'No. You will reveal it.' Hamlet pouts like a churlish child.

'Not I, my lord, by heaven!' swears Horatio.

'Nor I, my lord,' promises Marcellus.

'Nor I, my lord,' mumbles Bernardo.

'You will keep it *secret*?' Hamlet casts heavy conspiratorial glances over his shoulder.

'Yes, by heaven, my lord,' his companions chorus.

Hamlet draws them close, with the prurient air of a ten-year-old divulging Birds and Bees.

'There's never a *villain* dwelling in all Denmark that isn't an arrant *knave*.' Gleefully, like a logic student refuting proofs of God's existence.

'We need no ghost, my lord, come from the grave, to tell us this.' Horatio speaks seriously. Fears for Hamlet's sanity.

'Why, you are right,' the Prince trills. 'And so, without further ado, let us shake hands and part. You, as your business shall direct you. Myself, I shall go to pray.' This he delivers piously, like an oily fat bishop.

Horatio's friendly features frown. 'These are whirling words, my lord,' he protests, knowing that Hamlet hasn't prayed for fifteen years.

'I am sorry they offend you. Heartily.'

'There's no offence, my lord.'

'Yes, by Saint Patrick, there *is*!'

Horatio recoils.

'Much offence. This vision here is an *honest* ghost. I will tell you that. But your desire to know more you must overcome. And now, as you are friends, scholars and soldiers, grant me one poor request.'

'What, my lord?'

'Never make known what you saw here tonight.'

'My lord, we will not,' the companions promise together.

'*Swear* it.'

'My lord, I *do* swear.' Horatio is piqued at Hamlet's insistence.

'And I, my lord.'

'And I.'

Hamlet is not satisfied. He whips out his sabre.

'Upon my sword.'

Marcellus balks at this.

'My lord,' he protests, 'we have sworn already.'

'Upon my *sword*.' Royal authority rings in Hamlet's voice as he presents his blade.

Suddenly his command is echoed by the throaty voice of the Apparition, which seems to boom from under the ground.

'Swear,' rasps the voice.

'Ha, ha, boy!' Hamlet madly responds. 'Do you say so?' Cups hands to his ears. 'Are you there, old chap?' He gestures to his companions. 'Come on. You hear this fellow in the cellarage. Consent to swear.'

'Propose the oath, my lord,' stammers Horatio.

'Never to speak of this you have seen. Swear by my sword.'

'*Swear.*' The Apparition's voice creaks like a rusty hinge against the suicidal thundering of the far-below waves.

'A ubiquitous ghost!' mocks Hamlet. He strides some paces west. 'Let us shift our ground. Hither, gentlemen. Lay your hands upon my sword, and swear.'

His companions move to obey, but again:

'*Swear.*' The ghostly injunction sounds nearer, and half an octave higher.

'Well said, old mole!' taunts Hamlet. 'Dig through the earth so fast? Ho-hum! Once more, good friends, let us change our ground.' He retreats twenty paces down the cliff, towards the Castle.

His good friends follow.

'This is wondrous strange,' Horatio marvels.

'And therefore, as a stranger, give it welcome!' Hamlet's flippant retort reminds Horatio to be thankful he is not a Dane. 'There are more things in heaven and earth, Horatio, than are dreamt of in *your* philosophy.' Then Hamlet feels remorse for teasing his old friend. He takes Horatio aside, and whispers such that neither Marcellus and Bernardo nor the Apparition could possibly hear:

'But come,' he claps a reassuring arm around Horatio's troubled shoulder. 'From now on, however fantastic my behaviour, do not, by a knowing nod or a doubtful phrase, expose my antics.' He turns back to the two soldiers. Again presents his sword:

'Swear,' he insists.

All three companions comply.

'*Swear*,' the Apparition echoes, belatedly.

'Rest, perturbed spirit!' Hamlet jeers. Then, to his followers:

'Well, gentlemen, whatever such a poor man as I may do, to express his love for you, shall be done. God willing. Let us go in together.' He shepherds them Castlewards.

Through the eastern gloom a faint grey glimmers.

'Remember,' the Prince adds a final caution. 'Your fingers on your lips, I pray.' And a Parthian shot at the ubiquitous Apparition:

'The time is out of joint,' he calls ominously. 'Oh, cursed spite! That ever *I* was born to set it right!' Hearing no response, he rejoins his retinue. 'Come on,' he says. 'Let's go.'

7
FIRST INTERLUDE

The Apparition is counterfeit, yet Hamlet alone perceives this.

So what is going on in the Castle?

For three weeks Hamlet fishes to find out. Deliberately courting twilight unsanity, he becomes scruffier, dirtier, wilder. He drinks and shouts, whimpers and sulks. Speaks to no one.

Claudius asks Horatio what ails the Prince?

Horatio protests unhappy ignorance.

Claudius broods:

If Hamlet is mad, what treasonable atrocities might suddenly spill out of him? Claudius is constantly mindful of Hamlet's physical strength and skill with weapons. But . . . if *not* mad?

He is scheming!

And who but Claudius would Hamlet scheme against?

So Claudius sends to Copenhagen for Rosencrantz and Guildenstern.

Being of high intelligence and royal blood, Hamlet started university at the age of fourteen. Two older students, Rosencrantz and Guildenstern, were appointed to look after him. For a while Hamlet depended heavily on his mentors, and looked up to them. Later he saw what second-hand smarmers they really were.

When Rosencrantz and Guildenstern had completed their studies, they took posts in the civil service. Thus, Claudius summons them both as Hamlet's fellows and as employees. Of course, Claudius can't know that, as he briefs the messenger to fetch the lickspittles from Copenhagen, Hamlet is behind the brickwork, blinking red from lack of sleep and surfeit wine. He stifles a curdling belch as he perceives how Claudius intends to use Rosencrantz and Guildenstern:

Establish the Prince's madness, or unearth his dissimulation.

Hamlet's clandestine latenight prowls inform him also that, whereas initially Claudius pestered Gertrude, now the sexual predator is the Queen. She throws herself at Claudius like a shark at raw meat. Claudius' swelling reticence is (beyond Hamlet's ken) to do with Gertrude's teeth. Despite her otherwise trim fettle, primitive dentistry has left her with metallic breath. This dampens the Kingly ardour, which mortifies Gertrude herself.

One night Hamlet observes her gazing wanly into her dressing-table mirror. Pondering the wisdom of her recent marriage?

And why is Claudius so attentive to Ophelia?

Because Polonius keeps his daughter's public appearances scarce and well chaperoned?

Since inaccessibility fans desire?

Monitoring Polonius, Hamlet finds his own activities being monitored by one Reynaldo, agent to Polonius. Reynaldo is in his forties, oppressively anonymous, mercenary, a surveillance professional. One day, returning via his passageways from Ophelia bathing, Hamlet espies Reynaldo casing his room and copying from his cryptic diary. Smiling wryly, the Prince stands freezing behind the wall until Reynaldo departs.

One furtive transaction Hamlet misses:

Between Claudius and Osric.

Claudius is uneasy about the mission of Voltimand and Cornelius to Norway. He thinks he can trust them, but ... who knows with diplomats? So he dispatches Osric to Norway, to vet the ambassadors. Osric is ideal for this task because of his Norwegian estates. Whenever Claudius sends him ferreting, he can claim to be touring his properties.

In the nude Osric would excite no more interest than Reynaldo. Except, perhaps, for his plum pink buttocks. But his wealth and gay disposition are evident in his fanciful garb. His slight lithp and greasy drawl personify 'consenting adult'. Still, beneath his lush exterior, Osric is hard as nails. Not to be underestimated.

Across the sea from frozen flatland Denmark, past deep inscrutable fjords and valleys, sprawling glaciers and meandering dark forests, is the court of Old Norway, at Trondhjem. The castle is inset from the coast on the south side of Trondhjem's Fjord, where the northing body of Norway narrows.

Old Norway, throne vantaged, frowns sternly as he plays Diplomacy with Voltimand and Cornelius.

What, more than slimy platitudes, can pass between the Danish emissaries and the ostensibly Decrepit Norway?

Do they disclose the *real* instructions that Claudius secretly gave them *before* the Great Council meeting?

Though the Norwegian King is old, he is less derelict than Claudius made out. Years of competent kingship still burn blearily in Old Norway's creamy blue eyes. Why, then, did Claudius prime the Danish Great Council with a false impression?

In Copenhagen:

Amidst architectural splendour and bureaucratic indolence, Claudius' messenger requisitions Rosencrantz and Guildenstern, who pack their bags in immediate pawn obedience.

Back in Norway:

Voltimand and Cornelius at the court of Fortinbras, Old Norway's supposedly insurgent nephew. Fortinbras has his forces stationed at the castle of Fredrikstad, at the south tip of Norway, close to the border with Sweden.

Fortinbras is in his mid twenties. Medium height, heavily built; short-haired, clean-shaven. Pugnacious determination in his mouth; ruthless ambition in his eyes. As Laertes imagines himself. Conversing with Voltimand, Fortinbras betrays no emotion.

The ambassadors are ill at ease. They treat Fortinbras with the deference due to a dozing tiger.

In the background, the young general's sparring partner sits frowning over a chess table. The pieces, carved from reindeer antler, represent snarling monsters from Viking mythology.

Parades and manoeuvres in the castle grounds reveal a sharp difference between Fortinbras' soldiers in the flesh and the impression given of them by Claudius to the Great Council. Here are no outlaws, nourished on liquor and bloodlust, but disciplined cavalry, infantry, and commandos – practising their killing skills and caring scrupulously for their animals and equipment.

So what *can* Claudius be up to?

That question torments Hamlet, as, one isolated fine afternoon, he rides out on his great black stallion. Denmark is deep in winter, the weather increasingly arctic. While he pilots the snorting Woden between treacherous patches of maiden snow, discordances drone in the Prince's head. If the Apparition was a fake:

Who commissioned it? Who wants Hamlet to believe that Claudius killed his father? He (or she) also *seems* to want Hamlet to kill Claudius. But perhaps he (or she) only *really* wants Hamlet to *try* to kill Claudius. A trap? To make him compromise himself? Thus losing his claim to the throne, by ignominious default?

Indeed:

Might not Claudius himself be Author of the Apparition? To trick the Prince into punishable offences? This would square with the Apparition's insistence that Hamlet take no action against his mother. And yet . . . would Claudius be so considerate?

On the other hand:

If the Apparition was *not* sponsored by Claudius, why should it protect Gertrude from reprisals by Hamlet? Especially if it was so disgusted by Gertrude's lustfulness? These cogitations loop Hamlet back to the most important questions of all:

Is it TRUE that Claudius killed his father?

And:

Whether or not Claudius killed Old Hamlet, *did Claudius instigate the Apparition?*

Moreover:

How to answer such questions without creating a public outcry?

Hamlet's extramural monitoring has yielded little useful information in this area. Neither have the faithful scoutings undertaken by Marcellus and Bernardo.

One factor which bothers Hamlet – against Claudius having murdered Old Hamlet:

If Claudius was prepared to murder the King, main motives Gertrude and the crown, *why wait so long?* Years ago, he would have got Gertrude in her blossom, with less to fear from Hamlet. Why wait till now?

But, again:

Does that *really* argue Claudius' innocence?

Or a craven Hamletic hope that there was no murder at all? Hence no obligation to seek revenge? In fact:

Is Hamlet a moral coward?

Thus the doubts war in the Prince's lonely brain. He points Woden back towards the Castle, beneath clouds of scrambling snow. Twin cones of freezing vapour stream from the huge horse's flaring nostrils, as its rider frets on:

Is it *true* that Claudius seduced Gertrude long before the wedding? Hamlet doubts it. Surely he would have witnessed their illicit fornications from his subterranean grapevine. But if it is not true? Does the Apparition's suggestion that it *is* true imply that the Apparition was *not* authored by Claudius?

Or merely a Claudius scheme to goad Hamlet into premature folly?

Also:

Why did the Apparition give itself away so conclusively, by complaining of no last Catholic rites? Was this deliberate? An artful red herring?

Or sheer ignorance – so exonerating Claudius?

These wrestling possibilities make Hamlet's madness façade ever more convincing. Eyes red as smouldering coals in dark hollows, his sleep of late has been drained by a dreadful dream:

The Prince stands snooping behind the royal bedroom wall. His mother sprawls wanton across the bed, naked, legs apart. Claudius, also naked, pudgy puce, stalks the bed. His unsightly erection prongs squintly. As his uncle nears his itching mother, the royal tool expands and distorts horrifically. In seconds it balloons into a vast throbbing funnel of hungering tumescence. Gertrude's wide eyes scream in terror. A ghastly hoarse gurgle issues from the purple throat of Claudius' cavernous member. With a sadistic yell he lunges at her loins and sucks her into himself, genitals first, in a wet cacophony of snapping bones and gleety slurps. Hamlet howls in fear and rage, like an impotent small boy. Claudius whirls around, his eyes hellish scarlet and smoking. He heaves his belching megamember at the brickwork chink to which Hamlet is helplessly glued. Ingests his nephew's eyeballs through the wall.

Here the Prince awakes with a groan. Frozen, having kicked his coverlet to the floor, trembling, and steeped in icy sweat. Not since childhood has he had such dismal dreams.

Riding home, now, he shivers and shakes his head, to dislodge the nightmare memory. Around him flutter the first few flakes of a snowfall that soon will be severe.

Woden's hooves scrunch on the frozen cobbles of the carriage-way into outer Aarhus.

Quarter of a mile on, the Castle rises like the malignant crown of a gorgon's head, its reptilian turrets black-eyed with petrified menace.

Down a narrow cobbled sidestreet is the harbour, where labour the butchers and bakers and candlestick-makers, the unaspiring salt of Denmark's earth. Coarse unlovely housewives brave the cold and prepare their meals, as they have always done. Fishmongers sell their fish and curse their frozen fingers, as they have always done. In poky hovels toothless crones thaw brittle bones by homely hearths, and appraise the direst omens:

Whose favourite granddaughter had a miscarriage this week?

Whose chronic rheumatism betokens untold evils in the months to come?

Across the harbour snow falls blinding fast. All the vessels on the seafront are secured for the night. Sailors, dockers and all manner of men take willing refuge in the taverns. The arms build-up, the bruited ubiquity of secret police, political informers . . . all are forgotten for the stormbound night. Log fires crackle merrily. Brown beer bubbles warmly and exudes a nourishing aroma of burnt sugar.

In a dark corner sits Osric. Hot in dispute with two large bizarre characters in colourful clothes. These are tragedians from Copenhagen. Finding work scarce in the capital, they have followed the court to Aarhus, to grub some song-and-dance pennies. Round the bar, in odd pockets of busking pantomime, the other players perform for their supper. But pennies are not conspicuously forthcoming. Such is the state of the economy.

Osric's altercation is with the leader of the troupe and his son, two gruff and burly fellows of friable integrity. Osric is angry. His chubby pink cheeks flush danger crimson. Because his ship for

Norway has been delayed by the deteriorating weather?

Or is there some deeper difference between him and the senior players?

The latter keep their tempers, and the encounter ends abruptly when Osric stands, his complexion white with suppressed rage, hurls a purse of gold coin at the leading player, and storms out of the tavern.

In the next few days:

Laertes, in Paris, gives recitals of his latest lovesongs.

Ophelia, confined to quarters by Polonius, completes a savage tapestry.

Osric's ship, just short of Norway, meets that of Voltimand and Cornelius on its way back to Denmark. The boats heave to. Claudius' three emissaries swap notes.

Back in the cosy Aarhus tavern, the leading player and his son wrangle with Rosencrantz and Guildenstern, who have just arrived from Copenhagen. This confrontation is less acrimonious than that between the players and Osric:

The white-collar toadies outline a proposition;

The players affect reluctance;

A purse of gold changes hands;

The players' reluctance is overcome;

Rosencrantz and Guildenstern leave the tavern and head for the Castle;

The leading player gathers his team around him in an appetitive huddle.

Finally, in Norway, at the court of Fortinbras:

Osric speaks.

Fortinbras looks displeased. His eyes narrow. His heavy lips purse. He epitomizes the rational egoist sorely tried by errant underlings.

But Osric keeps his cool. He faces out Fortinbras' wrath, with qualities which Hamlet will later overlook.

8
PUBESCENT PRANKS

Polonius' study, before noon.

Polonius is briefing Reynaldo to spy on Laertes in Paris:

'Give him this money and these notes, Reynaldo.'

'I will, my lord.'

'You will do marvellous wisely, good Reynaldo, before you visit him, to make inquiry about his behaviour.'

'My lord, I did intend it.' Reynaldo pockets the documents.

'First inquire what Danes are in Paris. Where they live. At what expense. The company they keep. And if they know my son, then use your wits to tease their confidence.

'You might affect distant knowledge of him. Say, "I know his father, his friends – " Are you *listening*, Reynaldo?' Polonius is exasperated by Reynaldo's apparent glazed inattention.

'Indeed, my lord.' With the assurance of an infallible memory.

'Yes,' Polonius proceeds at double volume. 'Say *that* you know him. But not *well*. Feign that you remember him as very wild, addicted, and so forth. Indeed, charge him with what forgeries you please, but do not *dishonour* him. Keep to such wanton slips as youth is noted for.'

'Gambling, my lord?'

'Or drinking. Fencing, swearing, quarrelling. Whoring. You may go so far.'

'My lord! That *would* dishonour him.' But the agent doesn't look dismayed.

Polonius bridles:

'No,' he brays. 'Not if you are artful. Do not accuse him of total debauchery. That's not my meaning. But breathe his faults quaintly, as the mere extravagances of a fiery mind and untamed blood, to which young men are liable.'

'But . . .'

'Why do I bid you do this?'

Reynaldo nods curiously.

Polonius obliges:

'When you lay these slight sullies on my son, the other party will say, "I know the gentleman; I saw him yesterday . . .", and thus you will discover his behaviour and the company he keeps.'

Reynaldo nods admiringly.

Polonius beams like a tickled full moon. Accepts Reynaldo's tribute as a dry sponge accepts moisture. Rises from his desk and struts to and fro. His originally splendid but long-unwashed robes rustle over the rugs on the cold tiled floor.

'You will find out when he has been gambling,' the eloquence gushes. 'When the worse for liquor. When to a brothel. And so forth. In this way, a bait of falsehood hooks a carp of truth.'

Reynaldo yawns inwardly.

Polonius concludes:

'So shall you unearth my son's activities in Paris. Understand?'

'I do, my lord.'

'And make such direct observations as you can, when you visit him.'

'I shall, my lord.'

'And let him ply his music.' Polonius thinks of the arts as wonderful distractions for potential subversives.

'Indeed, my lord.'

'Farewell!'

Reynaldo bows. Marches out of his master's study. Departs for Paris.

A throaty chuckle issues like a moist eructation from Polonius' grey-whiskered maw, as he relishes his taste for power. He turns to the paperwork on the desk but is foiled by the sudden distraught entry of Ophelia.

She is pale, pink-eyed, and looks starved of sleep. Her stiff carriage, crumpled face, and frumpish dress (buttoned to the Adam's apple) radiate maidenly distress.

'What's wrong, Ophelia?' her father exclaims.

'Oh!' she groans. 'My lord, I have been so *affrighted*!'

'With what, by God?' Polonius seizes his dimpled daughter's

chin. Turns her head to meet his sceptical scrutiny. He trusts no one totally, and Ophelia less than most.

'My lord,' she gulps, 'as I was sewing in my closet, Lord Hamlet came before me. His doublet all undone, stockings ungartered around his ankles. His skin pale as his shirt. His knees knocking together. And he looked on me as if from hell, to speak of horrors.'

'Mad for your love?'

'Truly I do fear it.'

'What did he say?' Polonius is not convinced, but he releases his daughter's chin.

Tears glisten authentically in Ophelia's eyes. She unsleeves a dainty perfumed handkerchief, dabs her trickling cheeks, and relates:

'He took me by the wrist, and held me hard. His other hand against his brow, he perusalled my face as if to draw it. At last I ventured to shake my arm a little. He nodded three times, and raised a piteous sigh that seemed to shatter all his being. That done, he let me go. As he left, his head turned back over his shoulder, and his eyes to the last, bended their light on *me*.'

Polonius nods mechanically. Frowns thoughtfully.

Ophelia chokes a sob.

Has she convinced her father?

Polonius struts; tuts; muses plosively.

Ophelia sniffles bravely, remembering what really happened.

She had been touching herself, after her bath.

Hamlet, secreted and peeping, had been synchronously masturbating. He had been suffering for days from chronic erections, a by-product of his sleepless nights. As he watched Ophelia achieving her unsatisfying frenzy, he found himself unable. No matter how hard he pulled, his orgasm would not come. He was stuck, in fact, with an awful, dry, aching boner – such as only ravaging time or the thirsty thighs of a lubricated partner could succour.

Well, thought Hamlet. She wants it. I want it. And I am supposed to be mad. So? I am going to give it to her.

He peeled off his clothes in the passage behind the wall, retaining only his bearskin to parry the cold and conceal his nudity. Entered Polonius' house through the fireplace in Laertes' room, thus avoiding embarrassing encounters with Polonius' household staff. Finally, he crossed the landing from Laertes' door to Ophelia's, glanced quickly right and left, and slipped noiselessly into Ophelia's bedchamber.

Ophelia's nakedness spun round from her mirror on the wall. This great hairy blur in the corner of her eye she found alarming.

Oh, my lord, she gasped, seeing Hamlet and the hairy blur were one. Her left forearm flashed across her proudly jutting breasts and her right hand shot down to screen her creamy black bush.

Oh, my *lord*, she hissed incredulously, when Hamlet's bristling bearskin fell open to disclose his rearing shaft. Ophelia's excitement was not at the enormity of Hamlet's organ, but at its unheralded presence, visibility, and twitching stiffness – since she far prefers quivering keenness to horribly hanging hugeness. After her initial shock, accordingly, she sank gratefully to her knees.

Oh, my lord, she murmured. Cradled the royal scrotum in her cupped palms. Took his cranium of inflamed flesh between full red lips licked wet with anticipation.

Hamlet, saying nothing, flapped his bearskin about her shoulders. His crusted eyes defied his mirror image.

Ophelia's tongue combed the head of his hardness. Her lips compressed tightly. Rhythmically she rocked the roots of his fundament.

Hamlet was amazed by her aptitude. And disgusted. Bending gingerly, lest her sharp teeth wound him, he gripped Ophelia's ears. Pulled her upright. Slowly, almost tenderly, as in a hypnotic trance, he turned her round and folded her over the many-hued patchwork coverlet on her four-poster bed. Leant over her. Encircling her unprotesting trunk and squeezing her penduling breasts with his right hand. Sliding his left through her thighs, to establish moist receptivity. Electrifying the golden hair that tumbled down her back and over his pubes.

Entering her from the rear.

He felt her whole body bark with excitement.

Powerful muscles closed knowingly around his predatory prong.

Ophelia moaned. Her bulging eyes glistened like those of an ovulating rabbit. Across her breasts a roseate flush howled *Lust* twice as loud as a donkey's erection.

Then Hamlet went sexually berserk.

Poking and bucking, lunging and rearing, heaving and ploughing, on and on. All the fears and tensions of weeks' insomnia he shafted between her bouncing buttocks and up into her yearning emptiness.

Ophelia came almost immediately, in a riot of crescent yells and pelvic shudders. Hamlet had to hold her shoulders down, to prevent her bouncing right off him and over the bed. His erection was still dry as old camel bones, and he was determined to get a good orgasm out of it, after going to so much trouble. So, on and *on again*, he plunged and arched and thrust with all his might. Dribbles of pasty perspiration fell from his nipples to his navel, and sucked around Ophelia's dancing derrière, but still he felt no come to come.

And as he plumed and piledrove between Ophelia's whinnying hams, the Prince's mind's eye wavered back to the years of his sexual peak, in Copenhagen. He had a girl then with breasts like huge wild aubergines. Her big purple nipples would frot tantalizingly against his own, as she cavorted possessively on top of him. This erectile strumming mined a vein of pure pleasure from the Prince's puckered anus to some archaic anchor in his neck. As the fandango apexed in his loins, Hamlet would experience a volley of secondary orgasms in his Adam's apple.

Such frills of physical gratification he now finds wearisome. After rogering Ophelia for twenty solid minutes, and lifting her to a high plateau of nonstop whimpering climax, what gratification had *he* to show for it?

Intimations of exhaustion, burning genital discomfort, and dry unsatisfaction still.

Determined to consummate the violation, Hamlet renewed his exertions with unprecedented savagery.

Ophelia's melted whimpering steamed into a shameless shriek of debauched disbelief.

Blattering her already pulverized vulva, the Prince glanced jerkily around her room, hungrily scanning for an image to blissify his recalcitrant glands.

One of Ophelia's wall-hung tapestries caught his jumping attention:

Two muscular wrestlers – naked, entwined, tussling and gloatingly masturbating one another. This picture jolted the Prince to recollect Rosencrantz and Guildenstern, and the intense sexual fantasies and explorations of his teens.

In his early Copenhagen days the pubescent Hamlet was compulsively fascinated by all things genital. Was it possible, he wondered, to infer a man's gonadic endowment from his facial features and social deportment?

Or vice versa?

Lusting for knowledge, the licensed Prince threw a dinner party of outrageous opulence and ostentation. To this he invited his waggish contemporaries, and a complement of buxom chambermaids, dancers, and other ladies of manageable virtue. After a gastronomic experience of aphrodisiac splendour, the two parties were coaxed to the games room. This was divided down its length by a thick velvet curtain. Ladies to one side; gentlemen to the other.

All present to disrobe:

Gentlemen in modestly screened-off cubicles of tailored velvet, befitting their aristocratic standing; ladies in the communal nakedness of the socially negligible. Attention was then directed to cunningly flapped apertures, at pelvic height, leading from the cells of the men to the open prison of the women. The bucks had next to protrude themselves, anonymously, through these apertures.

Now:

Could the ladies judge whom they were servicing, by genitals alone?

In fact the giggling speculations were never collated, since the jest-crazed Hamlet suddenly opted to spoil his own experiment. Exercising his host's prerogative, he slunk round the velvet partition and joined the ladies. Shushing the gaping dames, the Prince, his own virile figure at half-mast, knelt between the pube-high apertures where evidence of Rosencrantz and Guildenstern should shortly appear. He indicated, pointedly, that all but two of the busty bawds should ply their contracted business, the remaining pair to stand by him.

Soon:

Predictable gasps and gulps and splutters began. The six asymmetrical marriage prospects of Rosencrantz and Guildenstern appeared hesitantly in their windows of wrinkled crimson, limply bourgeois and embarrassed. Hamlet tickled his buff apprentices into a suitable serenade. His own regal mitts took the proffered consortia of flaccid genitalia. Tenderly he teased the reluctant poles of Rosencrantz and Guildenstern into mediocre stiffness. These he then hauled gleefully, imagining the turgied indignation to come, while Playmate One crawled between his legs to nibble the furl of his yardarm and Playmate Two massaged his nipples and banged his ears with her enormous globular mammaries.

Those, then, were Hamlet's perverse associations as he plundered Ophelia against her groaning four-poster.

Aaah! Oooooh! she shrieked and wailed. Aaaaah! Ooooooooh!

Fixated on a double-image of Rosencrantz and Guildenstern coughing up their measly jissom, on the one hand, and their cold mean fishfaces when later apprised of the prank, on the other hand, Hamlet suddenly climaxed like a lost Greek tragedy.

Feeling as though his wilting loins had discharged a cannonball, the Prince disengaged immediately.

Might not Polonius have heard his daughter's caterwaul?

Hamlet left Ophelia without a word, but with a stinging spank on her streaming rump.

Abandoned, she lay face down on her patchwork coverlet for many minutes, twitching in helpless ecstasy.

Prowling back to his room, behind the Castle walls, Hamlet gave no thought to possible repercussions from Ophelia. His mind looped Rosencrantz and Guildenstern. They had never forgiven him for the light-hearted porno stunt he pulled in Copenhagen. So . . . why had they been sent for? Was Claudius aware of their grudges against Hamlet? If so, how would the King direct their oily services to his nephew's disadvantage? This question swung like a pendulum in Hamlet's mind until he sank gratefully into his first nourishing slumber for weeks.

While Ophelia lay awake and wondered.

She isn't convinced that Hamlet is mad, yet why should he fake derangement?

Either way, what a husband!

If he has gone cuckoo? Surely cuckoo intercourse is twice as nice. Especially when the cuck in question may soon be King.

And if Hamlet isn't mad?

Then, Ophelia reckons, his sexual indiscretion arms her with a big enough stick to beat him into the nuptial net.

Hence the tearful expurgation she recites to Polonius. He, in turn, is now less hostile to a lawful union between Ophelia and Hamlet. Now Claudius is securely throned. And provided the succession eventually reverts to Hamlet, as Polonius believes it must, a marriage between Hamlet and Ophelia would make Polonius unassailable:

Grandfather to Kings of Denmark!

Such are the beetling thoughts behind the bumptious brow that pirouettes agitatedly before the penitent posture of tear-stained Ophelia.

'Come,' Polonius decides. 'Come with me. I will go seek the King. This is the very ecstasy of love. Its violent nature undoes itself and . . . Have you given him hard words of late?'

Ophelia's gaze remains downcast. She dams a rolling tear.

'No, my good lord,' she replies. 'But, as you did command, I did repel his letters, and denied him access to me.'

'That has made him mad!' Polonius unites his desiccated palms in a thin eureka clap.

Ophelia notes with smug satisfaction that her father seems won to the prospect of royalty in the family.

'I am sorry', Polonius burbles, 'that I did not pay more serious heed. I feared he did but trifle, and meant to ruin you. Curse my jealousy! Come. To the King. This must be known.'

9
FORGERIES

A large official room.

Claudius and Gertrude, lavishly attended, are receiving Rosencrantz and Guildenstern.

Incinerating pine trunks perfume the air, yet the cold is cancerous. The royal couple are dressed as sumptuously as the temperature allows. Gertrude's magnetic bosom is well muffled. Exhalations freeze instantly. Claudius gestures expressively with his goblet of hot spiced wine.

An hour of Castle time has passed since Ophelia deceived Polonius.

'Welcome, dear Rosencrantz and Guildenstern!' Claudius booms. Belches.

No eyelids bat.

'You have heard something', the King continues, 'of Hamlet's transformation? What – other than his father's death – has deranged him so, I cannot dream of. So I entreat you both, who spent your youth with him and are familiar with his humour, stay in our court some time. Draw him on to pleasures. And gather if something unknown to us afflicts him. Which, if revealed, might be in our power to remedy.'

'Good gentlemen,' Gertrude diplomatically lies, 'he has talked about you much. To no men living does he more adhere. Help us and your visitation shall receive much thanks.'

Rosencrantz and Guildenstern bow from their ankles. They see through Gertrude's buttering bounty. But, such is her radiance, they are flattered and grateful nonetheless. Simpering in her limelight smile:

'Your majesties,' chirps Rosencrantz, 'might put your royal pleasure to *command.*'

'But we *obey*,' lisps Guildenstern, through narrow white nostrils, 'and lay our service freely at your feet.'

'Thanks, Rosencrantz and gentle Guildenstern.' Claudius swigs. His mind seems already elsewhere.

'Thanks, Guildenstern and gentle Rosencrantz.' Gertrude corrects the democratic balance in dulcet tones. Her thoughtful involvement reflects concern for Hamlet's welfare.

'And I beseech you,' she directs, 'visit my changèd son this instant. Go, some of you,' she waves imperiously at various attendants. 'Take these gentlemen to Hamlet.' A fading blonde wisp escapes from her disciplined coiffure and settles fetchingly on her forehead.

'May heaven make our presence helpful to him,' gushes Guildenstern, as he and Rosencrantz bow away, shepherded by expressionless courtiers.

'Amen!' Anguished sincerity powers Gertrude's sigh.

But her emotion is eclipsed by the bustling entry of Polonius, who has been braving the cruel corridor cold for several minutes. Partly to eavesdrop; partly to secure a richer reception.

'The ambassadors from Norway, my good lord,' he announces triumphantly, 'are joyfully returned.'

'Always have you fathered goodly news,' Claudius rumbles distantly.

'Have I, my lord?' Polonius, adept at dispensing flattery, is himself completely addicted. This applause for fathering good news diverts his thoughts to the other 'good news'.

'I assure you, my good lord,' he gabbles, 'I hold my duty important as my soul. And I do think, that I have found the *cause of Hamlet's lunacy*!'

'Oh! Speak of that!' Claudius snaps out of his reverie with a roar. 'That I do *long* to hear.'

Polonius is startled by the ardour of the King's response to his second disclosure. Why? Because he doesn't know that Voltimand and Cornelius have *already* reported to Claudius: while Polonius was hearing Ophelia's confession. Since Polonius had told Voltimand and Cornelius to report to *him* first, he cannot fathom Claudius' apparent lack of interest in the news from Norway.

'First, admit the ambassadors,' Polonius advises. 'My news shall be the fruit to that great feast.'

Claudius does not wish Polonius to suspect his private dealings with Voltimand and Cornelius, so he resigns himself to postponing the analysis of Hamlet's madness.

'Very well,' he assents. 'Bring them in.'

Polonius struts away to fetch the ambassadors.

Claudius launches a sarcastic aside at his wife:

'He tells me, dear Gertrude, that he has found the source of your son's distemper.'

'I think it only what we suspected.' She shakes her head uneasily. 'His father's death and our most hasty marriage.'

'We shall see.'

Clomp, clomp.

Polonius returns breezily.

Voltimand and Cornelius follow.

Voltimand, taking care not to trip on his trailing robes, carries their black dispatch-box.

Claudius drinks deeply. Braces himself for a convincing performance:

'Welcome, my good friends. Say, Voltimand. What news from our brother Norway?'

'Most fair,' Voltimand recites. 'He sent out immediately to suppress his nephew's armies. These had appeared to him a preparation against the Poles. Looking more closely, he found them truly aimed against your highness. Greatly grieved, his age and sickness thus abused, he orders that Fortinbras desist.

'Fortinbras, in brief, obeys. Accepts his uncle's rebuke, and vows never more to scheme against your majesty. Old Norway, in joy at this, bequeaths to Fortinbras three thousand crowns, and grants he lead his soldiers, after all, against the Poles.

'He further entreats your majesty,' Voltimand rummages in his dispatch-box and flourishes a scroll, 'to let his nephew quietly through your dominions in pursuit of this enterprise; on conditions, and with safeguards, as said herein.'

Claudius takes the scroll. Affects to peruse it with pleasant Kingly surprise.

(Across the grey waves, in Fredrikstad, Fortinbras is loading troops and equipment on to transport ships. A chilly aura of disciplined energy prevails. Terse orders are quietly spoken and effectively carried out. Occasional cavalry chargers snort and kick in highly-strung anticipation.)

Polonius and the courtiers applaud the Norway news.

Claudius voices the general mood:

'We are well pleased. Soon we'll read and answer. Meanwhile, thanks for your success. Go rest. At night we'll feast together. Most welcome home.'

Voltimand and Cornelius exit, bowing, bland as ever.

Claudius secretes the scroll, which he knows to be an artful forgery, within his voluminous robes. He burps again and turns to Polonius, who is agog to impart his other 'good news'.

'This business is well ended.' Polonius approves Voltimand's report. Then, with a deep breath:

'My lord, and madam, to discuss what majesty should be, what duty is, why day is day, night night, and time time, would merely waste day, night, and time. Therefore, since brevity is the soul of wit, I will be brief. Your noble son is mad. Mad, I *call* it. For to *define* true madness, need one not be mad oneself? But let that go.'

'More fire; less smoke.' Gertrude's rebuke is spoken sharply. Polonius is not her favourite person. Nor is she party to Claudius' reasons for staying in the old man's good books.

'Madam,' Polonius amplifies wounded humility, 'I swear I blow no smoke at all!' He bows innocently to Gertrude, who sniffs.

'Mad, let us grant him,' Polonius piffles on. 'It now remains to find the cause of this defect. For this defective effect can only be effected by some cause. Which nears the heart of the matter. I pray you, mark my words.

'I have a daughter, at least while she is still mine,' he refers obliquely to the property rites attending marriage, 'who in her obedience, has given me *this*.' He plucks a letter from his awning plumes. 'Now, I pray you, listen and surmise:

'"To the celestial, and my soul's idol, the most beautified Ophelia . . ." That's an ill phrase; "beautified" is a *vile* phrase. But I shall read you the rest. Thus:

'"In her excellent white bosom . . ."'

'From *Hamlet*? To *her*?' Gertrude is no poet, but her mother's intuition doubts that Hamlet could have penned such doggerel. She edges towards Polonius, to squint at the letter.

He shrinks back in stately horror.

'Good madam,' he blares indignantly. 'Stay awhile. I will be faithful.' He smooths his ruffled feathers. Shakes the letter out of Gertrude's reach, as though to dislodge a spider. And ominously reads:

> Doubt that the stars are fire:
> And that the sun's above;
> Doubt truth to be a liar;
> But never doubt I love.

Oh, dear Ophelia! I have not skill enough to versify my groans. But do believe I love you best; oh, most best! Adieu.

Yours evermore, dear lady, whilst this body is mine,

Hamlet.

Polonius sighs:

'Similarly have I heard of his solicitings, as they reached her.' He shakes his head heavily, like a reluctant pontiff.

The letter, needless to say, is a forgery. Who wrote it? Ophelia. Who devised it? Polonius. The old man is now so determined to mix royal blood with his own that he leaves nothing to chance. Since Ophelia could not produce any love-letters from Hamlet, ostensibly having repelled them all, Polonius decided, lest the King and Queen suspect the verbal testimony of an interested maiden, to dictate a love-letter and have Ophelia forge Hamlet's hand.

How?

She copied Hamlet's writing from some lyrics, wheedled from him under the umbrella of starry-eyed admiration in times of less intransigence. But her heart was afire with foreboding. How could she now confess to Polonius that there *never had been* any letters or tender protestations? Consequently, she realizes with growing trepidation, it is *she* who hardens Polonius' conviction that Hamlet is truly mad.

Of course, Polonius *wants* Hamlet to be mad. Otherwise? Love of Ophelia cannot have caused his madness, and Polonius' dreams of royal grandchildren dissolve. So? Duped by Ophelia's deceit into

85

having her forge a letter (for which, unknown to him, there were never any originals), Polonius thought it too dangerous for her to appear before the royal couple when he produced the bogus missive. In case her girlish gaucheness gave the game away. That's why he changed his mind and made her stay at home.

'How has she received his love?' Claudius inquires. *He* would prefer Hamlet to be sane, hence punishable. But, *if* Hamlet is authentically mad, Claudius is not averse to thwarted passion being the cause.

Gertrude frowns severely. Her noble brow wrinkles in silent anger. Ophelia, like Polonius, is one of the Queen's least favourite people.

Polonius senses the scepticism of the King and the hostility of the Queen.

'My lord,' he blares, man-to-King, 'what do you think of me?'

'As a faithful and honourable man.' Claudius gives nothing away in his gracious reply.

Polonius knows it:

'I would gladly prove so,' he acknowledges. 'But what might you think if, when I saw this hot love wing, I had ignored it?

'No! I went quickly to admonish my young mistress. "Lord Hamlet is a Prince, beyond your station," I said. "This must not be." And I had her lock herself away, admit no messengers and receive no tokens. He, repulsed, fell into a sadness, thence to a fast, to sleeplessness, distractedness; and by this declension, into the madness where now he raves, and we all mourn for.'

During this rhapsody by Polonius, Hamlet himself arrives behind the wall. Suffering from bad conscience and physical aches from his sexual exertions with Ophelia. Black rings his eyes, despite his recent slumber, and he has been drinking. As he eavesdrops, he fiddles furiously with his beard – twisting hairs from their follicles by the roots, leaving sore red eruptions all over his chin.

The Prince has missed Polonius' disclosure of the letter, but he is quick to catch the drift. And he sneers as Polonius labours to convince the royals that his daughter's inaccessible charms are the fount of Hamlet's disarray.

Claudius, unwilling to commit himself, invites Gertrude's opinion:

'Do you think it is this?'

'It *may* be.'

The Queen's cool aloofness generates heat beneath Polonius' grimy collar. He turns tempestuously to Claudius. Leans heavily on his reputation:

'Has there ever been a time when I have positively said, "It is so," and it turned out otherwise?'

'Not that I know,' Claudius automatically lies. His eyes flush with weariness and blurring befuddlement. He doesn't want to upset Gertrude, yet he mustn't offend Polonius.

Polonius pursues this advantage.

'Take this chain of office from my neck, if I am wrong in this,' he gambles carefully.

Hamlet is unimpressed by Polonius' impassioned bravado. He slinks away to a solitary fireplace through which to re-enter public space.

Claudius yawns.

'How may we test your theory?' he asks Polonius.

'You know he walks hours at a time, here in the lobby?'

'He does indeed,' Gertrude concedes.

Polonius proposes to Claudius:

'I will meet him with my daughter. You and I, if your majesty agrees, will be concealed behind a tapestry. If it transpire that love of her is *not* the feller of his reason, then let me keep a farm, and carters.'

'We will try it.' There is a tinge of menace in Claudius' throaty assent. But . . .

'Look!' exclaims Gertrude. 'The poor wretch comes reading.'

In shuffles Hamlet, apparently wrapt in writ. Certainly he looks mad enough, nosepicking and dishevelled.

As the Prince anticipates, his entrance panics Polonius. He believes Hamlet *is* mad, but *how* mad?

And what if Claudius and Gertrude quiz Hamlet on the love-letter he is supposed to have written?

'Away!' Polonius hisses at the royal couple with furtive urgency. 'I'll accost him.'

Claudius, aching for a snooze, gallantly takes Gertrude's hand. Leads the company out by the south door. This leaves Polonius to tackle Hamlet, who dithers distractedly by the north door.

Hamlet is apparently oblivious to the exodus south.

Polonius pulsates with relief. He approaches the poring Prince. Petitions ingratiatingly:

'How does my good Lord Hamlet?'

'Passing well.' Without looking up.

'Do you know me, my lord?'

Hamlet rolls a drunkard eye:

'You are a fishmonger.'

In Denmark 'fishmonger's daughter' is colloquial for 'whore'. But the slur is lost on Polonius.

'Not I, my lord,' he disclaims earnestly.

'Then I wish you were so honest.'

'*Honest*, my lord!?'

'Yes, sir. To be honest is to be one man in ten thousand.' Hamlet shambles past Polonius.

'That's very true, my lord.' Polonius pursues. The irony hits the wall beside him and falls writhing to the floor.

Hamlet leaps on a lunatic tangent:

'For if the son spawn simians in a succulent strumpet,' he roars and rounds on Polonius, causing the old man to shrink in terror, 'she being a sucker of substance . . .'

Then a pause.

Hamlet circles the hall in agitation, like a man whose memory threads have snapped.

Polonius follows at a nervous distance.

'Have you a daughter?' Hamlet asks suddenly. Kingly. As if . . . what greater misfortune?

Polonius is bewildered:

'I have, my lord.'

'Let her not walk in the sun,' advises Hamlet, ecclesiastically. 'Conception is a blessing. But, as your daughter may conceive, friend, take care.' *Again* 'sun' with 'son'.

Polonius does not notice the pun.

Or how Hamlet loads 'conceive': warning Polonius lest his daughter get pregnant, *and* hinting at Ophelia's risky schemes. The deluded manipulator continues up the wrong tree.

'Listen to that!' he mutters. 'Still harping on my daughter. Yet he knew me not at first. Said I was a fishmonger! He is *far* gone. As when in youth, *I* suffered much for love. Very near this. I'll speak to him again.'

Hamlet squats by the hearth. Flicks through his diary.

Polonius approaches:

'What do you read, my lord?'

'*Words!*'

'What is the *matter*, my lord?'

'Between who?'

'I mean the matter that you *read*, my lord?'

Polonius' soapy solicitudes finally goad Hamlet into definitive detestation. He leaps to his feet. Snaps shut his diary. Chases the First Minister round the room.

'Slanders, sir,' the Prince jeers. 'For the satirical rogue says here,' he thumps his diary, 'that old men have grey beards. That their faces are wrinkled. That their eyes excrete thick resin and plum-tree gum. And that they have a most plentiful lack of wit, together with most weak hams. All of which, sir, though I most powerfully believe it, yet I hold it not honesty writ thus. For yourself, sir, would grow old as I am, if, like a crab, you could go backwards.' Hamlet desists abruptly.

Polonius gibbers by the north door.

Hamlet returns to the fireplace with his diary.

'Though this be madness,' Polonius hisses, 'yet there is method in it.' He hems. 'May it please you walk out of here, my lord?' He calls as if concerned for the Prince's health.

'Into my grave?'

'Indeed,' Polonius puzzles, 'that *is* out of here.' He twitches by the door, uneager to be hounded round the room again. Mumbles:

'How pregnant his replies can be! A happiness that madness often hits, when sanity could not. I will leave him, and contrive his sudden meeting with my daughter.'

'My honourable lord,' his dignity reinflates, 'I humbly take my leave of you.'

'You cannot, sir, take any thing that I will more willingly part with. Except my LIFE!' Hamlet rises to a hysterical sob.

'Fare you well, my lord.' Polonius exits hastily.

Hamlet retches a gizzard-green gob into the fire's hissing heart.

'These tedious old fools!' he exclaims to the blaze.

10
FENCING

A dank corridor.

Polonius flusters into Rosencrantz and Guildenstern.

They have been wandering the Castle in search of Hamlet. Failing to find him has soured their tempers, but this they conceal from Polonius, who is enormously their superior.

'You seek the Lord Hamlet,' Polonius presumes. 'There he is.' He points pettishly and sweeps away.

Rosencrantz and Guildenstern bow after him.

'God save you, sir!' Rosencrantz calls respectfully.

He and Guildenstern then venture where Hamlet is harboured. They find him crouched by the fire, clasping his diary against his knees, watching phantoms in the flames.

'Mine honoured lord!'

'My most dear lord!' Rosencrantz choruses smoothly.

Long moments expire before the Prince stirs. He turns to his visitors slowly. It appears difficult for him to focus. Then, to their relief, he reverts to near normalcy.

'My excellent good friends!' He takes Guildenstern's hand. 'How are you Guildenstern? Ah, Rosencrantz! How are you both?'

What could be more cordial. Yet:

'We are as the children of the earth.' Rosencrantz's response is polite but cool.

'Happy,' expounds Guildenstern, 'that we are not *too* happy. On Fortune's cap we are not the bobble.'

'Nor the soles of her shoes?'

'Neither, my lord.' Rosencrantz takes refuge in negativity.

'Then,' Hamlet pounces like a brash young scholar, 'you live about her waist, or in the middle of her favours?'

'Yes,' allows Guildenstern, defensively. 'We are – '

'In the secret parts of Fortune?' – Hamlet mouths obscenely. 'Most true! She is a strumpet.'

Rosencrantz and Guildenstern exchange galled glances.

Is this the filthy-minded madman they must . . .

Hamlet catches them off balance:

'What news?' he demands quietly.

'None, my lord.' Rosencrantz pretends not to understand Hamlet's fishing. 'Except that the world's grown honest.'

'Then doomsday is near! But your news is not true. Let me question you more precisely. How have you, my good friends, offended Fortune, that she sends you to prison hither?'

'Prison, my lord!' exclaims Guildenstern.

'Denmark's a prison,' Hamlet announces resignedly, as if commenting on the weather.

'Then the whole world is a prison.' Rosencrantz suggests that since the whole world is *not* a prison, Denmark cannot be a prison either.

Hamlet is unmoved by such trivial wool-pulling.

'The whole world is, indeed, a goodly prison,' he concurs. 'Containing many dungeons and torture-chambers. Denmark is one of the worst.' He sighs.

'We do not agree, my lord,' Rosencrantz dissents optimistically.

'Why, then, it is no prison to *you*. For nothing is bad until thinking makes it so. To me, the world is a prison.'

'Why, then your *ambition* makes it so,' Rosencrantz hypothesizes. If *he* were Hamlet, and mad, it would be thwarted ambition which had made him mad. Therefore? Hamlet, if mad, *must* be mad because of thwarted ambition!

'The world', Rosencrantz projects fawningly, 'is too narrow for your mind.'

Hamlet smites his brow.

'Oh God!' he wails. 'I could be imprisoned in a nutshell, and still count myself a king of infinite space, were it not that I have bad dreams.' He heaves a hollow sob.

'But these dreams, my lord,' Guildenstern urges, 'are themselves ambition. For even the successes of the ambitious are but the shadows of their dreams.'

'A dream itself is but a shadow.'

91

Rosencrantz jumps at the Prince's baited abstraction:

'Truly,' he applauds. 'And ambition is but a shadow's shadow.' He and Guildenstern smirk like precocious schoolgirls.

Hamlet plays puzzled. Then he breaks into brutal burlesque:

'In that case, our lowly beggars are bodies. And our greatly aspiring monarchs and dead heroes are but the beggars' shadows . . . Shall we go seek the court?' The Prince bows a parody of the squirming pair before him. 'For, upon my word, I seem unable to reason.'

Rosencrantz and Guildenstern seek sanctuary in a courtly deference:

'We'll wait upon you.'

'Not at all,' says Hamlet. 'I will not class you with the *rest* of my servants. For, to tell the *truth*, I am most dreadfully attended. But tell me, for *friendship's* sake, what brought you here?'

Rosencrantz protests:

'We come to visit *you*, my lord. No other reason.'

Hamlet tuts in disgust. Pads round them like a hungry tiger. Draws his dagger. Thoughtfully tests its edge against his thumb. Appears to wrestle with some knotty problem. Then:

'Beggar that I am,' he rails. 'I am even poor in thanks. But I thank you. And you may be sure, my dear friends, that my thanks are not worth a halfpenny.'

Rosencrantz licks his lips.

Hamlet forestalls him in a menacingly friendly falsetto:

'Were you not *sent* for? Is it your *own* inclination that brings you here? Is this a *free* visitation? Come, come. Deal justly with me. Speak.'

'What should we say, my lord?' Guildenstern's question reflects his limp helplessness.

But Hamlet is not a compassionate man.

'Why, *anything*,' he insists. 'So long as it is to the point. You *were* sent for. And there is a confession in your looks which your modesties can't conceal. I *know* the good King sent for you.'

'To what end, my lord?' stalls Rosencrantz.

'That you must teach me. But let me *implore* you, by the obligation of our ever-preservèd love, and by whatever more eloquent appeal, be honest! Were you sent for?'

The Prince's sarcasm reduces Rosencrantz and Guildenstern to mumbling. Their reluctance to admit that they *have* been sent for is grounded in fear of Claudius.

'What shall we say?' Rosencrantz mutters to Guildenstern.

But Hamlet hears.

'I see through you,' he sings over his prowling shoulder. 'If you *love* me, don't *deceive* me.'

'My lord, we were sent for,' Guildenstern confesses.

'Very well,' Hamlet sighs. '*I* will tell *you* why. This way, your feathered secrecy to the King need not moult.

'I have of late (I know not why) lost all my mirth. Given up all my customs and exercises. My disposition is so jaded that this goodly earth seems nothing but a sterile promontory.' Hamlet warms to his smokescreen: puzzling prolixity to distract his auditors from the probing they have just received. He points at the tapestried walls. Lifts his gaze to the ancient-cobwebbed ceiling. And billows:

'This excellent canopy, the air;' he waves, 'this brave overhanging firmament, the sky;' he clasps his hands, 'this majestical roof of golden fire, the heavens?' he salutes. 'All a foul congregation of vapours!' He pauses to spit on the fire.

'What a piece of work is a man!' he next exclaims. 'How *noble* in reason!' He shakes his head in wonder. 'How *infinite* in faculty!' He gasps. 'In form, in moving, how well executed and *admirable*!' He sighs. 'In action, how like an *angel*! In understanding, like a *god*! The beauty of the world! The paragon of animals!

'And yet, to me, what is this quintessence of dust?' He spits again. Petulantly. Like a schoolboy. 'Man delights me not.' He scowls. 'Nor woman. Though your smiling seems to say so.' He rounds aggressively on Rosencrantz.

'My lord,' the smirker vows, 'nothing was further from my thoughts.'

'Why then did you laugh, when I said *man* delights me not?'

'Because, my lord, if man delights you not, the players will be disappointed. We passed them on our way. Coming hither, to offer you service.'

This comes like an icicle from the blue.

Hamlet freezes.

93

Behind his eyes a multitude of memories erupt.

He desperately needs time to think. To gain this, he mounts his Russian Bear charade. Goggles his eyes and snorts a great snort. Bends his elbows and knees, and capers round the hall, grunting and growling.

Gnumph, gnumph, he lumbers, pawing his chest. *Gnumph, gnumph, gnumph.*

Rosencrantz and Guildenstern are destabilized once more. As their faces crinkle in alarm at Hamlet's antics, his molten thoughts pour back to his prime obsession:

Who could have enacted the Old-Hamlet Apparition?

If not . . . the Player King?

The leader of the Copenhagen Tragedians!

Few men have the height, breadth, depth of voice, histrionic accomplishment, and sheer gall to impersonate his father, never mind his father's ghost. And who more splendidly qualified than the Player King of Copenhagen?

But if the Apparition was indeed the Player King, again, *who put him up to it?* Also:

Are Rosencrantz and Guildenstern involved?

Until now the Prince has been toying with his former comrades, secure in the knowledge that they couldn't *know* he knew Claudius had sent for them. He also knows he isn't mad, whereas they can only suspect this. Thus, Hamlet has been gambling on his presumed information advantage. But now the awful suspicion hits him that he has only been making a fool of himself. That his ostensible dupes have been playing along with him, to ensnare him all the more.

How to regain the upper hand?

As these high-pressure questions throb, Hamlet continues his lunatic ursine play for time.

Gnumph, gnumph . . .

He charges at Rosencrantz, clawing the air, until their noses touch.

Rosencrantz squirms. His eyes appeal sideways to Guildenstern, who fidgets and coughs. The last thing they want is a physical encounter with Hamlet, against whom they would fare worse than two poodles against a leopard.

The Prince senses that his antic aggression has won back some psychological ground. Accordingly, he diverts again, to a more dignified plane. Holds his head, as if suffering from a severe migraine. Sits down suddenly. Blinks like someone returning from a hypnotic trance.

Relief colours the pallor of Rosencrantz and Guildenstern.

Hamlet, to confirm that the players Rosencrantz mentioned are indeed the Tragedians of Copenhagen, proceeds with caution:

'He that plays the King will be welcome,' the Prince says bemusedly. 'The adventurous Knight will wield his sword. The Lover will not sigh in vain. The Clown will set easy lungs heaving. And the Lady will speak her mind freely, or not at all. What players are they?' He throws in the vital question as an afterthought.

'The very players you once would delight in, my lord,' replies Rosencrantz. 'The Tragedians of Copenhagen.'

Hamlet puzzles:

'Why do they travel? They were better off in the capital.'

'Their wandering is due to the recent upheavals.' Rosencrantz refers to the social and cultural agitations and displacements since the death of Old Hamlet, the coronation of Claudius, and the build-up of paranoid forces.

'Are they not esteemed as when I was in the city?' Hamlet betrays nothing but sympathy for impoverished actors.

'No,' answers Rosencrantz.

'Have they grown rusty?'

'No, my lord. But there recently appeared in the city a nestful of precocious squawkers whose shrill voices gain the most outrageous applause.' Rosencrantz overpaints the picture, pandering to Hamlet's residual Platonism.

The Prince rises to the bait:

'What!' he snorts. *Children?* Who maintains them? How are they looked after? Don't they see that their early flowering must end in premature withering? That their writers and managers only exploit their present ephemeral popularity?' Hamlet puffs indignantly. Behind the digression, his thoughts carve tougher meat.

Rosencrantz purrs, happy that his pink-herring ploy has hooked the Prince's interest.

'To be sure, my lord,' he explains, 'there has been much to-do.

But the nation does nothing to forbid the use of such youngsters.'

'Do these boys remain popular?'

'Indeed.'

'It is hardly strange,' muses Hamlet. 'For, since my uncle became King of Denmark, those who scorned him while my father lived give a hundred ducats for miniatures of his portrait!'

A far-off flourish of trumpetry reverberates off the Castle walls and down its arterial corridors.

'There are the players,' infers Guildenstern.

Hamlet relapses into temporary civility:

'Come, gentlemen. Lend me your hands! For the *appearance* of welcome!' He pumps their clammy paws. 'Lest you be offended by the warmth with which I greet the players!' And an irresistible taunt:

'But my uncle-father and aunt-mother are deceived.'

'In what, dear my lord?' Guildenstern asks eagerly.

'I am mad only in a northerly wind.' Hamlet giggles. 'When it blows southerly, I can still tell cheese from chalk.' Hysterical with mirth, he scampers round Rosencrantz and Guildenstern like an effervescent toddler delighting in the ignorance of adults.

Enter Polonius by the south door.

'Good day, gentlemen!' he calls.

Hamlet hides behind Rosencrantz, like a child afraid of a Big Bad Wolf.

'Look at this, my friends,' he burbles loudly, clutching Rosencrantz's pigeon shoulders in a vice-like grip. 'That great baby still in swaddling clothes!' He spits.

'He is indeed fortunate, my lord, to enjoy his second childhood,' Rosencrantz mumbles. He wants to humour Hamlet, but fears to offend Polonius.

'I prophesy', Hamlet whispers, 'that he comes to announce the players. Listen.' He stands erect. Affects normal conversation. Ignores Polonius.

'Quite right, sir,' he nods to Guildenstern. 'I had forgotten.'

'My lord,' booms Polonius, 'I have news!' Incensed at being snubbed in the presence of inferiors.

'My lord,' Hamlet mimics, 'I have news too: *There once was an actor of Rome –* '

'The actors are come hither, my lord!'

'Old hat!'

'Upon my honour – '

'*Whose wife had a child by a gnome . . .*'

Polonius draws breath to drown Hamlet's insolent extempore.

'These, my lord,' he roars, 'are the best actors in all the world. For tragedy, comedy, history, pastoral, pastoral-comical, or tragical-romantical, *these are the only men.*' He gasps triumphantly.

Hamlet wrings his hands like a virgin in terror. Appeals to the ceiling:

'Oh Jephthah, judge of Israel, what a treasure you had!' He winks slyly to Rosencrantz.

'What treasure, my lord?' Polonius' obsessive curiosity overcomes his irritation.

'Why,' trills Hamlet:

'*His lovely daughter: the apple of his eye.*' This is a quote from a popular song.

Polonius doesn't get the reference.

'Listen to that!' he invites Guildenstern. 'Still on my daughter!'

Hamlet pretends not to notice. He closes with Polonius. Tweaks his nose.

'Am I not right, old Jephthah?' he leers.

'If you call me Jephthah, my lord, I *do* have a daughter, and she *is* the apple of my eye.'

'That is not what follows.'

'What does follow, then, my lord?'

Hamlet sings:

'*She drank some dirty water, and soon . . .*'

Several players bound in, followed by four flustered flunkeys. An oboe pipes. A jingling tambourine thumps against a mannikin knee. The clown cartwheels dizzily around the imposing approach of the Player King.

Hamlet grins.

'Ah well, old Jephthah,' again he tweaks the Prime-Ministerial proboscis, 'to know what follows, you must learn the song yourself. But here comes better entertainment.' He gives Polonius a forceful prod in the ribs, and turns to greet the players.

11
COOKING THE SACRED COW

A friendly sharpness in Hamlet's voice recalls his previous dealings with these players. Years ago, in Copenhagen, the Prince tried his restless hand at theatre writing and directing, so he knows the foibles of the acting trade.

'Welcome, my friends!' he cries. 'I am glad to see you well.' And to the Player King:

'You have grown a fringe since I last saw you! Have you come to beard me, here in Denmark?'

The hulking Player King moistens with a hesitant tongue his hairy thick lips. Before he can respond, Hamlet moves on to his son.

When Hamlet last patronized them, in Copenhagen, the boy was barely adolescent, and still played mostly ladies' parts. Now he is a tall and sturdy young buck – clearly from the same cast as his deep-chested sire.

But Hamlet teases him.

'What!' he exclaims in apparent disbelief. 'My young mistress?' He offers to kiss the unladylike buck lips. 'By our lady, your ladyship is nearer heaven now, by the altitude of a good high-heel.' He offers to squeeze the young buck's codpiece. 'Pray God your voice has not cracked with loss of innocence, like a counterfeit gold coin.'

The young buck recoils in alarm.

Hamlet leaves him, chuckles, and cordially shakes all the players by the hand. To put them at ease, and off their guard.

'My friends,' he repeats, 'you are all most welcome. And as French falconers do: we'll fly at everything we see. Indeed, a speech forthwith!' Eagerly to the Player King:

'Come. A taste of your quality. Let's have a passionate speech.'

The Player King stares at him, inscrutably inquiring. Extravert but disingenuous. Exuding ingenuity and accomplishment, yet without integrity. He is a wandering thundercloud, charged with energy and disposable passion; devoid of self-direction. He fingers a tangle on his shaggy sheepskin waistcoat, and asks:

'What speech, my good lord?'

'Once I heard you do Aeneas' tale to Dido. Relating the slaughter of Priam. If it live in your memory still, begin at this line ...' Hamlet strokes his brow in concentration.

'Let me see,' he mutters. '"The rugged Pyrrhus like the tiger ..." No.' He shakes his head in irritation, then snaps his fingers and recites:

> The rugged Pyrrhus, whose arm and might
> And sooty aims resembled night
> When he lay in the Trojan Horse,
> Now has good reason for remorse.
> His dusky skin is blemished now
> And trailing gore from toe to brow.
> Steeped in shame and familial blood
> All mixed and caked with dusty mud
> From off the parched and sun-struck streets
> Which Pyrrhus' vilest murders greet
> And highlight with their searing glare,
> Thus fired by wrath and scorching air,
> With bulging red carbuncle eyes,
> The hellish Pyrrhus blackly tries
> Old hated grandsire Priam to find ...

Hamlet breaks from his furious declamation to snatch some breath. He has made several small errors, some deliberate, but all present are impressed by his memory feat. Not least the Player King, who gapes in amazement.

The Prince regards the Player King's astonishment with satisfaction.

'Proceed from there,' he commands.

The Player King scratches his uncombed head.

His discomfiture is respited by Polonius, who interprets Hamlet's ability to conjure snatches of dramatic verse from the cobwebs of yesteryear as confirmation of mental imbalance.

'Well spoken, my lord!' he applauds. 'Excellent intonation ...'
His encouragement dwindles into beardy mumblings, as Hamlet
scowls fit to shrivel a jellyfish.

By now the Player King has recovered his bearings. He shrugs
off his matted waistcoat, the better to colour his speech with
gesture, and continues where Hamlet left off:

> ... Soon he finds him, partly blind,
> His ancient cutlass vainly seeks
> The dancing heads of teasing Greeks
> And then falls from his palsied grip
> Leaving his defences stripped
> When Pyrrhus in his strength and rage
> And heedless of the old man's age
> Swings his sword to cleave his side
> And heaves a curse when he hits wide;
> But Priam is brought to his knees
> By Pyrrhus' weapon's deathly breeze
> And only gains a moment's grace
> When flaming Troy returns to base
> And vainly strives to save the day;
> His blow carves Pyrrhus' ear away
> Just as his sword, again swung high,
> About to fall on Priam's eye,
> Seemed for several instants quick
> To pause, and in the air to stick;
> Then, for a moment frozen still,
> Pyrrhus could not force his will
> To execute his dread desire.
> But, as when the heavens dire
> And dark stand still before the storm
> And cloud battalions freeze their form
> And bold winds hush and hold their breath
> And all the world is still as death
> Before the dreadful thunder bursts;
> So painted Pyrrhus' thorny thirst
> For vengeance overcomes his stall.
> And never did Cyclops' hammer fall
> Upon the armour plate of Mars,
> Forged to outlive all the stars,
> With less remorse and rue arrayed
> Than Pyrrhus' whirling bleeding blade
> Now falls and severs Priam's head.
> Out, out, Fortune, dripping red,

Look at all the blood you've shed.
Oh, you gods, look down, I pray,
And strip this wanton's charms away,
Smash her hub and rim and spokes
And thus curtail her vengeful jokes,
And then bowl her chastized remains
Down Heaven's Hill to Hades' Plains –

'This is too long.' Polonius pats the fungus round his mouth, smothering a mouldy yawn.

Hamlet rounds on him in a rage.

'Then take it to the barber's, with your beard,' he snarls, savagely yanking the old man's milky beaver. 'Continue,' he urges the Player King. 'That old ninny must have a bawdy jig, or else he sleeps. I pray you, skip to the passage concerning Hecuba.'

The Player King coughs in renewed vexation. He has just been getting into his stride, tripping delicately through labyrinth forgetfulness. Where the occasional phrase eludes him, he improvises with a metrical fluency not matched by cognitive synonymy. Just what Hamlet is looking for:

To test his theory that it *could* have been the Player King who imghostated his father. Why choose a passage from a deservedly neglected play?

First, to try the Player King's facility for ad-libbing with superficial eloquence. Second, to exercise his flair for injecting false passion into purple passages of loquacious vacuity.

As far as Hamlet is concerned, the Player King has passed the first test with flying colours. The second is still to come, in the lament for Hecuba, unfortunate Priam's unfortunate wife. This mind-clogging doggerel is an ideal platform for unscrupulous tear-jerking.

And the Player King begins.

'"But he that saw the mobled queen . . ."'

'The *mobled* queen?' Hamlet ejaculates incredulously. For it should be *noble* queen. The archaic 'mobled', arguably meaning 'muffled', is completely incongruous. Hamlet marvels at the blithe insouciance with which the Player King trades the obvious for the obscure.

Polonius, meanwhile, reasserts his Taste.

'That's good;' he bleats, thinking to humour Hamlet, "mobled queen" is good.'

His inanity falls on unsympathetic soil. Hamlet offers to thicken his ear, and he is forced to totter out of range.

Hamlet waves impatiently.

The Player King continues:

> ... Widowed thus by Pyrrhus' spleen,
> Running barefoot up and down
> Without her regal robes or crown,
> A hasty blanket round her thighs
> And blinding tears to swamp her eyes
> And fall to salt the fevered blaze;
> Whoever on this scene did gaze,
> However smooth and forked his tongue,
> Would have been moved to force his lungs
> And Fortune's treachery decry.
> And if the gods themselves stood by
> When she saw Priam, limb from limb,
> Torn and minced at Pyrrhus' whim,
> Unless they scorn *all* mortal coils,
> They would have felt their blue blood boil
> And seethe to hear her piteous cries.
> And milky tears from Heaven's eyes
> And sympathies from Heaven's tongue
> Would have, by her woe, been wrung.

'Look!' Polonius exclaims. 'He is pale; has tears in his eyes. I pray you,' he begs Hamlet, cooing like the tenderest dove of all humanity, 'no more!'

The Player King's tears are shed by the shallow trance into which he hams himself. Polonius feels the power of this. Finds it disturbing.

Hamlet is delighted.

'Very good,' he commends. 'We'll hear the rest of it soon.' He walks the floor for a minute, fingering his beard. Then, to Polonius:

'Good my lord,' he requests with ponderous courtesy. 'Please ensure that these players have comfortable lodgings, and good food and drink. Do you hear? Be good to them, for they are the mirror of our times.' He salutes the players.

They clap enthusiastically.

Polonius is offended.

'My lord,' he puffs, 'I will treat them as they *deserve.*'

'God's penis, man,' Hamlet expostulates. 'Treat every man as he *deserves*, and who shall escape whipping? Treat them according to your own *honour.* The less they deserve, the more merit is in your bounty. Take them away.' He pats Polonius' robed posterior.

'Come, sirs.' Polonius huffily leads off the players. He has had enough of Hamlet's crazy liberties. As they go, Hamlet buttonholes the Player King.

'Follow him, friends,' the Prince tells the other players. 'We'll hear a play tomorrow.' He waves them away, then herds the Player King across the floor, beside a crackling pine fire, out of earshot of Rosencrantz and Guildenstern.

'Hear me, old friend?' Hamlet whispers. 'Can you play *The Murder of Gonzago?*'

'Yes, my lord.' Fly-traps in the Player eyes.

What can he be thinking?

'Then we'll have it tomorrow night. You could learn a speech of some sixteen lines, to insert in the play?'

'Yes, my lord.' The fly-traps glisten.

'Very well. Follow that lord.' Hamlet aims a vulgar gesture after Polonius. 'And try not to mock him.'

The Player King exits like an ambulant orchid.

That leaves Rosencrantz and Guildenstern. Hamlet views them with weary distaste. The past few hours have overdrawn his psychic resources. He craves the balm of solitude. How then to be rid of Rosencrantz and Guildenstern most quickly?

The Prince fishes in his codpiece. Liberating his member, he approaches his unwanted audience as if to urinate upon them.

'My good friends,' he drawls darkly, 'I'll leave you till tonight. You are welcome to *Elsinore.*'

'Good my lord!' squeaks Rosencrantz.

Hamlet's threatening organ advances.

Rosencrantz and Guildenstern flee ignominiously.

'And God be with you!' Hamlet jeers after them. Alone, he relieves himself on the fire. This keeps his protrusion warm, and vanishes his micturate up the chimney in hissing steam. As Hamlet sprays the distillate of his earlier drinking and his recent nervous intercourse into the tonguing flames and wreathing reeky vapours, a pullulating pantomime of knobbly gnomes, gruesome gargoyles and oriental concubines clad only in spangled fans suck scornfully at his dribbling pizzle. They are playful, but ruthless. *Remember*, they seem to sing, *the wages of weakness are fear.*

My only constant companions, Hamlet sighs.

He tucks away. Prowls his cage for several minutes. The germs of many plans and the chaff of much information thresh among his thoughts. He is certain now that the Player King *was* the Apparition.

But *why*?

How to find out *discreetly*?

Taking his diary from his belt, and a charcoal scribe from the leather pouch beside his cod, the Prince settles by the fire and incites his consciousness to stream:

Now alone. What a peasant rogue am I! Is it not monstrous that a simple player can, in such a dream of passion, so force his soul that blood drains from his face, tears fill his eyes, distraction overcomes him, his voice breaks, and his entire being melts and moulds itself to the part he plays?

And all for nothing! For Hecuba! What is Hecuba to him, that he should weep for her? What would he do, given motives such as mine? He would drown the world with tears, cleave the ear of all mankind with horrid speech, and make the guilty mad.

Yet I, a dull and weak-willed rascal, pine like a heedless dreamer, and can say nothing. Not even for a King upon whose person, property and heritage the *foulest outrage* was committed.

Am I a coward? Who insults me? Who cracks my head? Plucks off my beard and blows it in my face? Tweaks my nose? Calls me a liar? Who dares? Ha!

God knows, I deserve it though. For if I were not pigeon-livered, lacking gall to oppress my oppressor, I should long ago have fatted all the vultures of the air with this slave's offal. Bloody, bawdy villain! Remorseless, treacherous, lecherous, most unnatural *villain*! OH! *Vengeance!*

Yet, what an ass am I! How brave: that the son of a dear father murdered, prompted to revenge by heaven and hell, must, like a whore, unpack his heart with words, and fall cursing like a scullion! To hell with it!

But now, my brain, to work! It has been said that guilty creatures, watching a play like their own vile crimes, sometimes do rise and confess through stricken appearance to all their murk. For murder finds miraculous tongues!

I'll have these players resemble the murder of my father, before my uncle. To probe the very core of his defective heart, whose tiniest flinch will clinch his guilt.

The spirit I saw, upon the cliff, may be the devil. In a pleasing shape, to profit from my melancholy. Perhaps to suck my soul into eternal fire, through the murder of my uncle. I must have proof, and the play's the thing, to catch the conscience of the King.

Of course this entry must never fall into snooping hands. Rather than tear the entire leaf from his journal, the Prince leaves a tantalizing serrated margin. Eloquent truncations such as *treac* and *Venge* remain to inflame the spying eye.

Hamlet, now decided, feels much better. He springs to his feet. Consigns the scrap of extracted diary to the flames. Leaves the lobby, and returns to his own chamber. He travels publicly this time, to not pop up mysteriously too often.

As he clatters the corridors, he notes with revulsion the abnormal numbers of sleek large rats scampering unconcernedly past him. Most of the Castle inmates have retired to bed, so the rats roam unmolested except by odd hunting kitchen cats. And some of these rats are such monsters that even the tomcats turn a blind eye to their sharp twitching noses and reptilian grey tails.

Suddenly:

Mad for a meaty chicken leg some glutton dropped on his lurch to bed, a superrat comes thundering between Hamlet's legs. Almost knocks him over. Sinks its yellow fangs in the decomposing fowl.

Quicker than thought:

Hamlet draws his dagger;

Zipp;

Splat;

His blade has shafted through the air and skewered the rapacious jugular.

From the screaming hissing bubbling bleeding dying mess that was the rat the Prince retrieves his blade. Wiping the wet weapon on his hair and in his beard, and whistling a popular song, he proceeds to . . .

Compose an insert for the Player King to slip into the play which will test Claudius;

Write a more arcane diary entry, to further confound the snoopers;

Sleep.

12
RIFTY HINTS

Cold tiled floors; flapping tapestries; crusty cobwebs in unbrushed lofty cornices.

Rosencrantz and Guildenstern, loose plumage flattering their pigeon chests, are reporting to Claudius and Gertrude.

Polonius and Ophelia are also present.

Polonius, Rosencrantz and Guildenstern are politicly bland.

Ophelia is chastely pale and simply clad.

The King and Queen wear opulent public benevolence over the rags of their mutual malcontent. In the past twelve hours, Claudius has, for the first time, experienced absolute impotence. In consequence it has become vividly apparent to the royal couple that, apart from the desiccating fast glue of lust, there is little to hold their marriage together bar reciprocal contempt.

Beneath her brave front of regal composure, Gertrude is desperately worried. Realizing that this second marriage was a dreadful mistake, she now fears for her future. Even for her life.

This atmosphere oxydizes Claudius' occasional shifty glances at Ophelia. There is nothing surer than sembling virginal purity to whet his jaded appetite.

As Gertrude perceives.

Claudius is quizzing Rosencrantz and Guildenstern.

The latter stand uneasily.

The King paces expansively in the limelight. It is morning but he is drinking already. Rainbow reflections flash from the jewelled goblet in his fleshy fist.

'And can't you,' he quaffs, 'through loaded conversation, find out why he mounts this lunacy, which contrasts so harshly with his former quiet?'

'He does confess himself distracted,' Rosencrantz replies. 'But will not gloss the cause.'

'Nor is he easily probed,' adds Guildenstern. 'But with a crafty madness keeps aloof.'

'Did he receive you well?' Gertrude.

'Like a gentleman,' Rosencrantz.

'Yet his behaviour seemed most strained,' Guildenstern.

'He asked few questions, but was most *free* in his replies to our demands.' As Rosencrantz bolsters the courtly falsehood, he and Guildenstern think back with feeling to the indignities they suffered from Hamlet.

'Did you lure him to some amusement?' Gertrude is the only person present not trying to manipulate the Prince out of sordid motives.

'Madam,' Rosencrantz puffs with pride, 'it so happened that on our journey here, we overtook a troupe of players. We told him of these, and he seemed pleased. They have arrived at court, and already have instructions to play this evening.' Rosencrantz and Guildenstern bask in anticipation of Approval. But why don't they also explain that they *commissioned* the players to court Hamlet's amusement?

Because they are obsessively cautious: something might still go wrong.

Polonius has been smouldering in fretful silence for some minutes. Now he bursts into conversational flames.

'Most true,' he whooshes, as if Rosencrantz's testimony could never suffice. 'And he beseeched me entreat your majesties to the show.' Beneath his snowy whiskers, Polonius exults at having outshone Rosencrantz.

'Gladly!' Claudius perks up. 'I am pleased that he is thus inclined.' He celebrates with a drink. Then, to Rosencrantz and Guildenstern:

'Good gentlemen, sharpen his appetite for these delights.' Like Polonius, he views the arts as harmless diversions for latent insurgents.

'We shall, my lord.' Rosencrantz and Guildenstern bow out.

'Sweet Gertrude,' Claudius purrs, 'leave us too. For we have secretly sent for Hamlet. That he, by accident as it were, may encounter Ophelia. Her father and myself, lawful observers, will so secrete ourselves that, seeing while yet unseen, we may judge frankly of their meeting. Our purpose is to gather if it is indeed rejected love has made him suffer so.'

'I shall obey you.' Gertrude would rather remain with the surveillance party. But, due to her deteriorating relationship with Claudius, she dare not insist.

Subtly, she vents her spleen on Ophelia:

'For your part, Ophelia,' the Queen offers her hand so that Ophelia is obliged to curtsey and kiss it, 'I wish your good beauties are the happy cause of Hamlet's wildness. And that your virtues will restore his former self, to both your honours.'

'Madam, I wish it may.' Ophelia alone feels the feminine malice in Gertrude's plurals: 'beauties' and 'virtues'. But what can she do except smile wanly, curtsey again, and lamely reply with the singular 'it'?

Gertrude sweeps out.

Polonius takes effusive charge of the surveillance team.

'Ophelia,' he takes her arm, 'you walk here. Graciously, if you please. We will hide ourselves. You read in this book,' he hands her a bible, 'so your loneliness seems not unnatural. We are often to blame in this, there are countless precedents,' he chuckles gleefully, 'that with the face of devotion we sugar over the devil himself.'

Claudius mumbles inaudibly into his goblet:

'How sore you lash my conscience with these words! The harlot's cheek, beautied with plastering art, is prettier naked than is my deed beside my painted word. Oh, heavy burden!'

A distant shuffling.

Faint declamatory snatches of Hamlet's voice.

Polonius bustles.

'I hear him coming,' he hisses. 'Let us withdraw, my lord.' He ushers Claudius behind an enormous hanging tapestry depicting the gory empire-building of King Valdemar I in the early thirteenth century. Behind the tapestry is an alcove, for the display of large statues in warmer times. Polonius has had the sculptings removed. Into the resultant vacancy he and Claudius now scramble.

Ophelia is silently frantic. Would she have suggested Hamlet was mad for her, if she had foreseen such complications? How can the coming encounter with the Prince fail to fiasco? Leaving her discredited!

Her only hopes are:

First, that Hamlet *is* mad, and correspondingly incapable of manipulating her. Second, that if Hamlet is *not* mad, she can still control his need to *appear* mad.

Such considerations now flutter Ophelia's devious breast. She scans her bible with misgivings, for Hamlet knows she is no cloister vestal. Polonius has instructed her to draw Hamlet out: elicit his inner feelings and holy intentions. To this end, she has brought along some lyrics which, in happier times, she persuaded him to lend her. She has told Polonius that these were love-songs, written by Hamlet to her. Polonius has ordered her to return them under the description *Love Tokens*.

The telltale chink of Polonius' office chain is savagely muted.

Hamlet ambles crazily in. Great blue-green pastures of shadow halo his eyes. Grimy clawmarks streak his complexion. His rat-stained hair and beard would send a scarecrow yelping over the fields in terror, and he is talking to himself.

Or so it seems.

Actually, Hamlet is reciting his second diary entry from yesterday. As he reads, the Prince makes punctilious corrections with a charcoal stub. The corner of his eye has spotted Ophelia, but he feigns absorption in his editing.

Ophelia, beside the screening tapestry, watches him apprehensively.

Hamlet groans, as in metaphysical anguish, and speechifies:

To be? Or not? Vexing! Is it nobler to suffer outrageous fortune, or take arms, oppose, and end it?

To die! To sleep, no more? If only the sleep of death were *sure* to end the heartache! It were a consummation to be wished.

To die. To sleep. To sleep, perchance to *dream*. That's the snag. For, in that sleep of death, when we have shuffled off mortality, what dreams may come? This question harrows long our lives.

For who would bear the scorns of time? Injustice? The proud man's contempt? Pangs of spurned love? The law's delay, and insolence of office? The indignities that patient merit suffers? Bear such wrongs as these?

Or *settle the account, with* but *a* humble *dagger*? Who indeed would grunt and sweat through weary Life, did not the dread of *AfterDeath*, that undiscovered country from whose frontier no traveller returns, puzzle the will, and make us rather bear those ills we have, than fly to unknown others?

Thus does self-awareness cowards make. And our great enterprises founder on indecision.

Are these the soulful ruminations of a potential suicide?

Or the cantings of a casuist contemplating murderous revenge?

Must the interpretation reflect the listener's own conscience? His understanding and interests?

What about Ophelia?

Has she been following Hamlet's utterance?

Or worrying about her own problems?

Hamlet closes on her. His shrubby beard gapes. His veined eyes sharpen. He drawls: 'The fair Ophelia!' He stares at the bible she is parading. 'Nymph, in *your* prayers may all *my* sins be remembered.' He sighs piously. Gestures lewdly with his hips.

She retreats nervously, not wanting more vigorous intercourse while her father and King are behind the tapestry.

'Good my lord,' she begins solicitously, 'how have you been keeping this many a day?'

'I humbly thank you,' the Prince nods, 'well.'

'My lord,' she plunges, 'I have remembrances of yours, to re-deliver. I pray you, now receive them.' She hands him his old lyrics.

In this instant:

Hamlet realizes what game she is playing. Also that they are being spied on. *Why* should she pretend his lyrics are love tokens? *Unless* to 'prove' that Hamlet is mad for love of her? This reasoning comforts the Prince. It implies that Ophelia either believes he is mad or needs to affect this belief.

He takes the lyrics from her. Scans them quizzically. Drops them to the floor.

'Not I.' He shakes his head vehemently. 'I never gave you anything.'

'My honoured lord! You know you *did*.' Ophelia's pale composure is sweating now. 'And with them sweet words, to make the gifts more rich.' She stoops to gather the scattered papers. 'As their perfume is now lost, take these again.' She offers him the lyrics once more. 'For rich gifts wax poor when givers prove unkind.' She presses the lyrics into his hand. 'There, my lord.'

This time Hamlet accepts the papers with a snort. Stuffs them into his doublet.

'Ha!' he grunts. 'Are you *chaste*?'

'My lord!' she gasps primly.

'Are you *beautiful*?'

'What means your lordship?'

'That if you be chaste *and* beautiful, your chastity should forswear intercourse with your beauty.'

'Could beauty, my lord, have better commerce than with chastity?'

'Indeed. For beauty will sooner transform chastity into a bawd than chastity can translate beauty. I had thought this a paradox, but now . . .' He hawks a huge hunk of mucus at the nearest fire. It splats on the iron grate. Sizzles like fatty bacon.

'I did love you once,' he nods musingly.

'My lord, you made me believe so.' Ophelia looks hopeful.

'You should not have believed me. For virtue cannot milk bad blood. I loved you not.'

'Then I was the more deceived.' Ophelia pouts, peeved at Hamlet's naughty play on 'love'.

'Get you *to a nunnery*,' he suddenly shouts. 'Why would you breed sinners?' He prods her womb. 'I am myself indifferent honest. Yet guilty of such things that it were better my mother had not borne me. I am very proud. Revengeful. Ambitious. I have more offences in my nature than thoughts to put them in. Why should such fellows crawl, between heaven and earth? We are arrant knaves, all. Believe none of us. Get you to a nunnery.'

Before this tempest Ophelia retreats until her bustled buttocks kiss the face of the great tapestry which conceals her father and the King.

Hamlet's invective abruptly lulls. His nose wrinkles. He sniffs. Comprehension swells his eyes:

'Where's your father?'

'At home, my lord,' Ophelia stutters in dismay.

But Hamlet knows Polonius isn't at home.

For the First Minister has rifted mightily in his concealment.

'Let the doors be shut upon him,' Hamlet roars through the tapestry. 'That he may play the fool nowhere but in his own house. Farewell.' He points for Ophelia to leave.

She is utterly desperate. Polonius' anal expulsion has penetrated even her well-scented nostrils, and she realizes that Hamlet has twigged. Terrified that Hamlet may savage Polonius (for she knows that Hamlet can't know that Claudius also is behind the tapestry), she:

Falls to her knees; clasps her hands; throws back her head; keeningly importunes the ceiling:

'Oh! Help him, you sweet heavens!' she wails.

Hamlet is not impressed.

'If you *do* marry,' he remarks acidly, 'I give you this dowry: Be you as chaste as ice, pure as snow, you will not escape calumny. Get you to a nunnery. Go. Farewell. Or if you must marry, marry a fool. For wise men know what monsters you make of them. To a *nunnery,* go. And quickly too. Farewell.'

'Oh, heavenly powers, restore him!'

'I have heard of your paintings too,' Hamlet scolds. 'God gives you one face; you make yourself another. You jig, you amble, and you lisp. You mock and abuse God's creatures; plead ignorance to excuse your wantonness. But I'll say no more about this. *It has made me mad.*' He thrusts his face hairily into hers, to drive the point home. 'I say: *no more marriages.*' He steps up to the tapestry and bellows:

'Those that are married already, ALL BUT ONE, shall live. The rest shall stay as they are. To a *Parisian brothel,* go.' Hamlet stalks off. Polonius may not be alone in the alcove, and the Prince doesn't want a confrontation which might hinder this evening's play. As he goes, he tugs the crumpled lyrics from his doublet and hurls them into the fire.

'Oh!' cries Ophelia, astutely remaining on her knees. 'What a noble mind is here overthrown. The courtier's eye. The scholar's tongue. The soldier's sword. The hope and flower of our fair state.' Her voice trembles. 'The envy of all observers, quite, quite *down*! And I,' sob, 'the most wretched of ladies. I, who sucked the honey of his music vows. I, who see his noble reason harsh, like sweet bells cruelly jangled. I, who gaze upon the face of perfect manhood

112

blasted with *madness*. Oh! *Woe is me.* To have seen what I have seen, and see what I see!'

Timely tears fall.

Claudius and Polonius re-emerge.

Polonius is flustered.

Claudius is in a filthy mood.

'*Love!*' he scoffs at Polonius. 'His emotions are not so inclined. And what he spoke, though it lacked form a little, was not like madness. There's something in his soul on which his melancholy sits brooding. And nothing will hatch out but danger. Hence he will forthwith to England, ostensibly to pay our overdue respects. The seas and change should shake this irksome matter from his heart and calm his madly beating brain. What think you?'

'A capital plan, my lord,' Polonius claques. 'But *still* I believe his grief is thwarted *love.*' He hoists his daughter from her knees. 'Come now, Ophelia! You need not tell us what Lord Hamlet said. We heard it all.' To the King:

'My lord, do as you please. But . . . let his mother summon him, after the play. To reveal his grievances to her alone. Let her be stern with him. I'll be placed, if your lordship agrees, secretly, to hear their conference. If *she* fail to prove me right, then send him to England. Or . . . confine him where your wisdom shall think best.'

'It shall be so,' the King concurs. 'Great madness must be watched.'

Claudius sails out, like a laded galleon.

Polonius follows.

Ophelia brings up an anxious rear. The colours of her world are flattening. Reds and whites and golds run into sludge. She glimpses the panic of chaos.

13
LUDICROUS POINTS

Eight in the evening.

A large hall in the Castle, shaped like a debating chamber, with a raised stage and sloped seating.

Hamlet is rehearsing the players. He is costumed as a clown. Red, yellow, orange, green and blue patches dapple his torso. Long floppy boots of burnished brown dribble down from his knicker-bockered knees and spread in shuffling puddles on the floor until they disappear in ludicrous points. Buckles of brilliant brass tinkle and squeak about his person in random time to the rattling clunk of the bauble bell twirling from the tip of his limp dunce hat. The visible patches of his complexion are powdered deathly white. Strapped across his eyes is a menacing mask, suggestive of blackmail, rape, murder and revenge. Around his loins is girded a bulging codpiece of lewd purple donkey dimensions.

While the deadly dagger hangs as ever from his snakeskin belt.

Feeling he needs a witness to Claudius' reaction to the play, lest his own observation be jaundiced, Hamlet has sent for Horatio.

(Elsewhere in the Castle: Osric, fresh from Norway, is confirm-ing to Claudius the communication recently brought by Voltimand and Cornelius from Fortinbras. Never a man to trust either his right hand or his left, alone, Claudius is exhilarated to hear Osric's corroboration of the ambassadors' testimony.)

Hamlet casts final pearls of directional wisdom before the players, and the King in particular, before they dress for the performance. So far the rehearsal has oscillated between lunatic raillery and disciplined seriousness. Now Hamlet stresses that even a cuckoo Prince will not tolerate a shoddy performance:

'Speak the speech, I pray you,' he bids the Player King, 'as I pronounced it: trippingly on the tongue. Do not *mouth* it, as so many players do. For it offends my soul to hear a blustering wiggy fellow tear a passionate speech to tatters, to very *rags*. And all for what?

'To split the sides of the rabble in the pit! Myself I would have such a fellow *whipped* for such excesses. Pray you, avoid them.'

'Have no fear, your honour.' The Player King grins his appetitive lips.

'Don't be too tame either,' the Prince adds. 'But suit the action to the word. Anything overdone betrays the purpose of playing. Which is? *To hold the mirror up to nature –* '

'I hope, my lord,' the Player King ventures, 'that we have more or less reformed such faults in us.'

'Reform them *altogether*!' Hamlet wallops his left palm with his right fist, causing his hat bauble to twirl and rattle. 'And let your clowns speak *no more than is laid down for them.*' He squints through his mask at the inscrutable Player King. 'Go. Get ready.' He waves them off.

The players amble away to dress and make up.

Hamlet inspects the stage. Scans for a seat which will enable him to scrutinize Claudius' every frown and flinch. As he ponders, he winces at the aesthetics he has just laid on the players. In fact, Hamlet is far from subscribing to a purely mimetic theory of art. But all he wants tonight is a straight performance of a simple drama.

His heavily costumed movements express great excitement. He is impatient for his private word with Horatio, before the court assembles.

Footsteps.

Hamlet turns.

Horatio?

Polonius.

Attended by Rosencrantz and Guildenstern.

Hamlet curses. Aloud:

'How now, my lord! Will the King hear this piece?'

'The Queen too. They are on their way.' Polonius is so pleased he almost curtseys. He construes Hamlet's bizarre attire and politeness as confirming all his optimistic theories. His untended nostril tufts bristle with pleasure.

'Bid the players haste.' Hamlet waves dismissively.

Polonius bumbles out.

Rosencrantz and Guildenstern fidget uncomfortably.

Hamlet advances on them, glinting blackly through his mask and fingering his gargantuan cod.

'Will you *help* to hasten them?'

'We will, my lord.' Rosencrantz and Guildenstern exit rapidly after Polonius.

'Now,' mutters Hamlet, 'where's Horatio?' He cones his hands: 'HORATIO!'

'Here, sweet lord.' Horatio scurries in. 'At your service.' In his plain brown robe he looks like a neurotic monk.

The Prince now lards Horatio with compliments. Partly to express sincere regard. Partly to expiate the guilt Hamlet feels about not taking Horatio *fully* into his confidence. And to butter for a favour:

'Horatio,' Hamlet flings a friendly arm round his friendly friend's shoulders, 'you are as *just* a man as ever I met.'

'My dear lord! – '

'Do not think I flatter. For what advancement could I seek from you? With no revenue but your good spirits? Why should the poor be flattered? No! But enough of this.' For the favour has still to be asked: 'This play tonight: the King will attend.' Hamlet waves vaguely round the hall, and at the stage. 'One scene touches those circumstances of my father's death I mentioned earlier. When the time comes, focus upon my uncle. If no hidden guilt runs yelping forth during the crucial speech, it is a devil that we saw, and my imaginings outfoul a blacksmith's oxter. Let us fix upon his face, and later compare our judgements.'

'I will, my lord.'

Tumultuous buzzing whispers approach.

Kettledrums roll.

Sundry trumpets, bugles . . .

'They come,' Hamlet exclaims excitedly. 'I must fool. Get you a place.' He bundles Horatio into a seat. Scoops up a tambourine. Leaps up on to the stage. Shakes and beats the tambourine while kicking high his elongated boots.

The court enters, led by Claudius and Gertrude. All the Castle is present. Except the kitchen staff, who are busy getting drunk while preparing a midnight snack of mammoth proportions.

An atmosphere of gaiety and eager anticipation eases the chronic Castle chill, even if only through the palpitating presence of so many expectant bodies. Rumour says the players have cured the melancholy of the Prince, and, consequently, the ill-humour of the King.

Claudius certainly looks jovial. He is pleased with the news (brought by Voltimand and Cornelius, and now corroborated by Osric) from Norway. Indeed, he is still briefing Voltimand and Cornelius for their imminent return to Norway.

The ambassadors pace patiently behind him.

Gertrude, in a dazzling gem-studded gown of deep velvet green, is exotically radiant and full-breastedly Queenly.

Polonius exudes smug self-satisfaction like a snail trail from his capacious rift-raddled robes. His chain of office hangs like a golden albatross about his neck.

Ophelia, in a plain white dress of stunning simplicity, projects pale prim aloofness through her irrepressible physique.

Hamlet is politely ignored by the rank and file as he skips, kicks, bangs and rattles on the stage. Apart from its clowning value, this exercise dissipates the nervous tension he has built up around the drama to come.

Gertrude bestows a benevolent beam on her capering son. She interprets his antics as healthy showmanship.

Claudius steps forward to the stage, to set the ball rolling and make contact with Hamlet. With the King goes his brimming silver goblet. He has been drinking steadily throughout the day, but is not yet drunk, having had to concentrate on what reply to send Fortinbras.

'How fares our cousin Hamlet?' he calls up heartily.

'Hugely, thank you.' Hamlet kicks. 'Of the chameleon's dish.' He skips. 'I eat the air,' he bangs his tambourine, 'promise-crammed.' He jinglejangles. 'You cannot fatten turkeys thus.' He skips, kicks, bangs and jinglejangles.

Claudius is not affected by the Prince's pun. He has other things on his mind.

'I can make nothing of this answer, Hamlet,' he replies. 'These words are not mine.' As if he were sole proprietor of the Danish language. He beckons Voltimand and Cornelius into a diplomatic huddle in a far corner of the hall, anxious to prime them to deal with Fortinbras, and to set them sailing for Norway on the next tide.

Hamlet sneers at his uncle's retreating back:

'Nor mine, now!' He jumps down from the stage and socializes as normally as any refugee from a cuckoo circus could:

'My lord,' he accosts Polonius, 'you played once in the university, did you not?' Everyone in the Castle knows this.

'I did, my lord. And was accounted a *good* actor.'

'What did you enact?'

'Julius Caesar. I was killed in the Capitol. Brutus killed me.'

'Bully for him,' Hamlet sympathizes. Turns impatiently to Rosencrantz. 'Are the players ready?'

'And waiting.'

The lower orders are now seated.

'Come hither, good Hamlet,' Gertrude smiles. 'Sit by me.' She takes a celebrity chair in the centre stalls, and pats the plush beside her.

But such a seat would prevent Hamlet from observing Claudius.

'No, good mother.' He bounds across to Ophelia and throws his arm around her waist. 'Here's metal more attractive.'

Gertrude bridles stormily.

Ophelia is demurely taken aback.

Polonius crows:

'Oh ho! Do you hear that?' he calls hopefully.

But Claudius ignores Polonius. The King is still deep in discourse with Voltimand and Cornelius.

Hamlet propels Ophelia to the front stalls, close to the entrance through which the players will appear.

She acquiesces with mixed feelings. She hasn't a clue what Hamlet is up to, but how can it harm her to appear high in his affections? She sits, stiff-backed and tense.

Hamlet lies down on the bench beside her. His head forms a right angle with her left thigh. This posture enables him to view the stage and the celebrity seats simultaneously. He gazes up and asks Ophelia's nostrils:

'Lady, may I lie in your lap?'

'No, my lord,' she replies distantly. She looks round the faces behind her, hoping Hamlet won't come on overtly lewd.

'I mean, my *head . . . upon* your lap?'

'Yes, my lord.'

The Prince wriggles to pillow his head on her thigh. Inhales deeply through his mask. Beneath the liberal tinsel of Ophelia's bottled perfume lurks the stronger musk of her pervasive sexuality. Hamlet rubs the back of his head gently in the triangular concavity between her thighs and lower belly. His dunce hat comes off and falls rattling to the floor.

'Do you think I meant *cunt*ry matters?'

'I think nothing, my lord.'

'That's a fair thought to lie between maids' legs.'

'What is, my lord?'

'Nothing.' He chuckles.

'You are merry, my lord.' Ophelia smiles glassily.

'Me?' He continues his cranial caressing.

'Yes, my lord.'

'Oh, God! Am I your only jester?' He stares suddenly, straight up into her eyes.

Ophelia looks away, disconcerted by Hamlet's mask.

'What should a man do but be merry?' he laments. 'Look up there. How cheerful my mother looks, and my father died two hours ago.'

'No, my lord. It is twice two months since his death.'

'So long?' His yelp of astonishment mocks her tactful exaggeration. 'Oh, heavens! To have died two months ago, and not forgotten yet? Then there's hope that a *great* man's memory may outlive him by half a year. But, by our lady,' he waves his left hand; the knuckles brush Ophelia's breast, 'he will have to build churches, or he won't be remembered at all. Like the hobby-horse, whose epitaph is . . .' he sings:

'For, Oh! For, Oh! The hobby-horse is FORGOT!'

From behind the stage comes oboe piping.

The players are about to enter.

Lackeys round the hall douse all lights except those illuminating the stage. Reflections from this are sufficient to let Hamlet monitor the celebrity seats.

But still Claudius is huddled with his ambassadors in a far corner.

The stage lights flicker.

Spooky dramatic shadows are cast.

The piping oboes gain in volume.

Two pipers enter the hall and mount the stage.

The expectant buzz dwindles to a rustling hush.

Enter the dumbshow:

Two junior players, clad symbolically as king and queen. They follow the pipers on to the stage. Their mime enacts:

Enter a *King* and *Queen*, very loving. The *Queen* embraces him, and he her. She kneels, and makes show of protestation unto him. He takes her up; declines his head upon her neck; lays him down upon a bank of flowers. She, seeing him asleep, leaves him. Anon comes in a fellow, takes off his crown, kisses it, pours poison in the *King's* ears, and exit. The *Queen* returns; finds the *King* dead; makes passionate action. The *Poisoner*, with three Mutes, comes in again, seeming to lament with her. The dead body is carried away. The *Poisoner* woos the *Queen* with gifts. She seems loath awhile, but soon accepts his love. (Exeunt.)

Hamlet, beneath his mask, turns white with foreboding fury.

Why have the players disobeyed his instruction to *omit* the dumbshow?

The dumbshow scampers off.

Hamlet squints round apprehensively, to see if Claudius has been watching.

Fortunately, the King is still cornered with Voltimand and Cornelius.

But Ophelia's curiosity is aroused.

'What means this, my lord?' she asks Hamlet.

'This?' He points vengefully at the parting dumbshow. 'Snivelling wickedness. It means mischief.'

'Perhaps this plot foreshadows the play?' Ophelia's inflection needles Hamlet. But he is saved by the *Prologue*:

A plain-dressed youth mounts the stage.

'We shall know by this fellow.' Hamlet tries to distract Ophelia from the dumbshow. 'Players keep no secrets. They'll tell all.'

'Will he tell us what *this* show meant?' Her persistence irritates the Prince.

'And any show that *you* show him.' Hamlet hisses viciously, his mind rolling over images of Ophelia stupendously naked after her bath and touching before her mirror. 'If *you* show *him*, *he*'ll not shame to tell *you* what it means.'

'You are *lewd*,' she rebukes him. 'I'll confine myself to the play.'

The *Prologue* walks forward to the cape of the stage. Bows to the general assembly. Delivers in a loud nasal monotone:

> FOR US AND FOR OUR TRAGEDY,
> HERE STOOPING TO YOUR CLEMENCY,
> WE BEG YOUR HEARING PATIENTLY.

He bows again and leaves the stage.

Claudius concludes his intercourse with Voltimand and Cornelius. He crosses the hall and takes his place beside Gertrude. Unostentatious as possible for a fleshy middle-aged king in heavy, shoulder-exaggerating robes.

Voltimand and Cornelius leave the hall, bound for Norway.

Hamlet grumbles again about the players:

'Is this a prologue, or a nursery rhyme?' he gripes.

'It is brief, my lord.' Ophelia's tone suggests that brevity is the soul of drama.

'As a woman's love,' Hamlet counters.

Enter two principal characters.

The hall hush contracts to fevered silence.

In the cornices far above an adolescent spider feels threatened by the tension. Scuttles back in alarm to the thin grey security of his web.

The Player King ascends the stage. His imposing stature vibrates with chimerical majesty. His robes and crown are grander far than those of Claudius. He is followed by a boy got up as a beauteous queen.

And the nested play begins:

P. KING   Full thirty times the sun's gone round
               Our cold grey sea and great green ground,

And nine score moons with borrowed sheen
Twice around the world have been,
Since love our hearts and law our hands
United in most sacred bands.

He embraces her tenderly.

P. QUEEN   Then may another thirty suns
Go round the earth ere love be done!
But woe is me! For you, of late,
Have fallen from your former state
Of strength and health, and I do fear,
At times, you will not last the year.
But, though I fear, be not distressed,
For women never know what's best,
Since women's fear and women's love
Go hand in hand, like hand in glove.
I love you dearly, that you know;
All my fears inform you so.
Where love is great, small doubts are fear,
And tiny doubts grow greatly here.

She pats her heaving bosom.

P. KING   I must leave this world ere long;
My bones below the ground belong.
And you, alas, must learn to live
Without me; and in time you'll give
Another husband your sweet hand,
To take the helm of this fair land . . .

P. QUEEN   I pray you, do not speak the rest;
Such love must needs pollute my breast.
Wives who wed again are cursed,
And like as not have *murdered* first.

'Woodworm!' Hamlet breathes an oblique comment on the
bitterness of the irony.

Only Ophelia can hear him.

P. QUEEN   Whichever woman marries twice
Loves not the man but just the price;
A second time I'd kill you dead
If other limbs should scale my bed.

122

P. KING   I doubt not that you are *sincere*,
            Yet for your *resolution* fear;
            For purpose is to memory
            As closely tied as leaf to tree,
            And whereas in the green of spring
            Our leaves to trees do tightly cling,
            In autumn's mellow golden brown
            The slightest breeze will blow them down.
            And often it is for the best
            When hot resolves fail action's test,
            Once they have cooled from white to grey
            And passion's fires have died away.
            The violent acts of grief and joy
            Only their own selves destroy;
            Where joy sings out, grief follows on,
            And revelling eyes grow quickly wan.
            Our lives are short, and it's not strange
            That our loves with our fortunes change.
            Our thoughts are tailored to our needs,
            And we believe love fortune leads;
            But there's no proof: we may be wrong,
            And all be singing fortune's song.
            Most often, when a great man dies,
            His woman weeps but quickly flies;
            And he who hopes some power to seize
            Fakes friendship with his enemies;
            And countless friends will fawning wait
            On he whose wealth and power are great;
            While he who begs a hollow friend
            For help must with his hate contend.
            In such ways we see love led,
             A mindless maid, to fortune's bed.
            But . . . where I started, let me close:
            Our wills and fates are so opposed
            That we have no real power to choose;
            To this extent we're bound to lose.
            So, *think* you will no other wed;
            But *change* your mind when I am . . . *dead*.

As the speech closes, the Player King expresses ancient dignity and wisdom combining with unutterable shoulder-sagging weariness and resignation.
   His nettled Queen makes passionate action and fervid protestation:

P. QUEEN   Starve me of food and heaven's light
            And worldly pleasure, both day and night!

Turn my hope and trust to fear
And chain me to a hermit's cheer!
Turn the heart from my desires
And feed them to infernal fires!
Curse me with eternal strife
If, once widowed, I be wife!

She throws her arms around the Player King.
He staggers sideways, unable to support her deadening emotion.

The atmosphere in the hall is supercharged.

Hamlet is keyed to brainstorm pitch. His fists are clenched. He is sweating profusely in his jester's costume.

'If she should spoil it now!' he mutters hoarsely, like a man watching a race on which he has staked his life's savings.

The Player King breaks loose from the claustrophobic embrace of his agitated Queen, and lies down.

P. KING I'll take your word. But leave me here
Awhile, my sweet; I'm tired, I fear.
My brain works slow, my spirits dull,
And I my heart with sleep would lull.

He stretches out, as on a cushioned couch. Pillows his head on his hands. Closes his eyes. Sinks into aspect slumber.

P. QUEEN May you sleep as babies do,
And *nothing* come between us two!

She kneels. Tenderly kisses his dormant brow. Rises. Casts a glance of ambiguous uncertainty round the hall. Exits.

This marks a pause in the action, and Hamlet invites responses.

'Madam,' he calls to Gertrude, 'how do *you* like this play?'

'I think the lady's protestations extreme.' Gertrude replies coolly. The correspondence with her own recent past has not escaped her.

'Oh, but *she*'ll keep her word!' Hamlet chortles and throws his head back into Ophelia's scent-laden lap.

'Do you *know* the story? Is there no *offence* in it?' A scowling edge to Claudius' questions.

'No, no,' Hamlet scoffs. 'They do but jest. Poison in jest. No offence in the world.'

'What do you *call* the play?' Claudius still sounds suspicious.

'*The Mouse Trap*. Figuratively!' Hamlet chuckles. 'This play portrays a murder done in Vienna. The duke's name is Gonzago. His wife is Baptista. It is a knavish piece of work, as you will shortly see. But what of that? Your majesty, and all of us with consciences unsullied, have nothing to fear. Let the guilty wince. *We* have nothing to hide.' Hamlet delivers this with nonchalant jocularity.

Claudius glowers suspiciously at his nephew.

A startled gasp animates the audience.

Another player has made a dark and silent entry.

The tall lithe son of the Player King:

A flowing figure in swirling robes of midnight black, topped by a spine-chilling witch's hood which conceals the player's features.

The sinister spectre steals across the stage.

'This is one Lucianus,' Hamlet announces loudly, 'nephew to the king.'

'You are a good chorus, my lord,' Ophelia murmurs.

'I could interpret between you and your lover,' hisses Hamlet bitingly, 'if I could see the puppets dallying.'

'You are cutting, my lord.'

'It would cost you a groaning to take off my edge.'

'Still better, and worse.'

'So you mistake your husbands.' Before Hamlet can develop his attack on marriage vows . . .

Horror echoes round the hall.

On the stage, stealthy Lucianus stands over his sleeping uncle. His folded-back hood reveals a horrendous skull-mask. Tiny shards of coloured glass embedded in his staring eye-sockets reflect stray beams of light in the shapes of seething worms and maggots.

This prospect contorts Hamlet's caution into blinding fury. The skull-mask touch is absolutely contrary to his instructions, and . . .

'*Begin*, murderer!' he howls at the stage, electrifying the audience. 'A pox on your damnable faces. BEGIN. Come, the croaking raven bellows for REVENGE.' He vows to have the players flogged, if the climax is not as planned.

This punitive resolve penetrates Lucianus. He peels off his skull-mask. Under it he is wearing a black bandit mask, identical to Hamlet's. And:

Lucianus minces round his recumbent uncle. Pulls a glass phial from the folds of his cloak. Holds it up to the audience. Slowly the fingers of his left hand unfasten his cloak. To heighten lust for climax, he chants in time to his quickening predatory footfalls:

LUCIANUS My thoughts are black, my hands are apt,
     The time is right, my course is mapped.
     Oh, mixture rank, of midnight weeds
     Distilled and boiled to aid my deeds
     And by three witches blackly cursed,
     I conjure you to do your worst,
     May your magic take this life
     More surely than the sharpest knife.

Lucianus swoops down and pours poison in the sleeper's ear. The sleeping figure writhes, screams, convulses. Collapses in a lifeless heap.
 Lucianus spits triumphantly on his uncle's corpse. Steps over it. Walks to the front of the stage. Throws off his cloak. Bows as to thunderous applause.

But the audience is paralytic with silence.

Because?

Lucianus stands costumed as a clown. Red, yellow, orange, green and blue patches dapple his torso. Long floppy boots of burnished brown dribble down from his knickerbockered knees, and spread in shuffling puddles on the floor until the toes disappear in ludicrous points. About his loins is girded a bulging codpiece of lewd purple donkey dimensions, which he now rubs suggestively.

Exactly like Hamlet.

Who leaps up from Ophelia's lap and interprets the murder:

'He poisons him in the garden for his estate,' the Prince explains. 'His name's Gonzago. It's a true story, and written in very choice Italian. You will see shortly how the murderer gets the love of Gonzago's wife.'

'The King rises.' Ophelia understates the general wonder at Claudius' appearance.

He starts to his feet. Even in the gloom-dark hall his florid drinker's face shows ashen white and his eyes pop dreadfully, as if he had just soiled his pantaloons.

'What!' exclaims Hamlet sarcastically. 'Frightened by fireworks?'

'What's wrong, my lord?' asks Gertrude, fearfully. She rises and tugs vainly at her thunderstruck husband's arm.

Claudius ignores her. He lurches from his seat. Stumbles across the hall.

Polonius dodders to the stage and shoos the players away.

'Stop the play,' he bleats.

Alarmed by the havoc they have unwittingly wreaked, the players are glad to obey.

'Give me some *light*!' Claudius finally croaks. 'Away!' He reels out of the hall.

Exode of babbling lackeys, vexed courtiers, and thwarted theatre-goers.

'Lights, lights!' they clamour. Like sheep crying, 'Baa, baa!'

Seeing his public melt away, Hamlet retrieves his tambourine and leaps jingling on to the stage.

14
THE RECORDERS

After the flabbergasted King, Hamlet savagely sings:

> Let the stricken stag go cry;
>   The hart ungallèd play;
> For some must live, while others die;
>   So runs the world away.

The last lackey follows the pandemonium out.

Hamlet tails off a jeering chorus of *la*.

Only Horatio remains with him, sitting in the stalls, frowning uncomfortably.

Hamlet addresses him grandiloquently:

'Would not this production, sir, and a great plumed bonnet, and pink Provençal rosettes on my ludicrous shoes, make my fortune as a player? If the rest of my fortunes turn traitor? Sir?' He pretends to doff the twirling dunce crown which no longer tops his tousled brown locks – burlesquing the convoluted manners that sheathe Danish treachery.

Horatio rises. Steps to the stage.

'Half a fortune,' he suggests. Literal as ever.

'A whole one, surely,' Hamlet scoffs, and snatches another song:

> For you must know, my darling dear,
>   This realm has never heard
> Of light or love; and now reigns here
>   A bloated, lustful . . . puddock.

'You might have rhymed.' Horatio misses the point.

Hamlet doesn't trouble to unpack it. Unable to contain any longer:

'Oh, Horatio! I'll take the ghost's word for a thousand pounds. Did you perceive?'

'Very well, my lord.'

'At the talk of poisoning?'

'I did very well note him.' Horatio nods gravely. It disgusts him to consider that great monarchs and powerful political leaders may secretly be abominable villains and filthy murderers.

Re-enter Rosencrantz and Guildenstern. Subtle differences in their posture. Their attitude to Hamlet has revised. Like hyenas smiling at an injured lion.

'Ah ha!' roars the Prince. 'Come. Some *music!*' He goosejumps down from the stage, thumping the tambourine against his thigh. 'Come. The recorders!' he shouts over his shoulder. Then he improvises at Rosencrantz and Guildenstern:

> For if the King like not the play,
> The Queen can kiss his tears away!

'MUSIC!' he bellows again through the players' exit.

All this clowning gives Hamlet time to think. His life has just taken an irreversible meander (how often can one discover *for sure* that one's uncle is indeed one's father's murderer?) and his brain is madly remapping.

'Good my lord,' Guildenstern rubs an imaginary greasespot on his oil-green sleeve, 'vouchsafe me a word.'

'Sir, a whole history.' Hamlet bows his sarcastic nose to the floor.

'The King, sir – '

'What of him?'

'Is extraordinarily upset.'

'With drink?'

'No, my lord. Rather with choler.'

'Then wisdom would inform his doctor. For *me* to minister his purgation might plunge him rather deeper into choler.' Hamlet's teeth suggest the sound of necks breaking.

'Good my lord,' menace rides on Guildenstern's fluty admonition, 'put your discourse in some order.'

'I am tame, sir. Pronounce.'

'The Queen, your mother, in great affliction of spirit, has sent me to you.'

'You are welcome.' Hamlet chortles. Throws wide his arms. Invites hugs and kisses.

'No, good my lord. This courtesy is not of the right breed. If you make me a wholesome answer, I will do your mother's commandment. If not – '

'Sir, I cannot.'

'What, my lord?'

'Make you a wholesome answer.' Hamlet pats his head. 'My wit's diseased. But, sir, such answer as I can make, you shall command. Or rather, as you say, my mother shall command. But enough of this. To the point. My mother, you say . . .'

'She says your behaviour has struck her into astonishment.' Rosencrantz.

'Oh, wonderful son, to so astonish a mother!' Hamlet's hands congratulate his breast. 'But is there no hound at the heels of this mother's amazement?'

'She desires to speak with you in her closet before you go to bed.'

'We shall obey,' Hamlet parodies Claudius' *We*, 'were she ten times our mother. Have you further trade with *us*?'

'My lord,' Rosencrantz shiftily mumbles, 'you once did love me.'

'So I do still,' Hamlet jibes. 'As sworn by these pickers and stealers.' His fingers mime theft and treachery.

'Good my lord, what causes your distemper?' Rosencrantz's unction is seeded with malice. 'You surely endanger your freedom, if you vault your grievances from your friend.'

'Sir,' Hamlet wails, 'I lack advancement.'

'How can that be, when the King has guaranteed the succession to you?'

'Yes, sir,' Hamlet hums. 'But "While the grass grows . . ." I fear the proverb musts in my memory.'

Two young players return, blowing a nervous melody.

'The recorders!' Hamlet takes one and pipes a few notes. To Guildenstern:

'Tell me now,' he urges in a stertorous whisper, 'why do you circle upwind from me? To drive me into a snare?'

'Oh, my lord,' Guildenstern protests, 'if my *duty* seem too *bold*, it reflects my *love* too *eager*.'

'I am not sure I understand that.' Hamlet seems lost in thought. Then he offers Guildenstern the recorder. 'Will you play?'

'My lord, I cannot.'

'I pray you.'

'Believe me, I cannot.'

'I *beseech* you.' Hamlet waves the instrument under Guildenstern's apprehensive nose.

'I know no touch of it, my lord.'

'It is as easy as lying,' Hamlet breathes softly. 'Cover these holes with your finger and thumb, give it breath with your mouth, and it will pipe most eloquent music. Look, these are the stops.'

'But, my lord,' Guildenstern recoils, 'I cannot command them to harmony. *I have not the skill.*'

'Then how unworthily you think of me.' Hamlet's head shakes sadly. Shoulder-length hair swirls round his mask. 'You would play upon me. Seem to know my stops. Pluck out my mystery. And yet, though there is excellent voice in this little organ,' he brandishes the recorder, 'you cannot make it speak.' He chews his lower lip. Suddenly roars:

'GOD'S BLOOD! You think *I* am easier to play on than a *pipe*? Call me what instrument you will: though you fret me, you cannot play upon me.'

Hamlet's venomous contempt looks dangerous.

Guildenstern seems near to wetting himself. His discomfiture is alleviated by the flapping arrival of Polonius, who is bursting with stale news.

'God bless you, sir!' Hamlet's mask blinks at the newcomer.

'My lord,' the premier neighs, 'the Queen would speak with you, and soon.'

Hamlet nods thoughtfully. Directs attention to the ceiling:

'Do you see yonder cloud, shaped like a camel?'

Polonius peers obediently up.

'Upon my word,' he agrees, 'it is indeed like a camel.'

'A *weasel*?'

'*Backed* like a weasel,' concurs the aspiring father-in-law.

'Or a *whale*?'

131

'*Very* like a whale.'

'Then I will come to my mother by and by.' Hamlet wheels. Walks behind Horatio. 'They fool me all the way,' he murmurs pregnantly. 'I will come *by and by*,' he shouts at Polonius, waving him away.

'I will say so.' Polonius bows and departs.

'*By and by* is easily said,' Hamlet calls after him. 'Leave me, friends.' His request is an order.

Rosencrantz and Guildenstern, the pimply players, and even the stalwart Horatio retire respectfully.

Hamlet waits, checks the doorways, then executes a fireplace exit.

As he steals back to his chamber, all peripheral issues (such as the identity of the Apparition) are vaporized by the white-hot malignance of the central question which the Prince feels eating his entrails like a ravenous cancer:

Should he take revenge on Claudius?

How and when?

Seek justice openly? Expose the villain's true colours?

Or kill him clandestinely, then claim the succession?

But what if he should be caught?

Moreover:

Now Hamlet knows Claudius knows that he knows Claudius murdered Old Hamlet, the Prince's own life must be in constant danger from Claudius.

Back in his room, frosted breath foams like steam from Hamlet's troubled nostrils, but he leaves unlit the fire neatly laid in the grate. Sits at his writing-table and scratches in his diary:

Now is the witching time of night, when churchyards yawn and hell itself breathes out contagion. *Now* could I drink hot blood, and do such bitter business as would quake the day.

But I must go to my mother. Oh, my heart, be strong. Cruel; not unnatural. I will speak daggers to her; use none. Oh, my soul . . .

Sucking the feather of his quill, Hamlet winces in disgust. Hurls his journal against the wall. He feels like a poet with toothache who tries to ease the pain by writing a poem about toothache. And fails.

Frustrated thus, the Prince jumps up for *action*:

Sheds the grotesque codpiece from his loins; changes his ludicrous clown points for a pair of stout boots; but leaves his jester apparel untouched, since it justifies the mask.

Finally, Hamlet looks out a miniature of his father. It was given to him by Gertrude twenty years ago, to hang around his neck like a crucifix and treasure always. The likeness portrays Old Hamlet at his virile best. The brow is high and noble. Chin firm and brave. Eyes blue and stern. Hamlet has not sported this trinket for years, but now he hangs the fine gold chain around his neck and tucks the hallowed icon beneath his multicolour blouse.

Then he sets off to visit Gertrude.

15
WHAT HAMLET DOESN'T KNOW

Yes, Claudius *did* assassinate Old Hamlet.

But *why*?

And *why wait so long* before taking the murderous plunge? Until Old Hamlet was nearly dead of old age anyway?

In fact the precipitator was Young Fortinbras.

Not that Claudius had never thought of killing Old Hamlet. Indeed, the adult Claudius had seldom *not* thought of burking his brother.

But it was Fortinbras who finally jolted him into villainy.

Having established through meticulous screening that Osric was Claudius' most intimate confidant, Fortinbras nobbled Osric during the summer, while the latter was touring his Norwegian estates.

Duly suborned, Osric returned to Claudius with a sealed package of great furtiveness:

Fortinbras remarked to Claudius that Old Hamlet was obviously not long for this world, and that Hamlet would shortly be of age to succeed. Knowing no love was lost between Hamlet and Claudius, Fortinbras observed that Claudius would be even more powerless and frustrated under Hamlet than under Old Hamlet. Well then, Fortinbras reasoned, let's strike the following bargain:

Claudius was to dispatch Old Hamlet, disguise his passing as due to natural causes or misadventure, and make himself regent of Denmark. He would be assisted by communications from Fortinbras, threatening war on Denmark if the disputed territories (originally won by Old Hamlet from Old Fortinbras) were not returned to Norway forthwith. Then, consolidated overlord of Denmark, Claudius was to engineer the marriage of Fortinbras to Gertrude, establishing Fortinbras as titular King of Denmark. Claudius, however, would maintain a life regency, thereby depriving Hamlet of his birthright. This, Fortinbras supposed, would hardly grieve himself or Claudius, and should assure Claudius a rosier future than if Hamlet became King. Finally, the monarchy of Denmark would, after Claudius, go to Fortinbras (or his heir, if Claudius were to outlive him).

Thus propositioned, by Fortinbras through Osric, Claudius at last rose to the murder bait. His motivation was complex. Besides the persuasive arguments of Fortinbras, Claudius feared that if he did not liaise with the Norwegian prince the latter might go it alone via some alternative route. Leaving Claudius doubly ditched.

But the last straw, for Claudius, was the horrible churning fear that Fortinbras might snaffle Gertrude. The busty object of his barren aching lust for all those covetous years carried off and briefly bedded by that insolent pup over the water! This spectre was too much for Claudius. Especially when, he felt sure, Fortinbras' seedy intention was to parade Gertrude around for a few years then have her quietly replaced by some pink young buxom princess ripe to lay heirs.

So?

Claudius sent word, again through Osric, that he would axe Old Hamlet, and would Fortinbras please threaten via the ambassadors, Voltimand and Cornelius, as soon as Old Hamlet's death was made public, that Norway would war on Denmark if the disputed territories were not returned immediately? Claudius would then endeavour, aided by Fortinbras' threat, to secure overlordship of Denmark. Once he was established they would negotiate the marriage of Fortinbras to Gertrude at their leisure. Likewise the question of succession after Claudius.

In due course:

Osric returned from Norway with the news that Fortinbras was agreeable and that Claudius should proceed.

Claudius proceeded:

Old Hamlet was relieved of his already faltering existence.

Claudius, needless to say, never intended to meet Fortinbras' demands. Instead, he used Fortinbras' promised threat as a lever to persuade Polonius and the Council to sanction his marrying Gertrude and taking the throne. He also cited Fortinbras as justification for huge increases in defence spending and conscription. Claudius deemed this military build-up necessary lest Fortinbras seek redress by force.

But having recently decided, following a crosscheck of the evidences provided by Osric, and by Voltimand and Cornelius, that Fortinbras is not a serious strategic threat, and only needs a good old pillage to let off some steam and blood, Claudius now feels secure *vis-à-vis* his diplomatic position and military strength. This is why he was so breezy about sending Voltimand and Cornelius back with permission for Fortinbras to march a small force through Denmark on its way to persecute some unfortunate Poles.

Presently:

Claudius feels more threatened within. The focus of his guilt and paranoia has shifted dramatically from Fortinbras to Hamlet. Now, in addition, he has his rapidly crumbling marriage to fret about.

These, then, are some of the empirical facts that Hamlet the philosophical prodigy doesn't know, as . . .

16
MUMBLES AND MURMURS

On his private pathway to visit Gertrude, the Prince pauses behind the wall of Claudius' office. This involuted oubliette is heavily fortressed and it tantalizes Hamlet to think how easily he could penetrate his uncle's privacy: sneak in through the fireplace and wreak lethal requital at his leisure.

Claudius is seated at his desk. He looks pale, shaken, red-eyed. The worse for drink, but not drunk. Not quite. His goblet silvers reflections of the blazing fire, the torches round the walls, and the candles on the desk. Is the King attempting to banish horrid thoughts and dire imaginings by means of warmth and light?

If so, he is not succeeding.

His meaty baritone is tremulously frayed as he dispenses orders to Rosencrantz and Guildenstern:

'He worries me. It is not safe for us to let his madness rove. Therefore prepare. I will write your commission forthwith. You will accompany him to England. It is essential that our office, as King and Head of State, is not exposed . . . to the dangers which grow hourly . . . out of his lunacies.' Claudius trails off in a choking quaver.

Behind the wall, Hamlet smiles coldly.

Rosencrantz and Guildenstern leap loquaciously into the hole of Claudius' temporary speech impediment, to bolster the dyke of his majesty:

'We will prepare *immediately*.' Guildenstern. 'It is a holy fear, to keep those many bodies safe that live upon your majesty.'

Claudius takes grateful advantage of this servile respite. He rises heavily. Swallows back the turmoil in his gorge. Walks over to the fire.

Rosencrantz glibly enters this race to save the King's face:

'Even the *ordinary* life is sacred,' he purrs at the royal shoulders. 'Yet nothing! Compared with the Spirit upon whose health depend the lives of many. Majesty is like a giant wheel, atop the highest mountain. To its spokes ten thousand lesser things are bound. And if that majesty rolls and falls, dependent multitudes fall too.'

This seems to revive Claudius. He turns. Favours his adulators with a haggard smile.

'Make ready, I pray you, for this speedy voyage,' he rumbles thickly. 'To fetter this fear, which now goes too free-footed.'

'We haste.' Rosencrantz and Guildenstern leave.

Alone, the King's haggard smile collapses into weary folds of evil desperation.

Dark within his burrow of secrecy, Hamlet nods knowingly.

Claudius' lips pucker.

What is he muttering?

He takes a generous swallow from his goblet. Sits awkwardly at his desk. Sets out a quill and a virgin scroll. Buttocks his brow. Begins to write.

For several minutes Hamlet toys with the ungainly image of Claudius slumped, scribbling and slurping spiced wine. Then the Prince glides away. The intelligence he has gleaned from the exchange between Claudius and Rosencrantz and Guildenstern necessitates a speedy transaction of his own:

With Marcellus and Bernardo.

Accordingly, the visit to Gertrude must wait, and Hamlet goes roaming in quest of his trusty officers.

Claudius, frowning unawares, continues writing.

Shortly after Hamlet moves off, Polonius knocks on the inches-thick oak which portals Claudius' sanctum. As he bumbles in, the premier is smiling with toothless pleasure beneath his beard, for he is about to spy.

'My lord,' he spouts, 'he goes to his mother's closet. I'll conceal myself behind the tapestry. I'm sure she'll get the truth from him, and pull him to his senses. As you so wisely said, nature makes mothers partial. Wherefore some more audience than a mother must overhear the speech. Fare you well, my lord. I'll call before you go to bed, to tell what I have learned.'

'Thanks, dear my lord.' Claudius exhumes his haggard smile,

but he doesn't pay much attention to Polonius. His principal concern is that the old man shouldn't inquire into the scroll he has been scribing. Were he more alert, Claudius might react to Polonius' skilful imputation to *him* of what is entirely Polonius' own idea:

That Polonius should spy on Hamlet and Gertrude.

Anyway, Claudius injects an echo of gratitude into his farewell wave to Polonius, who exits like a geriatric sprite.

Claudius sinks more liquor. Shakes his head as if to dislodge a fly from his nose. His jowls flop obscenely. He resumes his writing. Signs the scroll with a weary flourish. Rolls it up and ties it. Takes a nugget of scarlet sealing-wax and an impressive seal from a drawer in his desk. Candles a generous dribble of wax on the scroll, and ciphers the molten red fluid with the Danish seal.

Next:

From another drawer he removes a sturdy dispatch-box, carved from blackest ebony and gold-embossed with the Danish crest. He unlocks the box, fits the scroll inside it, relocks the box, melts more wax over the keyhole, and repeats his performance with the royal seal.

So there, secured, is the commission which Rosencrantz and Guildenstern are to safeguard over the waves, together with Hamlet, to England.

Claudius heaves a great sigh. Drains his goblet. Stands unsteadily. Lurches to the fireplace. Refills the goblet from a large earthenware jug.

He takes a further swallow, rubs his dazed brow, breathes laboriously, and mumbles:

'My offence is rank. It smells to heaven. The curse of Cain upon it. A brother's murder! My inclination and my will are strong, yet I cannot pray. My strong intent eclipsed by towering guilt. I am a man in double-bind, pulled hither and thither; unable to move.'

His tortured eyes proclaim that he too once burbled and gurgled and took loving suck from a warm mother's breast. He raises the open palm of his right hand to his eyes, regards it with stark horror, and rambles:

'This cursèd hand so thick with brother's blood! Is there not rain enough in the sweet heavens to wash it white as snow? What does mercy serve, if not the souls of sinners? And why do we pray, if not to be forestalled before we sin, or pardoned once fallen? Well, then, I'll look up. My fault is past.

'But, oh! What prayer can rescue *me*? "Forgive me my foul murder"? That will not do, since I am still possessed of all that made me murder: my crown, ambition, and my Queen.

'May one be pardoned, yet retain the prize for which one sinned? In the corrupted currents of *this* world, the criminal may buy the judge. Power, once seized, may put a man above the law. But it's not so . . . *above*. There is no shuffling there: no deception. There our acts appear in nakedness. And each must testify against himself: to bare the very privates of his thoughts.'

Is there maudlin moisture in the King's eyes?

Unlike Hamlet, Claudius has never thought through religion. He has always assumed, at some oceanic depth of self-deception, that forgiveness would be forthcoming when required. Now, torn between horrendous guilt, the blinkers of his childhood conditioning, and the Cassandra of his dulled intelligence, he is not so sure:

'What then? What remains? When one *cannot* repent? Oh, wretched state! Bosom black as death! Soul ensnared, that, struggling to be free, is more enmeshed! Help, angels! Help me try. Bow, stubborn knees. And . . . heart with strings of steel, be soft as the newborn babe. All may be well.'

Claudius' goblet falls splashing to the floor. He drops to his knees with a graceless thud. His eyes close. His hands supplicate.

While the King prays, Hamlet returns silently behind the wall. Having transacted with Marcellus and Bernardo (who even now are mounting for an icy ride west), the Prince is again en route to visit the Queen in her closet. Beside his dagger now hangs a sword. Its cold hilt he grimly grips as he scowls at his kneeling uncle, and breathes:

'*Now* could I do it. Now he is praying. And suppose I did? And he went to heaven? Would I be revenged? A villain kills my father. And I this villain send to heaven? No! Up, sword. Take him at a fitter time. When he is drunk asleep. Or in his rage. Or the incestuous pleasure of his bed. Gaming, swearing, or about some act with no salvation in it.

'*Then* trip him, that his heels may kick at heaven. And may his soul be damnèd black as hell, whereto it goes. Meanwhile, my mother waits. And this medicine but prolongs your sickly days.' Whispering this last unheard threat to Claudius, Hamlet turns, still holding his sword to keep it from jangling, and melts darkly away.

Claudius wakes from his studied petition. Clambers to his feet. Horrified credulity milks his bloated features.

'My *words* fly up,' he rasps in strangled tones. 'My *thoughts* remain below.'

The heady brew of religion having failed him, Claudius must borrow his unreality from reality. He totters to the fireplace. Collects the jug of tepid wine. Shambles miserably from his comfortless sanctum.

Breathing like a pig with terminal tuberculosis.

17
OEDIPUS WRECKED

Polonius has arrived in Gertrude's closet, bristling with self-importance and free advice. His beard straggles over his chest like an ungroomed baby's bib.

Gertrude resents Polonius' presence, but she is eager for a heart-to-heart with Hamlet. She is distressed by the news of his probable departure to England, both because of maternal concern for him, and, now, because of fears for her own future.

Closet.

This small private room for the Queen adjoins the large bedchamber where Hamlet first saw Claudius and Gertrude getting to grips. It is tastefully furnished. Two fires blaze voraciously, one on each side of the bed, making Gertrude's the cosiest closet in the Castle.

The Queen is wearing a loose crimson velvet robe over flimsy night attire. Her feet are snug in ankle-length soft-felt boots, lined with polar-bear fur. Her nordic gold hair is down. She has been brushing it. Summer sunlight might reveal odd flecks of wiry grey in the burnished yellow.

But summer sunlight is far away.

Across the small doorway to the royal bedchamber hangs a tapestry of Claudius. Head and shoulders. He is fond of his image, and one of his first acts as King of Denmark was to replace all portraits of Old Hamlet with portraits of himself. The tapestry shows Claudius as young and vigorous. Perhaps he is twenty-eight in the image. Yet on his head sits Denmark's crown.

The intended function of the tapestry is to keep warmth in Gertrude's closet, and draughts out.

But:

'He will be here soon,' Polonius informs Gertrude. 'Speak to him sternly, I pray you. Say his pranks have been too much. And that your Grace has screened him from much anger. I'll hide here,' he points to the Claudius tapestry. 'I pray you, be *firm* with him.'

'Mother, mother, mother!' Sounding like 'Hello, hello, hello!', Hamlet's approach echoes along the corridor outside.

'Have no fear.' Gertrude favours Polonius with a wintry smile. 'Now, withdraw.'

Polonius scuttles behind the tapestry with the dignity of a ruffled pheasant cock.

Gertrude sheds her robe and throws it across a small couch to the left of the tapestry. Her nightdress is of a strange sheeny material. It is full-length, but thin and sheer, to emphasize the lavish protuberances and monumental rotundities of her Queenly figure. Her plan is to lecture Hamlet from the impregnable fortress of soft maternal vulnerability. She sits at her dressing-table. Takes up a hairbrush.

A loud knock.

The Queen doesn't answer.

A moment passes.

The door is thrown open.

Hamlet enters in a clanking, tinkling jangle of boots, sword, and dagger. Still in his dappled jester's outfit and mask. He marches up behind Gertrude. Stamps to attention. Salutes in a mockery of military panache.

His mother frowns sternly in her dressing-table mirror.

'Now, mother, what's the matter?'

'Hamlet, you have greatly offended your father.'

'Mother, *you* have greatly offended my father.'

'Come, come. You answer with an idle tongue.'

'Go, go. *You* question with a *wicked* tongue.'

'Why, Hamlet!' She turns and regards him severely.

'What?'

'Have you forgotten me?'

'No, by the cross. Not so. You are the Queen. Your husband's brother's wife. And – would it were not so! – you are my mother.' He seizes her wrists and pulls her to her feet. None too gently.

Gertrude tries to break free. Things are not going at all as planned, and she is fearful for Hamlet's sanity.

143

'Let me be,' she cries. 'Or I'll turn you over to those that *can* tame you.'

Hamlet is unmoved.

He perches on the dressing-table stool. Pulls her unceremoniously towards himself.

'Come,' he cajoles. 'Sit you down. You shall not budge, till I have set you up a mirror of your inmost parts.'

The Prince's intention is to bend Gertrude over his knee and spank her.

Gertrude misconstrues his behaviour. Panics:

'What are you *doing*?' she protests, struggling frantically. 'You will not murder *me*? HELP!'

'What? Help, *help*! HELP!' Polonius, hearing Gertrude's distress, bleats in muffled alarm from his hiding place.

This has an electrifying effect on Hamlet.

He dumps Gertrude like a sack of rotten potatoes, leaps to his feet and whips out his sword.

'What?' the Prince roars. 'A rat? And dead!' He rams his rapier through the tapestry, impaling Claudius' portraited throat.

'AAAAAAAAAAAAARRRRGH!' A ghastly shriek issues behind the hanging, followed by a crumpling fall. 'I am slain.' Polonius' last words sound like a rabbit screaming.

A gravid silence.

Gertrude falls to her knees and hugs her bouncing breasts.

'Oh me!' she moans. 'What have you done?' She looks in terror at Hamlet's sword, now hilted in Claudius' depicted Adam's apple.

On the weaving, round the blade, is a rich dark smear of blood.

Hamlet quietly retrieves the sword. Wipes it on his multicoloured blouse. Sheathes it at his hip. Turns once more to whimpering Gertrude.

'I know not,' he answers. 'Is it the King?'

'Oh!' she wails. 'What a rash and bloody deed is this?'

'Bloody deed!' Hamlet scoffs. 'Almost as bad, good mother, as kill a King, and marry with his brother.'

'As kill a King?!'

'Those were my words.' He pulls the tapestry aside.

Polonius lies in a rigid heap. Evidently he died in agony, Hamlet having skewered his left eye. From its socket black blood oozes mixed with globules of green and yellow brain mucus.

The Prince is unremorseful.

'You wretched, rash, intruding *fool*,' he rebukes the corpse. 'Farewell! I took you for your master.' He drapes the nastiness and faces Gertrude.

She is still in a sobbing posture.

Hamlet grapnels her armpits. Hoists her upright.

'Leave off wringing your hands,' he commands.

She struggles. Inflates her magnificent chest with breath for a scream.

Hamlet clamps her mouth.

'Peace!' he hisses. 'Sit you down, and let me wring your heart. If sordid habits have not hardened it against all feeling.' He perches on the dressing-table stool and pulls her down beside him.

'What have I done,' she sniffles, 'that you dare wag your tongue so rude against me?'

'An act to blur the blush of modesty. Call virtue a hypocrite. Make marriage vows as false as dicers' oaths. From it *Heaven turns her face away*!'

Hamlet is trying to needle Gertrude's conscience in language she will understand: to resonate the religious strings from which she dangles.

But:

'Ah me!' She rubs her nose miserably. 'What act? What have I done that merits such wrath and thunder?'

Hamlet unchains from his neck the miniature of Old Hamlet.

'Look here. Upon this picture.'

Gertrude silently obeys.

'And this.' Hamlet switches attention to the punctured portrait of Claudius which screens the remains of Polonius.

'See,' the Prince taps the image of his father. 'What dignity reigned upon this brow. Apollo's brain in human house. An eye like Mars', to threaten and command. This *was* your husband. Look now what follows.'

Gertrude hides in the long whispering blinkers of her hair.

Hamlet forces her chin to gaze at the Claudius tapestry.

'Here *is* your husband,' he sneers. 'Like a mildewed apple, rotting his wholesome brother. Have you eyes? How could you descend from this fair mountain, to slurp upon this moor?' The Prince lunges his forefinger through the sword hole in Claudius' throat. 'Ha! Have you eyes? You cannot call it love, for at your age the blood is tame. And what judgement would step from this to *this*?' He holds the picture of Old Hamlet beside the wound in Claudius' gorge.

Sob, sob.

Undeterred by maternal mawkishness, Hamlet presses on. To alienate Gertrude from Claudius for ever: 'What devil has bested you? Eyes without feeling! Feeling without sight!'

Sob, Sob. Gertrude's averted shoulders heave.

'Oh, SHAME!' thunders Hamlet. 'Where is your blush? Rebellious hell! Proclaim no shame when sunny youth breaks loose, for frosty middle-age burns just as hot, and reason panders to its will.'

'Oh, Hamlet!' his mother beseeches. 'Speak no more. You turn my eyes inside my soul. And there I see such black ingrainèd spots as never will wash clean.' She looks up at him in tearful hope.

He, thoughtfully, strokes her shimmering mane, as if she were a distraught child.

She pillows her grateful cheek on his thigh.

'Nay,' he murmurs, 'but to live in the rank sweat of a greasy bed. Stewed in corruption. Honeying between your thighs . . .'

'Speak no more!' Gertrude squeezes Hamlet's knee in desperate treaty. 'These words like daggers pierce. No more, sweet Hamlet!'

But sweet Hamlet can't stop. His course is determined by the unexpected development of:

A granite erection.

Yes. Beneath his mother's sorrowful majestic head and his own scanty hose, the Prince is hard as a petrified cucumber.

Hypertense sleeplessness?

Or fruit of desire to be revenged on Claudius? To sauce the bloat King by gandering his Queen?

To fuck Mummy, or not to fuck Mummy?

As he wrestles with this prickly dilemma, Hamlet plays for time by prolonging his self-righteous harangue:

'A murderer, and a villain,' he scolds. Squirms on the stool as his swollen totem jerks autonomously under Gertrude's cheek. 'A *clown* of kings. Pickpocket of the empire, that stole the precious diadem from a shelf.' He looks down and with a penile start sees through the neck of his mother's nightdress the deep dark valley of her inviting cleavage, while promontory nipples project stiffly through her filmy garment like sentinels on twin high hills calling cannon from the plain.

'No more!' Gertrude begs Hamlet's masked eyes.

His masked nostrils twitch at a critical whiff of the metallic halitosis that has ground relations between Gertrude and Claudius to a rancid stalemate. This tinny olfactory trace reminds him as sharply as a dead cat stinks of that near-hysterical coronation glimpse of the inflamed organ which coughed him bawling into the world thirty years ago.

So the Princely erection wilts.

'A king of shreds and patches . . .' Hamlet's slur on Claudius fades as his boiling mercurial consciousness surfaces the spirit of his father's ghost. On the fateful tapestry whereon skewered Claudius leers, Hamlet sees superimposed a lurid twisting image of Old Hamlet:

Crimson-robed; pale-faced; stern-gazed.

The spectre hovers between dimensions.

Hamlet feels it flowing out of him like smoky filaments of coloured fire from a magic lantern. Following Faust's Rule (that to flee such visitations courts instant shipwreck) the Prince takes a vigorous stand.

Leaving Gertrude deposited rudely on the floor.

'Save me! Protect me with your wings, you heavenly angels!' Hamlet appeals to the ceiling. Then he feints at the ghostly image, which retracts. 'What would your gracious figure?' the Prince inquires courteously.

The gracious figure frowns.

'Alas! He's *mad*!' Gertrude observes only Hamlet's behaviour. Never has she voyaged in the Mind's Other Kingdom. Hence her despairing whisper.

Hamlet ignores her.

'Come to chide your tardy son?' he asks encouragingly. 'Who, letting passion cool, neglects your dread command? Oh, say!'

'Do . . . not . . . forget!' The phantom's voice comes from deep in Hamlet's own throat, unnaturally bass and harsh:

'This visitation is to whet your . . . blunted . . . *purpose.*'

Hamlet stands spellbound by his externalization.

Gertrude is beside herself with uncomprehending terror.

'What's the matter with you, lady?' Hamlet murmurs distantly.

'Alas!' she laments. 'What's the matter with *you*, that you bend your eye on vacancy and converse with the empty air? While your hair starts up and stands on end, like soldiers attacked in their sleep, or flesh-flies on excrements. Oh, gentle son! Upon the heat of your distemper, sprinkle cool patience. Whereon do you look?' She stands beside Hamlet.

The Prince fixates his eidolon.

'On *him*!' Hamlet points mischievously at his simmering projection. He knows Gertrude can see nothing, but:

'Look!' he urges. 'How pale he glares,' he whispers confidentially, putting a comforting arm around her shoulder. 'His appearance and his grievance together, preaching to stones, would blast them into life.' He jumps forward suddenly, hand on sword, to keep the 'ghost' on its toes.

It dances back in disarray, almost out of existence.

'Do not look upon me,' Hamlet shouts. 'Lest you dilute my stern resolve. Then might I draw mere tears where *blood* must run.' He draws his sword, half playfully.

The spectre pales. Its bubbling hints of rainbow dimensionality attenuate to gossamer grey.

'*To whom* do you speak?' Gertrude tugs anxiously at Hamlet's jester sleeve.

'You see nothing there?' He feigns surprise.

'Nothing at all. Yet . . . all that is, I see.'

'And did you *hear* nothing?'

'Nothing but ourselves.'

'Why, look you here!' He points his blood-stained blade at the dissolving vision. 'Look! How it steals away. My father, dressed just as he lived.' Hamlet turns away from the tapestry. Slowly he rotates the dwindling demon round the walls, etiolating it to meek tattered wisps. 'Look! There he goes, even now, out through the door.'

The tattered wisps cluster into a small grey tornado and vanish through the keyhole of the main door like dirty water down a drain.

'This is but the coinage of your brain!' Gertrude cries unhappily.

'Madness!' snorts Hamlet. 'It is not madness that I have uttered. Not my madness, but *your own sins* do speak.'

Gertrude shakes her head. Without conviction.

'Confess,' Hamlet hounds her. 'Repent what's past. Avoid what is to come. Do not manure your weeds to make them ranker.'

'Oh Hamlet!' Gertrude wails. 'You have cleft my heart in two.' She seizes his right hand. Hugs it to her thudding bosom.

'Oh!' he mocks, beating his left hand against his chest. 'Throw away the baser part, and live more purely with the other. Good-night.' He disengages her neurotic embrace.

She shivers with misery.

Hamlet sermonizes:

'But spurn my uncle's bed. *Enact* a virtue, if you don't possess it. Refrain tonight,' he pats his genitals, 'and the next abstinence will be more easy. For Custom can *almost* recast Nature.

'Once more, good-night.' Hamlet makes as if to leave. 'When you are truly penitent I'll ask your blessing. For this same lord I do repent.' He points at dead Polonius. 'But heaven has pleased it, so I must be their scourge.' His gesture includes punctured Claudius. 'I will take him away, and in good time account in public for his death.' He stalks to the tapestry. Flings it aside. Takes the body by its decomposing armpits.

In Polonius' rapiered eye vile jelly congeals, like the custard bile that squelches from a bluebottle belly when it squashes.

'Again, good-night.' Hamlet drags the body across the floor. 'I must be cruel only to be kind. Thus bad begins, and worse remains behind!' With this cryptic comment on the nature of tragedy, Hamlet is about to leave. He shoulders Polonius. Reaches for the door-knob.

Gertrude panics. Throws herself at Hamlet's feet, embracing his knees. Her hair is rumpled, her eyes suggest a haunting hangover.

Hamlet sighs. 'One word more, good lady.' He drops his rotting burden to the floor behind him, where it lands with a sickening crunch.

'What shall I *do*?' Gertrude moans.

'Not this!' Hamlet leers:

'Let the bloat King tempt you again to bed; pinch wanton on

your cheek; call you his mouse. And let him, for a pair of sleazy kisses, or paddling in your neck with his toad paws, get you to reveal that I am only *mad in craft*.'

Because his mother is so hysterical, Hamlet's nastiness attempts to revive her discretion.

Gertrude sobs into his kneecaps.

'Let him know!' Hamlet lards the sarcasm. 'Why should a mere Queen – fair, sober, and *wise* – hide such secrets from a goat?'

'Rest assured,' Gertrude pledges brokenly. 'I have no life to breathe what you have said.'

Hamlet strokes a strand of hair from her eyes.

'I go to England,' he announces tenderly. 'Did you know?'

'Alack! Is it decided?'

'The letters are sealed, to be carried by my schoolfellows. For they must sweep my way, and marshal me to knavery. It will be hard, but I will dig below their mines, and blow them at the moon.'

Gertrude frowns in puzzled anxiety.

Hamlet pushes his mask up his forehead. Smiles grimly:

'How sweet! When in one line two crafts directly meet!'

What can this crafty pun imply?

Gertrude doesn't even notice it.

'This man shall set me packing,' Hamlet puns again. 'I'll lug the guts elsewhere. Mother, good-night.' He flings Polonius' corpse back over his shoulder, causing a weal of blood and brain to splash his back, and presents his cheek for a kiss.

Gertrude hugs him with disturbing ardour.

'Indeed,' Hamlet dodges her feeling, 'this counsellor is now most still. Secret and grave! Who was in life? A foolish prattling knave! Come, sir,' he pats Polonius' lifeless buttocks with his free hand, 'let's end with you.' He opens the door. 'Good-night, mother.' He gives her shoulder a last comforting squeeze, then carts his cadaverous bag into the yawning corridor dark.

18
ACCELERATION

One Castle hour has passed.

Gertrude, having prayed, has decided that Polonius' death must be communicated to Claudius. In her velvet robe she lies on a couch in the antechamber to Claudius' sanctum. Head in hand, she syncopates a symphony of sighs with sobs.

The imported oak door throws open.

Claudius appears.

Rosencrantz and Guildenstern follow. They are clad and shod in travelling leathers, and even sporting swords. Ready for England.

Claudius has concluded their brief.

Rosencrantz lovingly cradles the sealed dispatch-box.

Claudius' haggard baritone buzz breaks off when he spots his prostrate wife.

'There's something serious behind these weighty heaves,' he exclaims. Sits on the couch. Pats Gertrude's shoulder. 'You must translate,' he wheedles. 'What's wrong?'

Gertrude sobs louder.

Claudius abandons his ponderous tenderness. Roars:

'WHERE'S YOUR SON?'

Gertrude looks round. Sits up. Epitomizing tearful desolation, she asks:

'Leave us for a little while.'

Rosencrantz and Guildenstern withdraw.

'Ah!' wails Gertrude. 'My good lord, what I have seen tonight!'

'*What*, Gertrude?' Claudius struggles with his frowning black temper. 'Where is Hamlet?'

'Mad as the sea and wind contending. In his lawless fit, hearing something stir behind the tapestry, he seized his rapier, cried "A rat!" and *killed* the unseen good old man.'

'Oh, heavy deed!' Claudius' complexion drains. 'Likewise with *us*, had *we* been there,' in a flustered yap. 'His liberty imperils all. Yourself; us; everyone. Alas! This bloody deed will be blamed on *us*, whose foresight should have kept this mad young man restrained. But our love forbore, like the owner of a foul disease, to shield him from the public.' As he smarms Gertrude with these unctuous lies, the King's pulse races with paranoid exhilaration:

What better justification for Hamlet's deportation than this? The *mad* slaughter of poor old Polonius?

'Where has he gone?' Claudius asks guardedly.

'Somewhere with the body. In this his madness shows pure. He weeps for what is done.'

'Oh, Gertrude! Come away. The sun no sooner shall touch the mountains than we shall ship him hence. And this vile deed we must, with all our majesty and skill, excuse.' He squeezes her hand, as a cat caresses a mouse, and rises.

'Ho! Guildenstern!' he shouts.

In they ooze again, like haunting sewage from the sea.

'Friends both,' booms Claudius, 'go summon guards to your assistance. Hamlet, in his madness, has slain Polonius and dragged him from his mother's closet. Go seek him out. Humour him, take care, and bring the body into the chapel. I pray you, haste in this.'

The sewage departs.

'Come, Gertrude,' Claudius overflows. Inscrutably uxorious. 'We'll tell our wisest friends what has been done and what we mean to do. Slander whispers round the world at twice the speed of cannonballs. This way, his poisoned shot may miss our name, and hit the empty air. Come. My soul is full of discord and dismay.'

But Claudius, as he departs to rouse the Castle, looks bright with new life.

Gertrude has nothing to say. She is overwrought by Polonius' violent demise, and, especially, the prospect of Hamlet's banishment. At the same time, she would rather Hamlet were sent to England than brought to severe justice in Denmark. She senses, of course, that Claudius desires Hamlet's absence, but she also believes that Claudius, in his selfishness, will be acting in Hamlet's best interests.

So her milken motherhood misleads.

* * *

As Claudius and Gertrude bring bleary wakefulness to the bar-
nacled eyes of snuftering counsellors, Hamlet, along countless
convolutions of statue-lined corridors and up several flights of
spiral stairs, returns to his room after secreting the remains of
Polonius. He is hot and panting. His armpits soggy; mask stained
with brow sweat.

'Safely stowed,' he mutters.

Heavy footsteps approach.

'Lord Hamlet!'

He recognizes fluty Rosencrantz.

'What noise?' he responds. 'Who calls?'

The door creaks open.

'Oh!' groans Hamlet, as in disgusted surprise. 'Here they
come.'

Rosencrantz and Guildenstern march in, unasked.

A squad of armed guards stand ready outside.

Hamlet revives his Russian Bear act. Leaps on to his writing
table. Bounds to his bed. Swings his fists and grunts like a furious
hedgehog.

Rosencrantz tries an initiative:

'What have you done, my lord,' he inquires politely, 'with the
dead body?'

'Compounded it with dust, whereto it is kin.' Hamlet follows this
with an ear-splitting howl.

'Tell us where it is,' Rosencrantz persists. 'That we may bear it
to the chapel.'

'Do not believe it.' Hamlet jumps down from the bed. Smooths
his dappled chemise. Abandons his ursine charade.

'Believe what?'

'That I can keep your secrets and not my own.' The Prince
smiles with his mouth, but not with the slits in his mask. 'Besides,
to be questioned by a sponge!'

'A sponge, my lord?'

'Yes, sir. That soaks up the King's patronage, his rewards, his
authorities.' Hamlet crowds Rosencrantz. Takes the little man's
pasty jowl between thumb and forefinger. Shakes it reprovingly.
'But such officers do the King best service in the end. He keeps
them, as an ape keeps nuts and berries, in the corner of his jaw:

ingested first, they are swallowed last. When he wants what you have gleaned, he need only squeeze you, and, being a sponge, you will be dry again.'

'I do not understand you, my lord.'

'Good!'

A scowl of knowing malice flashes between Rosencrantz and Guildenstern.

'My lord, you *must* tell us where the body is, and go with us to the King,' Rosencrantz threatens.

Hamlet is unmoved.

'The body is with the King,' he mystifies, 'but the King is not with the body. The King is a thing . . .'

'A *thing*, my lord!' Guildenstern ejaculates in outrage.

'Of nothing,' quips Hamlet. 'Take me to him.' He walks slowly, soberly to the door. Then whirls and thumbs his nose in a timeless gesture:

'Hide, fox. And all away!' he cries, opening the door, exiting, and banging it shut behind him.

The jellied hearts and gaping mouths of Rosencrantz and Guildenstern rush after Hamlet, fearful of Claudius' wrath, and are galled to find the Prince standing calmly outside the door, chatting amiably with the guards.

Meanwhile:

Claudius is holding forth.

Around the King flock anxious courtiers.

The floor is thick with sleepymen dead before dawn.

Claudius has packed Gertrude off to bed with a spiritous sedative. His manner is more aggressive than it might be in her presence.

'I have sent to seek him,' the King orates. 'And to find the body. How dangerous that this man goes loose! And yet we cannot treat him to the full severity of the law, for he is loved by the distracted multitude. They, the people, like not with their judgement but with their eyes. So, the offender's *punishment* is broadcast to the heavens – but never his *offence*! Hence . . . a tolerant delay in calling him to account.'

Sycophantic nods. Murmurs of approval.

Claudius' next splurge is pre-empted by the self-important entry of Rosencrantz.

'How now!' raps the King. 'What news?'

'Where the dead body is bestowed, my lord, we cannot get from him.'

'But where is *he*?'

'Outside, my lord. Guarded, to know your pleasure.'

'Bring him before us.'

'Ho, Guildenstern,' warbles Rosencrantz. 'Bring in my lord.'

In marches Hamlet, with Guildenstern tripping behind him.

Like a bear with a whippet at his heels.

Though Hamlet is 'guarded', no one has relieved him of his sword and dagger.

As Claudius notes with frowning apprehension.

'Now, Hamlet,' the King ventures, 'where's Polonius?'

'At supper.'

'At supper? *Where?*'

'Where he is eaten. We fatten other creatures, that they may fatten us. And we fatten ourselves for? Maggots! Your fat king', the Prince pokes Claudius playfully in the belly with an accusing forefinger, 'and your lean beggar are but two different dishes: all served to the same table in the end.'

'Alas!' Claudius affects dismay at his nephew's mental condition.

The courtiers look glassily on.

'A man may fish with the worm', Hamlet continues, 'that has eaten of a king, and eat of the fish that fed on that worm.'

'So?'

'Nothing,' Hamlet waves airily, 'but how a king may progress through the guts of a beggar.' He chuckles, and whistles a popular air.

'WHERE IS POLONIUS?'

'In heaven,' Hamlet hypothesizes mildly. 'Send thither to see. If your messenger does not find him there, seek in the other place yourself. Failing there, you may nose him upstairs in the lobby.'

Claudius realizes with a gurgle of fear that Hamlet has stashed the rotting prime minister behind the enormous hanging tapestry depicting gory Danish history up to the establishment of the hereditary succession by Hamlet I. In other words:

The Prince has returned Polonius to the very alcove from which he and Claudius spied on the engineered confrontation between Hamlet and Ophelia before Polonius' rifting gave the game away.

'Go seek him there,' Claudius blusters to several attendants.

'He will wait for you,' Hamlet advises them.

'Hamlet,' Claudius lectures hurriedly, 'we cherish your safety as dear as we lament your deed. And so you must with fiery quickness prepare. The ship is ready, the wind favourable. Your companions are waiting, and everything is bent for England.'

'For . . . *England*!' Hamlet seems astonished.

'Yes, Hamlet.' Claudius seems so kind.

'Good.'

'You would say so again, if you knew our purposes.'

'I see a cherub that sees them.' Hamlet pretends to hold a mirror to his face. Gaily smooths his hair. He thinks of all his private peep-holes, and lights a mental candle to the perverse prodigality of his grandfather.

Then he snaps into businesslike action:

'But come,' he exclaims. 'For England! Farewell, dear mother.' He moves to kiss Claudius on the lips.

'Your loving *father*, Hamlet!' Claudius starts back, aghast.

'My *mother*,' Hamlet explains. 'Father and mother is man and wife. Man and wife is one flesh. And so; my *mother*. Come,' he beckons curtly to Rosencrantz and Guildenstern, 'for England.' And he speeds away, to collect his belongings.

'Follow him *immediately*,' Claudius orders. 'Tempt him aboard with *speed*. Don't delay. I'll have him hence *tonight*. Away!'

Rosencrantz and Guildenstern retire with spring in their step.

Slavering counsellors voice admiration of the King's handling of the Hamlet problem.

Claudius himself . . .

19
LAST ENTRY

The King returns to his sanctum. Pours yet another brimming gobletful of hot spiced liquor. Drains it in one greedy swallow. Refills. Sips more slowly.

Angels, devils; virgins, witches; lions, unicorns; and other gleaming twisting foaming frolicking protagonists of the mind's antipodes fertilize and fragment and ferment and reform in the furiously fizzling flames of the fire into which the King stares.

But the fireworks are lost on Claudius. He experiences nothing but dead hope and flat dread.

He wipes his wet fleshy mouth on a long-stained sleeve. Sighs. The searing spicy drink burns through his tattered stomach to broth his blood and haze the hopeless halls of his brain. His features sag into lumpy yellow irredeemable evil.

And he mumbles:

'Oh, England! If you value my love at all! If you heed my great power, you will execute our royal desire ... the instant *death of Hamlet*.

'Do it, England. For like a fever in my blood he rages, and you must cure me. Whatever fortune now may bring, I never can be happy till I know it is done.'

Claudius has intended all along that Hamlet be executed immediately he reaches England. But no one else yet knows this. Not even Rosencrantz and Guildenstern. For Claudius, holding that any unnecessary access to information is dangerous access, has committed the contract only to the sealed dispatch-box.

Now, the murderous King clambers off to the cold warm comfort of Gertrude's frustrated arms, breasts, itching fearful loins, and halitoid mouth.

* * *

Later the same morning, on the edge of the plain, a mile west of Aarhus:

In the cold grey half-light of a wintry dawn, a gentle fluff of fresh snow falls over the stale crust of packed ice.

Arcticized horse nostrils snort and steam indignantly.

Ominously in the thin gelid light two mounted figures loom.

One is Fortinbras, the other his captain.

For two hours Fortinbras has been busy unloading the soldiers, horses, and equipment of his vanguard. Now his impassive features scan the snowscape down to Aarhus harbour:

The market place; the meandering sidestreets; the sad sloughing slaps of the liquid iceberg sea, relentless against the harbour wall.

Further out, disappearing in a wave-kissing shroud of mist, are the departing empty hulks of Fortinbras' troop-ships.

Closer in, a huge black reptile wriggles up from the town: a gigantic python with eight thousand white labouring nostrils writhing up the shallow snowy slope to the plain. It is Fortinbras' advance-army crocodile, creeping to join him.

No flicker illumines his cold grey eyes. No shiver weakens his thick square jaw. Yet exhalations are freezing fast on his travel-stubble beard and moustache.

'Go, captain.' Fortinbras instructs his ambassador in a voice both self-assured and lifeless, like the weather.

The captain snaps to attention.

'From me greet the Danish King,' Fortinbras continues. 'Tell him Fortinbras claims his promised march across this kingdom. You know the rendezvous. If his majesty wishes, we shall express our duty in his presence. Be sure to make this clear.'

'I will, my lord.'

'Go now,' Fortinbras commands with a thick gauntlet forefinger. 'But *take your time.*'

The captain nods, spurs his mount, and trots back down the advancing caravan of soldiers, steeds, and light artillery.

Meanwhile, in the market place:

Hamlet is stomping moodily about the snowy square, attended by Rosencrantz and Guildenstern. They could have reached the jetty by carriage, but Hamlet has insisted on a nostalgic look round before sailing. His future is uncertain. Will he ever step on Danish soil again?

He, in his huge Russian bearskin, is dressed for the part. Rosencrantz and Guildenstern, in their heavy but impractical travelling leathers, are not. The spring frozen in their step, they drag along miserably behind the Prince, as his eyes and lungs drink deeply of the icy morning scene.

In the centre of the market square (where life would crowd, and stalls selling ripe earthy vegetables, lush fruit, and hand-made leather goods and pottery from the provinces would abound in warmer times) the children of the town have rolled, dressed and decorated an enormous snowman. Ten feet tall, four feet wide at the shoulder, this snowman is a daunting figure.

A soldier snowman.

On his head sits an upturned coalscuttle: his helmet. His eyes and nose are chunks of coal, as are his buttons. His doublet is a moth-eaten hide draped over his shoulders. And his weapon? A double-edged seven-foot wooden sword lodged under a belt of frayed rope.

Hamlet reflects on the cool aloofness of snowmen everywhere, and pictures into clearness a snowman of his own long-past creation:

Little Hamlet's snowman too had been a soldier, though smaller and more subtle. A bowl of newly slaughtered bullock's blood from the cooks in the kitchens had daubed his snowman's sword a deadly crimson and poured before him on the virgin snow the warm puddling proof of his prowess in battle.

And the Prince pessimistically ponders:

Why are children so cruel? So bloodthirsty? Children wish for death, and parents wish for children. Paradise would consist of memories and dreams, yet who would return to life at an earlier age? But why not? In our different ways, he gloomily concludes, we are deathwishers all. Yearning for the cold silent peace of eternal still.

Approaching heavy hooves crunch snow crystals into ice.

Hamlet turns.

In the dwindling distance he observes the reptilian progress of Fortinbras' military caravan, and it pricks his curiosity. There have been many army exercises in Denmark in recent months, ordered by Claudius' guilt-ridden paranoia, and yet . . .

Clip, clop; muffled. *Clip, clop* . . .

Fortinbras' captain trots into the market-place.

'Good sir,' Hamlet hails him, 'whose troops are these?'

The captain kicks his unenthusiastic mount round the towering snowman, and halts in front of Hamlet. He is happy to obey Fortinbras' admonition that he should take his time before approaching Claudius.

'Of Norway, sir,' he replies.

'Where bound, sir?' Hamlet enjoys the captain's ignorance of his own Princely identity.

'Against some part of Poland.'

'Who commands them?'

'The nephew to Old Norway, Fortinbras.'

'Do you proceed against Poland itself, sir? Or against some outpost?'

'Truly to speak,' the captain spits, 'we go to gain a little patch that has in it no profit but the name. For a rent of five ducats a year, I would not farm it. Nor will it bring to Norway or the Pole a greater sum if sold outright.'

'Why,' Hamlet scoffs, 'then the Polack will never defend it.'

'Yes,' the captain frowns. 'It is already garrisoned.'

Hamlet gazes after the soldiers retreating into the distance like ants on cream cheese.

'Two thousand souls and twenty thousand ducats will not settle the question of this straw,' he murmurs. 'This is the cancer of much wealth and peace, that breaks inwardly and gives no outside sign of why the man dies.' Again to the captain:

'I humbly thank you, sir.'

The captain realizes with a shock that he is being absent-mindedly dismissed by someone of high station. 'God be with you, sir.' He inclines his head respectfully, pulls wearily on his reins, and clops away.

Never one to roughshoe Fortinbras, the captain intends to find comfortable lodgings, a comfortable sleep, and perhaps even a comfortable Aarhus trollop, before he presents himself in the Castle. These prospects cheer him for a moment, but the cheer runs shallow. His heart of hearts acknowledges that he is getting old, may never return from his present mission, and would sooner be snug at home with his fat jolly wife and lusty bawling brats than bound for fruitless battle at Fortinbras' headstrong instigation.

Hamlet leaves the market-place without a backward glance. The information gleaned from the captain has disturbed him.

Rosencrantz and Guildenstern follow him like unwanted brides-maids gone brown and rancid from age and mould.

Hamlet leads down a narrow sidestreet to the harbour. Here, later in the day, will toil the humble townsfolk, the butchers and bakers and candlestick-makers. The unaspiring salt of Denmark's earth. The simple souls who were unambitiously going about their business long before Hamlet began, and who will continue long after he has ended.

But no such life is stirring yet.

On the harbour front two taverns are open. Now that Claudius is King there is always some defence-oriented activity on the seafront, hence a market for warm refuge and refreshment.

When Hamlet reaches the quay he watches his belongings being transported from the carriage to the ship.

'Will it please _you_ to go, my lord?' Rosencrantz's chilled marrow hopes.

The Prince rounds with disfavour on the chattering interruption: 'Presently,' he snaps. 'You go on ahead.'

Rosencrantz and Guildenstern, like parrots in a frozen zoo, are in no condition to argue. They hobble to the ship (a rugged threemaster, square-rigged, built for safety rather than speed), and climb aboard.

Hamlet watches them.

A solitary seagull lands on the rigging of the centre mast, like a flying maggot seeking warmth on a terrier's tail.

Hamlet turns his back on the salty scene and wanders vaguely into a tavern, for a last taste of nostalgia.

The fire burns low. The landlord is asleep at the bar, his fat head snoring on the counter. Somnolent sailing heads and guttural grunts inhabit sundry corners. An aged flea-bitten hound whimpers before the flagging fire as it goes the ghastly round of dreams and death.

Hamlet chucks a log into the grate, provoking an instant blaze, seats himself at a nearby table, bangs on it loudly to summon the landlord, and orders a jug of punch.

The drink arrives.

The Prince pays the landlord, takes a deep draught, delves inside his bearskin, produces his diary and a crayon. Then scribes to soothe his sorrows:

How everything seems to conspire against me, and spur my dull revenge! What is a man, if his chief goods are eating, sleeping and fornicating? A beast, no more. Surely he that endowed us so *generously* with rational thought, looking into the past and future, did not intend us to leave this god-like power, like a lute in a cellar, to moulder unused.

So why do I still live to say, 'This thing is still to do'?

Perhaps I am swayed by the siren song of sheer bestial oblivion. Or daunted by dreadful consequences? Containing one part wisdom, three parts cowardice?

I do not know.

Certainly, I have reason, will and strength to do it. Examples obvious as excrements exhort me. Witness this army, so strong, brave, and determined. Led by a tender prince, whose spirit thumbs its nose at the outcome. Thus the fortunes of so many, so mortal and unsure, exposed to danger, fate, and death. And all for an egg-shell.

Clearly, to be great is to battle over a straw when *honour* is on trial!

What does all this make of me?

My father is murdered, my mother stained. Motives fire my reason and my blood, and yet I let all sleep. And here, to my shame, I see the imminent death of twenty thousand men. For the chimerical crown of gory glory, they go to their graves like beds. They fight for a plot of land not large enough to house their battle; not rich enough to bury their slain.

Oh! From this time forth, *my thoughts will be bloody*; or worthless!

And yet:

As Hamlet leaves the haven tavern, and trudges blearily to his sojourn on the sea, he hardly *looks* ablaze with bloody thoughts.

Why not?

20
SECOND INTERLUDE

As Hamlet rolls and plunges through the parlous troughs and crests of icy seas, Fortinbras' taciturn captain reports to Claudius. Quietly grave, suavely deferential, he executes his mission with precision.

Claudius, grey and anxious, has little time for Fortinbras' adolescent military gewgaws. His principal concern is the fate of Hamlet. He pines for news of the Prince's death as if this would restore his virility. Still, the King has not lost his paranoid caution. He decides that though Fortinbras no longer constitutes a threat to Denmark, and Denmark's illustrious Head, he must nevertheless be checked and tagged, like any other migrant carnivore.

So Osric is dispatched to ensure that Fortinbras and his imported soldiers behave.

Osric inspects and approves Fortinbras.

Fortinbras and his army march south.

Osric advises Claudius that all is well.

Claudius sniffs, farts, orders regular checks on Fortinbras until he leaves Danish soil, and descends into more grey craving for news of Hamlet's death. Now that the King can't service his wife, he neglects his personal appearance. An odour reminiscent of Polonius haunts him – like a rotten mushroom in a damp cupboard.

For appearances, and due to compliance born of fear, Gertrude consents to sleep in her closet whilst Claudius, whenever wasted weariness and wine make this possible, snores through the door in the royal bedchamber. But nothing passes between them. Not even the ghost of a dead bent sperm.

Sometimes, as she lies cold and lonely and sleepless, Gertrude gazes by draught-crazed candlelight at the tapestried caricature of her husband that screens the door between herself and him. Streaks of faded blood brown cluster like veins in a Cyclops' eyeball around the puncture in Claudius' throat. Gertrude shivers, sighs, and silently weeps.

During the days she finds some solace in the comfortable company of Horatio. Staying on in the Castle at the behest of Hamlet before his departure, and at Gertrude's subsequent invitation, Horatio irrigates the Queen with a stream of solid sense and innocuous anecdote. He tells her glowing stories of Hamlet's academic and athletic prowess. Assures her incessantly that all will be well (for this is the best world possible) and that Hamlet will soon return.

At the same time, Gertrude stays close to Claudio, her Italian Switzer. Deeply imbrued in suspicion that her future is adrift on treacherous expediency and malice, she would even have her trusty bodyguard sleeping in her closet, like a devoted wolfhound, were it not for fear of calumny.

Claudio takes this all in excellent Sicilian spirit: stoically accepting that his destiny is either to mortgage his immortal soul in the execution of Gertrude's interests, or to lay down his own life in defence of hers. Or both.

And Ophelia?

Now mistress of her household, is she not happier, freer, revelling on pageboys?

No. There is a snag.

Ophelia is pregnant.

By whom?

Yes, by Hamlet.

How little did she think, as he furrowed between her eager thighs, that remorseless new life was blasting through the acid secretions of her animality, to fertilize her disappointed womb.

How cruelly unfair, she wails within, that this should happen to *me, now,* so late in my life. With my father so tragically slain, in anger, by the getter of my child-to-be. Oh, *woe.*

Indeed.

And who can she tell?

Not Polonius; he's dead.

Not Laertes; he's in Paris and can't be trusted.

Not Claudius or Gertrude; her pregnancy might fall dangerously foul of their succession plans.

Nor can she tell Hamlet; she has no means of contacting him (or reason to suppose she will ever see him alive again).

So what does she do?

First, she sends a messenger to summon Laertes from his Parisian luxuriana with the angry hint that Daddy Polonius has been savagely disposed of and buried without inquiry, revenge, or reparation. This carrot she spices with the rumour that the plebs are clamouring for Laertes' return. The common people are turning against Claudius, Ophelia implies, now that their Prime Minister has been deleted and their Crown Prince banished, all under cover of darkness and official obfuscation. Nor is the rumour groundless. There *are* factions who, in the absence of Hamlet, would sooner follow Laertes than Claudius.

Second, Ophelia goes 'mad'. Having been rogered at close quarters by the ostensible lunatic himself, she concludes that Hamlet's 'madness' was merely a clever charade. And if Hamlet can use the mask of madness to fool (so far as she can tell) everyone but her foxy self, why shouldn't she gambit likewise? Has she not more grief than Hamlet ever had? Her father dies horribly, killed by the Prince who is mad for love of *her*! Her profligate brother is debauching in Paris. She has no other kin to turn to. How natural, then, that she should break down!

Thirdly, she exploits her publicly deteriorating mental state to attract Claudius. Sensing that relations between Claudius and Gertrude have collapsed, Ophelia calculates, rightly, that Claudius will be anxious to prove his virility elsewhere. And that the sordid city of his mind will crawl with bright young buxom queens . . .

So pretty Ophelia assumes (not slavering lunacy, but) innocent derangement. Heart-rending, but acutely fetching. Pregnant with the possibility of happy recovery. Doubly licensed, bereaved and unsane, she meanders aimlessly about the Castle. Skipping and dancing in manic ecstasy. Then shuffling hangdog in depressive despair. And trilling gravid snatches of antic lays and gnomic runes.

And on her distracted sallies she wears?

Nothing more concealing than a wispy shift, with all her ingenuous appeals transparently displayed. Childish and charming, she will kneel by Claudius' feet like a helpless cherub looking up to a grizzled Gabriel, warmed only by the muted heat of Gertrude's broiling displeasure.

Claudius is hardly proof against such attentions. He views Ophelia's apparent plight with a sympathetic, avuncular, barely Platonic eye, and?

More than a few well-wishing Pats on Ophelia's all-but-unclad rump take place.

These events lead into the darkest arc of the coldest Danish winter. Climate and conditions become excruciatingly alien. Sprawling wastes of endless blinding whiteness blanket a treacherous marriage of rock and frozen mud. How then could Fortinbras have marched his army south?

The answer lies in Denmark's essential flatness, which, even when arcticized, does not entirely preclude motility, either military or personal.

And, indeed:

What of the common people?

The gentle peons and humble townsfolk?

The butchers and bakers and candlestick-makers?

The salt of Denmark's earth and snow?

At the moment they are less unanimously unaspiring than usual. Murmurs, frets and agitations buzz abroad. Since the rumour-raddled death of Polonius and exodus of Hamlet, factions have developed. Their grievances are several, yes, but all converge on the person and appendages of Claudius.

Who is responsible for such particular malignancies as:

The crippling taxation?

The prodigious expenditure on 'defence'?

The cruel conscription of mere stripling lads into military service which no longer provides against any clearcut threat from another nation?

So, people mutter, our hard-earned money is leeched from us. Our beloved sons are plucked from us. Our Prime Minister has disappeared. Our magnificent Crown Prince exiled overseas. Things are getting worse, not better.

Who to blame?

Claudius inevitably becomes the target of speculation, defamation, even underground aggression. Numbers of his private secret police disappear unaccountably in the night, or are found brutally murdered in public places. He finds to his horror that his intelligence services are becoming increasing impotent, as if invisibly contained by an enormous goldfish bowl or spider's web.

The King has suspicions, and liberal reprisals are taken. Suspected seditionaries are seized in the night and disappear in a blaze of rumour, never to be seen again. Or their mutilated bodies are left as glaring warnings, outside their homes or in the market-place, their frozen blood tracing hieroglyphs in the hardpacked snow, like the ominous ciphers of some clandestine brotherhood.

Torture too is much in vogue.

Rumour has a loathsome stench of burning flesh belch forth from the Castle dungeons from time to time, like the nauseous putrescence of frazzled rancid bacon. Some claim the deadest hours of night see slop buckets full of swilling blood, sundered limbs and severed genitals being hurried from the dungeons in the hooded anonymity of institutional shame. And, it is said, the distant hollow wails, and shrieks and tortured echoes from the Castle's deepest, dankest, rat-infested hellholes are so peripherally incessant that soon they fade below the wavering penumbra of conscionable awareness.

These entropic escalations have several consequences for Claudius.

First, his hands and neuroses fill to brimming. He loses confidence in his armed forces. As a result, he also loses a measure of real control. He distrusts everyone bar Osric, and even he is often kept in the dark. At the same time, discontent spreads from the civilian population to infect the forces, soon providing Claudius with retrospective justification for his paranoia. So the King's harrowed entrails inflame with gnawing pains, and his bowel movements feel like broken bottles undigested.

Second, suspicious of his own Danish troops, Claudius drastically cuts the Castle garrison, to reduce the risk of a military coup. For personal protection, he relies on his mercenary Switzers.

Thirdly, because of the current pan-Danish gaggle of subversive and rebellious factions, and the newly weakened Castle garrison,

Laertes, when finally he returns, finds himself in an unexpectedly strong position. Sophisticated dissidents and moronic mobs alike flock eagerly to him, as if he were a hero.

But is he?

Does Laertes have true killer instinct?

Or is he a mere pansy in stud's clothing?

21
SOME GRUDGING MORSELS

A public room.

Gertrude and Horatio.

Horatio is reciting a warming anecdote about the excellence of Hamlet's Master's Dissertation on logical moods.

Gertrude, inwardly, is worried sick. About her own situation and about Hamlet. Although barely time has elapsed for him to reach England and dispatch a letter back to Denmark, she constantly frets at his not having written. Horatio's chore is to reassure the Queen that Hamlet *will* write, *soon*, and all will turn out *best*.

Horatio is putting on weight. Apart from bolstering Gertrude's morale there is little for him to do in the Castle, except eat. The common folk of Denmark go hungry (though Horatio is not aware of this), but the Castle kitchens continue to disgorge:

Vast venison steaks, all steaming spices and sweating bloody protein; huge whole pigs, deliciously spit-roasted, exquisitely stuffed, garnished with lashings of baked apple and . . . Claudius, despite his sexual incapacity and ulcerating duodenum, is determined to maintain his gourmandy.

So Horatio fattens, far from the spartan cloisters and inkwells of Wittenberg. Today he is clad in the sombre clerical browns and greys he deems appropriate to a Queen's confidant.

Now the intercourse between Gertrude and himself is interrupted:

Enter an anonymous Gentleman.

To Gertrude the Gentleman announces that Ophelia is present without and begs an audience. This mediated request is necessary because Gertrude has ordered that she will not see Ophelia in any circumstances (thus expressing her fury at Ophelia's recent behaviour, especially in relation to Claudius).

'I will *not* speak with her,' snaps Gertrude, looking all her age. Small lines cluster her mouth and brow like new contours on a map showing weather erosion.

Her hair is severely bunned.

'She is importunate. *Distracted*,' croons the Gentleman. 'Her mood cries out to be *pitied*.'

'What does she want?'

The Gentleman unites his scented palms.

'She speaks much of her *father*,' he purrs. 'Says she hears there are *tricks* in the world. Hesitates in her speech, and beats her *breast*.

'She makes mountains out of molehills. Explodes at trifles. Utters things in doubtful tones which *almost* make sense.

'Her words themselves amount to nothing. Yet her incoherent use of them moves her hearers to infer. They *aim* at her speech, as at parables, and botch the words up to fit their own thoughts.

'And she nods, winks, gestures with such feeling, as to make one think there *must* be thoughts behind her words. Perhaps not cogent, but *surely unhappy*.'

Horatio gently rubs with the middle finger of his right hand the crown of his coming baldness. Coughing self-effacingly:

'It might be well to speak with her,' he ventures humbly. 'For she may strew dangerous conjectures.'

Gertrude exhales an exasperated tut and rises suddenly.

The Gentleman falls back.

Gertrude walks the floor angrily.

'Let her come in,' she finally hisses.

The Gentleman departs.

'Such is the nature of sin!' Gertrude cries with more hot feeling than Horatio finds comfortable. 'To my sick soul each vulgar trifle portends some royal disaster. So full of artless jealousy is *guilt* that it *spills itself* in fearing to be spilt.'

Horatio stirs uneasily on his stool. He assumes Gertrude is feeling remorse over her evidently abortive marriage to Claudius.

Gertrude, though frantically feeling, is not sure precisely *what*. Her lips purse and tremble.

Horatio gulps in panic lest the Queen break down and weep on his shoulder.

The situation is saved by the re-entry of the Gentleman.

With Ophelia:

'Where is the beautous majesty of Denmark?' she trills.

Inquiring after Hamlet?

Claudius?

Or a cunning conflation?

Certainly she is not inquiring after Gertrude.

'How now, Ophelia!' Gertrude snorts with indignation at Ophelia's appearance.

The younger lady is naked beneath a long billowing yet clinging white chemise which limelights and shadows her pertest protuberances and the darkest mysteries of her coolest valleys and warmest innermost recesses. The full nordic splendour of her golden hair floods carelessly down to her shoulders and cascades like a mountain spate in spring till it bounces spuming against her animated buttocks.

Cradled to Ophelia's breasts is a baby lute.

Glowing in the brilliant June of her beauty, she puts Gertrude to the shame of early October, when leaves are cruelly falling.

Just as a young rangy bitch will whimper and bare its genitals to a more heavily armoured animal (accepting its lowlier yapping rank, and extorting the stronger dog's protection), so Ophelia now sinks to her knees, beseechingly, at Gertrude's feet.

She gazes imploringly up into the Queen's fuming eyes. Strokes a minor chord on the lute. Her frail but not unpleasant voice sings:

> How should I your true love guess
> If we should ever meet?
> By his lowly pilgrim's dress,
> And the sandals on his feet.

'Alas!' Gertrude looks at Horatio for support. 'Sweet lady,' she attempts auntish benevolence, 'what does this song *mean*?'

'What say you?' Ophelia looks puzzled. 'No, I beg you, listen:

> Lady, he is cold and dead,
> Buried all alone.
> Mindless flowers mark his head,
> And at his heels, a stone.

Oh, Ho!'

'No, but Ophelia . . .' Gertrude pulls the kneeling girl upright. The Queen's generation considers it improper for young ladies to appear so scantily clad before gentlemen.

Ophelia wards off Gertrude's prudish attentions:

'I pray you, *listen*.' Wandering and strumming raggedly around the room, she sings:

> His shroud was pure as mountain snow . . .

Claudius stomps in.

He resembles a cunning worried sleepless pig. The natural pink plumpness of his features is creasing into blotchy puce. It takes him a moment to register that he is not alone.

'Alas!' Gertrude calls to him. 'Look here, my lord.' Hoping Ophelia's condition may re-establish communication between herself and her husband.

Claudius ignores her. His eyes, like blunt bloodshot gimlets, are glued to Ophelia's cold-hard nipples.

Ophelia, apparently unaware of the King, concludes:

> His brow was white in keeping.
> But no one mourned except for show;
> No true-love stood a-weeping.

Endearing tears fill her eyes. She chastely lowers her gaze.

Claudius walks up to her.

'How are you, pretty lady?' he asks, patting her shoulder. Even here, essaying tender warmth, his motive remains dominantly lecherous and manipulative.

Gertrude seethes. Silently.

Ophelia, as in a dream, takes Claudius' left hand and moulds it to her left breast. Seeming to want him to *feel* the demoniac drumming of her poor demented little heart.

Gertrude seethes. Almost audibly.

Ophelia breaks away from Claudius, affecting dismay at the attitude in which she finds herself.

'Well, God bless you!' she finally answers the King's question. 'They say his mother *was* a virgin. Lord! We know that we *are*, but not what we may *become*. May God be at your table!'

'She mourns for her father,' Claudius mumbles lamely.

Ophelia seems hurt:

'I beg you,' she pets, 'do not talk like that. But when they ask what it means, you may say this.' And she chants to a bawdy melody:

> 'Tomorrow is Saint Valentine's day,
> The moon is shining bright.
> And I at your window have come to be
> Your Valentine tonight.'
> Then up he leapt, from where he slept,
> Unlocked the chamber door;
> Took in the maid, and made the maid
> A Mayhoyden . . . no more.

'Pretty Ophelia!' Claudius advances a restraining avuncular arm.

Ophelia dances out of his reach, like a wilful filly.

'Indeed!' she exclaims, as she backpeddles, 'I shall *finish* it. *No one shall stop me!*' And she proceeds:

> By Jesus and Saint Charity,
> Alack and fie for shame!
> Young men will fuck, if they have such luck;
> By Cock they are to blame.
> Said she, 'Before you tumbled me,
> You promised me to wed.'
> (*He answers*)
> 'So would I have done, by yonder sun,
> If you had not come to my bed.'

'How long has she been like this?' Claudius soothes his embarrassment by adopting the mad image Ophelia is labouring to project.

Ophelia saves Gertrude and the others the discomfiture of replying to Claudius:

'I *hope* all will be well,' she murmurs. Draws herself up stiffly. Graciously. Like an elderly aristocrat. 'We must be patient. But I cannot help but weep,' she smiles bravely, 'to think that they should lay him in the cold, cold ground. My brother shall know of it. And so, I thank your good counsel. Come, my coach!' She snaps her fingers, as to a servant.

All eyes are on her.

No one moves.

Horatio fidgets.

'Goodnight, ladies.' Ophelia offers a regal wrist to Claudius.

He kisses it. As if reluctant.

'Goodnight, sweet ladies,' Ophelia blows kisses to Gertrude. 'Goodnight.' She walks out with the short mincing steps of a senior widow, pressing her lute like a bible to her bosom.

Claudius snaps at Horatio:

'Follow her closely. Ensure she is not left alone.'

Horatio exits monkishly.

Gertrude stands primly. Eyes downcast. Eloquently silent.

Claudius clears his throat irritably. Despite his Kingly powers, and much to his annoyance, he feels compelled to tender Gertrude some grudging appeasement.

'This', he exclaims in conciliatory tones, *vis-à-vis* Ophelia's charade, 'is the poison of deep grief. It springs from her father's death. Oh, Gertrude! Sorrows come not as single spies, but in battalions. First, her father slain. Next, your son gone. Even though his dreadful deed deserved it. And the people! Muddied, thick and unwholesome in their whispers. They gossip round Polonius' death. I fear we acted hastily, when we buried him so secretly.

'Now poor Ophelia is divided from herself, and last, but worst, her brother has come secretly from France. He flits under cover of night, and everywhere finds malice to stoke pestilent suspicion about his father's death.' Claudius moves close to Gertrude.

A calculating arm encircles the Queen's waist.

She stiffens in revulsion. Despite the cold she can smell stale alcohol on her husband's breath, and the nauseous emetic of his unwashed body. But does it occur to her that her own molar mouldering is repulsive to Claudius?

'And it cannot be wondered at,' he continues at arm's length, 'with so little truth released, that they lay Polonius' death at *our* door. Dear Gertrude!' he exclaims self-pityingly, 'this, like a murdering-piece, is killing me slowly, through a hundred super-fluous wounds.'

A murdering-piece is a small deadly handgun, like a sawn-off blunderbuss. With its lethal load of old nails and scrap metal, it is ideal for close-range dirty work. The simile comes easily to Claudius because, in recent weeks, his paranoia has required *two* such weapons beneath his pillow. One, he considers, is not enough – the powder might fail to ignite.

Now comes a tumult of shouting and scuffling in the corridor outside:

Violence offered, resisted, and overcome.

The cacophony approaches.

Above it soars a choking yell.

Gertrude draws away from Claudius. Wringing her hands:

'Alack!' she wails. 'What noise?'

Claudius doesn't answer. Turns deathly pale. His wind is snatching in asthmatic gasps.

Girding goblins gather unnoticed in the corners of the three huge fireplaces, like clusters of predatory sleepymen. It is late afternoon and the fires are sluggish. No one has tended them for hours. In their smouldering hearts mythic heroes mate unseen with transient nymphomaniacs. Ageless sages wager scorn on Claudius' selfish trepidation. Flickering candles burn low around the walls, melting in long lumpy dribbles of promiscuous wax like warty witches' fingers all grey and blemished dark with speckled sin.

The corridor violence approaches crescendo.

A sudden blast of chill invades the room. Blows the candle flames at crazy angles.

Creak, sob.

The doors throw open.

A second Gentleman staggers in. Frenziedly slams and bars the doors behind him. His feathers have been savagely ruffled. A bloody swelling eggs his forehead, and his eyes can't focus.

'Where are my *Switzers*?' Claudius croaks. 'Let them GUARD THE DOOR! What is the matter?'

'Save yourself, my lord,' the Gentleman wheezes. 'No tidal wave could break the shore with more impertinence than young Laertes, with a riotous band, overcomes your officers.'

He kneels. Sobs:

'The rabble call him *lord*. Ignoring history and tradition, they cry:

'"*Laertes* shall be King! We choose *Laertes*!" Caps, hands, and tongues applaud it to the clouds:

'"LAERTES, KING!"' The Gentleman shakes his battered head in loyal helpless sorrow.

'How cheerfully they bark at red herrings!' rages Gertrude. 'Oh, *treason*! You false Danish *dogs*!'

Her Swedish indignation is quelled by:

BANG, BANG, BLATTER, SPLINTER.

'The doors are breaking,' stammers Claudius.

22
MINCED LYRICS

In the corridor outside:

A serpentine throng.

Headed by four bruisers with sledgehammers and crowbars.

Glazed fervour, moist lips, throbbing temple veins.

The rabble is aged fifteen to twenty-five. It includes:

Self-styled intelligent youths, fugitives from Claudius' military conscription, and professional troublemakers.

Strung out behind this hammer mob, like bloody lumps of constipated serpent stool, lie the vanquished hulks of Claudius' Switzers. Some merely cut and bruised. Others mortally wounded and slowly dying.

Bang, crash.

With a creaking splintering thunderclap the huge doors fall. *Crash, bang.*

The jeerleaders surge forward like a greedy serpent's tongue – quick and deadly, but stupid.

Laertes springs to their head.

'Where is the King?' he cries stoutly. 'Sirs, I beg you, wait outside.' He turns. Faces the callous crocodile. Spreads his arms beseechingly, to halt its advance. How could his cause (whatever it is) benefit by allowing a gang of blood-crazed hoodlums to butcher the King?

'No! Let's come in.' Fists are shaken. Clubs are raised. On one, held high, is a bloody flap of Switzer scalp.

Laertes feels the mob mood bubbling like milk round the edge of a saucepan, about to boil over. He draws his sword and scars the nearest jeerleader cheek.

'We will. We will.' The sauropoid retracts its grumbling tongue.

'I thank you.' Laertes sops his hounds. 'I pray you, guard the door.' He motions them back, turns, and . . .

Claudius and Gertrude, seeing Laertes' dripping sword aloft, quail in horror.

'Oh, you *vile* King!' Laertes rushes at Claudius. 'Give me my father.'

Claudius cringes fearfully.

Gertrude flusters forward. Tugs Laertes' sword arm.

'Calmly, good Laertes,' she begs. Despite her tattered marriage, she doesn't want her husband murdered by an arrogant upstart with an imagined grievance.

Laertes rounds on her, his visage bulbous with passion.

'I am a *bastard*,' he howls, 'and my mother a harlot, if there is one calm drop of cowardly blood in all my body.'

But Laertes is a poor actor, his forced grief not convincing.

Claudius, even in the throes of his quaking, is quick to feel Laertes' uncertainty.

'Tell me, Laertes, why your rebellion struts so giant-like?' The King draws up to full height. Inflates. The studs on his gown flash gold. 'Let him go, Gertrude,' he gestures imperiously at his wife.

Who is still hanging like a protective harrier on Laertes' sleeve.

'Do not fear for our person.' Claudius reclaims his authority. 'So much divinity protects a King that it is easier for a camel to pass through the eye of a needle than for treason to harm him wrongfully. So, tell me, Laertes, why you are so incensed. *Let* him *go*, Gertrude.' Irritably Claudius waves Gertrude away. Opens his arms to Laertes. 'Speak, man,' he urges.

Gertrude releases Laertes. Drops back, doubtfully.

Laertes flexes his sword with an ominous swish.

'Where is my father?' he snarls.

'Dead.' Claudius shakes his head in sorrow.

'But not by him,' Gertrude earnestly protests.

'Let him demand his fill,' Claudius silences her.

'*How* did he die?' Laertes hisses. Feeling his advantage slipping away, he tries to retrieve the edge by magnifying his filial grief:

'I'LL NOT BE JUGGLED WITH,' he screams, brandishing his naked blade. 'To hell with allegiance! To the devil with holy vows! To the deepest sewer with conscience and grace! I dare damnation. And not one fig shall I give for this world, or the next, till I am revenged most thoroughly for my father's death.' He pauses for breath. Hoarse throat; purple face.

'Who can dissuade you?' the King asks mildly.

'Nothing in this world,' Laertes brays. 'Except my *will*.' He scowls threateningly.

'Good Laertes,' Claudius tries, 'is it writ in your revenge that, indiscriminately, you massacre both friend and foe?'

'None but his enemies.'

'Would you like to know them?'

Laertes contorts anew. Flings his arms like a strumpet's legs.

'To his good friends,' he vows, 'I'll open my arms thus wide. And feed them with my blood.'

Claudius pounces:

'Why,' he exclaims, 'now you speak like a good child and a true gentleman. That I am guiltless of your father's death, and deeply grieve for it, your judgement shall perceive as clear as your eye sees day.' The King's gelling plan is to bounce Laertes' aggression at the banished ogre of Hamlet's villainy. Given time and privacy, might he not even gain Laertes' confidence and support?

By explaining how *he too* (!) all but fell victim to Hamlet's murderous scheming?

Trump card (should he need to play it)?

Explain to Laertes how Hamlet has been sent to his death in England!

But not in the presence of Gertrude.

Claudius' castellating cogitations are crumbled by a dissident hubbub from the rebellious Danes guarding the fallen door.

'Let her go in,' comes the dominant bleat.

'How now!' queries Laertes. 'What noise?'

In sleepwalks Ophelia. Barely clad, as before. Hugging her lute. From her right wrist dangles a drawstring calfskin purse. This she dips into. Extracts thin handfuls of fluttery white fragments. Scatters them about her. Like a beautiful blind girl sowing snowflakes on flagstones.

Her glorious hanging fleece catches firelight and candlelight into one great heady mane of golden misfortune.

Laertes shatters the hush by falling to his knees.

Klonk.

His throat issues a protracted outraged gurgle.

Nnnnnnnnnaaaaah.

'Oh heat,' he yelps, 'dry up my brains!' He drops his sword and milks his hands. 'Tears, seven times salt, burn out my eyes! By heaven, your madness shall be paid for heavily, till the scales tip back in our favour.' He crawls towards Ophelia, groaning with sibling sorrow. 'Oh, rose of May! Dear maid, kind sister, sweet Ophelia!'

Ophelia turns blankly away from him.

Laertes beats his rejected chest and declaims to the ceiling:

'Oh heavens! A young maid's wits? Mortal as an old man's life?'

Ophelia ignores her tortuous brother. She frets her lute, strokes a sad chord, and trills:

> They bore him barefaced on the bier;
> Hey ninny, ninny; hey ninny non.
> And in his grave rained many a tear . . .

She breaks off suddenly. Seems surprised to have been singing. Dips into the little purse at her wrist. Strews some white flutter lovingly on the floor, as though dropping rose petals on a coffin.

'Fare you well, my dove!' she coos.

The white fragments are the ripped-up remnants of her copper-plate copies of Hamlet's lyrics. But . . .

'If you used sly wits to goad my revenge, you could not move me thus.' Laertes tries again to attract his sister's attention. How, he wonders, should he react to her performance?

He has heard, from his grapevine following, that Ophelia has been strange of late. But why? He is cynical enough to suspect that his sister may be shamming. And certainly he doesn't believe she has been driven insane by the loss of Polonius. On the other hand, if she *has* lost her sanity, whatever the reason, well, why should Laertes worry? Women, he believes, are naturally fickle and disposable creatures, and if one falls by the wayside? There are always plenty more to restock one's bed.

Ophelia cuts him dead again with song:

> You must sing, a-down, a-down,
> And you call him, a-down-a.

She stops short. Frowns petulantly.

'Oh, how *apt* the chorus is!' She looks down sadly, as into the mouth of a grave. 'It is the false steward that stole his master's daughter.'

'How loaded her nonsense is,' mutters Laertes, suspiciously. Habitually he scours even Ophelia's most innocent remarks. For veiled taunts.

Ophelia turns to him. A maiden smile flutters behind her eyes and hovers about her lips, ephemeral as a butterfly at dusk. She dips into her wrinkled reliquary.

'There's rosemary,' she says. 'That's for remembrance.' She drops a flurry of Hamlet's minced lyrics into Laertes' reluctant cupped hands.

Why?

'Pray, love, remember,' she adds. 'And there are some pansies. They are for thoughts.' She graces him with more white fragments.

Why?

'A document in madness: thoughts and remembrance fitted?' Laertes mutters again. He can make nothing of his sister's behaviour. But it must be in his interest for *others* to believe that her father's violent end has driven her insane. Mustn't it? For so his family grievance doubles.

Ophelia tours Claudius. So close that their bodies touch.

The King is acutely aware of the pillow power of Ophelia's caressing curves. Deep beneath the deceptive gold and crimson splendour of his drapery, and miles below the heady indigestion of his moral and political embroilment, he feels the twitch of a ghost.

While thunder brews unheard in the rasping rusty cauldron of Gertrude's impending menopause.

'There's fennel for you.' Ophelia showers Claudius with a lyric spray. Fennel may symbolize flattery, but Claudius, being a man, can be expected not to know this. 'And columbines.' More cipherous confetti bedecks the King.

Signifying?

Ophelia leaves Claudius. Rushes to Gertrude. Like a little girl remembering she has a present for Auntie too.

'There's rue for you,' she rhymes, as she dusts white paper on the Queen's stiff shoulders. 'And some for me,' she adds. She holds a fistful above her head and lets it fall down the gilden slopes of her hair.

Gertrude's impotent anger steams.

'We may call it herb of grace on Sundays.' Ophelia rues the Queen again.

Gertrude, being a woman, is more *au fait* than Claudius and Laertes with the folklore symbolism of flowers and herbs. She knows that rue represents either sorrow or repentance.

Ophelia plays on this duality:

'Oh!' she cries. '*You* must wear *your* rue with a *difference*.' Hinting that, while Ophelia only has cause for sorrow, Gertrude has good reason for *repentance*.

And Gertrude gets the point.

'There's a daisy.' Ophelia gives Gertrude a well-known emblem of deceit. 'I would give you some violets,' she explains apologetically. 'But they withered when my father died.'

Violets stand for faithfulness.

So is Ophelia deliberately slurrying Gertrude's character?

Certainly she is, thinks Gertrude.

Previously it was in Claudius' interest to believe that Hamlet's 'madness' was feigned. Now it suits Gertrude to believe that Ophelia's 'madness' is a ruse. This way, she can feel self-righteous about 'punishing' Ophelia's malicious impertinence.

'They say he made a good end . . .'

Who? Polonius? But . . .

Ophelia pirouettes from the loose end into another tangent song:

For bonny sweet Robin is all my joy.

'Melancholy and affliction! Suffering! Hell itself! She transforms all to prettiness.' Laertes grinds his teeth and pulls his hair in dissembling despair.

Ophelia waltzes round Claudius. Lovingly brushes some confetti from his shoulders. Steps back. Fingers her little lute. Sings a sweet swan song:

And will he not come again?
And will he not come again?
No, no, he is dead;
Go to your death-bed,
He never will come again.
His beard was white as snow,
His robes were black as coal.
He is gone, he is gone,
And we, stranded, pray on:
God have mercy on his soul.

She curtseys modestly, like a ten-year-old after her party-piece. 'And for all Christian souls, I pray,' she lisps. 'God be with you!' She curtseys again and exits dreamily, rocking the baby lute against her bosom.

Laertes' ragamuffin followers stand silently aside to let her pass.

Gertrude's narrowed eyes fire hatred at Ophelia's back.

Claudius eyes the silhouetted globes of Ophelia's parting buttocks. He feels his penis gulp.

Laertes gags:

'Do you see this, oh *God*?' Clenches his fists. Wracks his squat frame with hollow sobs. Howls his embarrassing woe to the fusty ceiling.

Claudius coughs appeasingly.

'Laertes,' he condoles, 'I feel most deeply for your grief. But let me speak my piece.' He summons a sad, weary smile. 'Go now. Choose your wisest friends, to judge between you and me. If they find us guilty, then we will give our kingdom, crown, and life to you.

'If not, you must lend patience to *us*. And we shall jointly labour with your soul, to give it satisfaction.'

Why can Claudius climb back from his insecure *I* to the confident Royal *We*?

Because he now has a strategy for dealing with Laertes.

But he can't unfold it in front of Gertrude.

Laertes seems to overcome his righteous frenzy.

'Let this be so,' he concurs. 'The cause of his death; his obscure burial; no trophy, sword or epitaph over his bones; no noble rite or ceremony. These things cry out to be explained. And so I have to call his death in question.'

'So you shall,' Claudius reassures him. Applies a Kingly squeeze to the younger man's shoulders. 'And where the offence is, there let the great axe fall.' Here Claudius winks heavily to Gertrude. As if to persuade her:

First, that Laertes is now under control; second, that he, Claudius, would not dream of feeding Laertes inflammatory information concerning darling Hamlet!

'I pray you, come with me,' the King requests but almost commands. And he exits with Laertes in a state of truce.

On his way, Laertes disbands his rowdy retinue, sopping them with vague promises of bigger bones to come.

Gertrude sails out by a different port, her features frozen in a stormy frown, to transact urgent business with her personal Switzer, Claudio.

23
SALTY MISSIVES

Framed against a narrow, forbidding window stands the muffled homely figure of Horatio.

Before him, a menial.

The servant informs Horatio that two visitors wish to see him.

'What sort of people?' inquires Horatio, dubiously.

'Sailors, sir. They say they have letters for you.'

Horatio's kindly brow rumples in perplexity. His right hand comforts his thinning crown.

'Let them come in,' he decides.

The menial exits.

Horatio gazes unhappily around his room. He is high in a turret on the Castle's north-west flank. If he unshutters the one slit window on a stormy night, he can hear the waves grind against the cliffs in the icy distance. His room is sparsely furnished and bereft of sumptuous decor. A lone grate fire in the wall combats the relentless chill of embattled winter, but Horatio still lies awake at nights, shivering.

His status in the Castle troubles him.

He knows the King is a murderer. Yet? He has to sit at the King's table, eat the King's food, drink the King's wine, politely ignoring the King's revolting personal habits, and console the King's fretful Queen. These are roles for which Horatio is poorly fitted.

Why does he stay?

Sense of duty. To Hamlet and to Gertrude.

Nevertheless, in the gloomy self-questioning vigil of his long dark hours alone, as he hears the howling winds of winter rage like jingles on the joys of death, Horatio often pines for the light cosy life of academic Wittenberg.

And it worries him that he hasn't heard from Hamlet.

Thinking now of his imminent visitors:

'I do not know', he murmurs anxiously, 'from whom I should be greeted, if not from Lord Hamlet.' He rubs his hands and holds them vainly over the little grate fire, as if toasted palms could dispel the gnawing chill of death from frozen bones.

A knock at the door.

Two sailors enter:

Clad in skins; ungentle in aspect.

Sailor One has a serrated cutlass scar from his right eye to his mouth, like a humourless vertical grin.

Sailor Two's mouth is a toothless gash.

Horatio stares misgivings at them.

'God bless you, sir,' rasps Sailor One, awkwardly.

'Let him bless you too,' Horatio responds coolly.

'He will, sir,' Sailor Two cackles like a happy fish out of water, 'if it please him!' He heaves a nautical cackle at this unlikely prospect. Then he gets to business:

'There's a letter for you, sir.' He offers Horatio a waterproof package. 'It comes from the ambassador that was bound for England. If your name be Horatio, as I am told.' He holds back the package for an instant, as if doubting Horatio's identity.

Horatio tuts at him. Seizes the package in feverish excitement. Tears open the letter, and eagerly reads:

Horatio,

When you have read through this, give these fellows access to the King. They have letters for him.

Before we were two days at sea, a pirate of warlike appointment gave us chase. Finding ourselves too slow of sail to escape, we were forced to resist their attack. In the grapple I boarded them. Seconds later they got clear of our ship, so I alone became their prisoner. They have dealt with me like thieves of mercy; but they knew what they did. I am to do a good turn for them.

Let the King have the letters I have sent; and haste to me as you would fly death. I have words to speak in your ear which will strike you dumb. These good fellows will bring you to me. Rosencrantz and Guildenstern hold their course for England. Of them I have much to tell you. Farewell.

Yours,
Hamlet.

Horatio glances up in agitation. Scours the raffish sailors for salty deceit. Scans again through Hamlet's letter. Tosses it impatiently on his bed, and rustles brownly to the door.

'Come,' he beckons. 'I will show you where to take your letters, and do it all the quicker, that you may direct me to him who sent them.' And Horatio bustles away with his head in a whirl. His first thought is to hand the letters over to Claudio, so the Switzer can inform Gertrude of Hamlet's impending return, leaving Horatio free to hurry back to dress for his journey to meet the Prince.

Who must be still alive!

Mustn't he?

24
HATCHING THE ROTTEN EGG

In the heart of infamy:

Claudius' private sanctum. Here, in the bowels of false security, the fires blaze and crackle, the candles flicker and gutter, the air is yellow with deceptive warmth and unnatural light.

Claudius is dispensing hot spiced wine to Laertes. The King's features are drawn. Jowls grey. Reports have come in during the past hour of ghostly warships lurking and vanishing in the freezing fog that rolls on the sea like a vast bubble of mercury.

Whose ships?

Or are they hallucinations in the minds of hysterical lookouts?

Light-headed alarms triggered by the same political uncertainty and social turbulence that unsettles Claudius himself?

To answer these questions the King would pay dearly, but for now his attention is occupied by Laertes.

Laertes is subdued. His sword hangs safely sheathed. His plan? To corner Claudius into appointing him successor to Polonius. In other words? Laertes now sees himself as Prime Minister apparent.

This aspiration Claudius has fostered by careful (but never committal) cultivation. The King has described to Laertes how nasty Hamlet was, at the time of Polonius' foul dispatch, plotting against his Royal Self also. But he hasn't disclosed that Hamlet, when he gored Polonius, was probably intent on goring Claudius.

The King takes a deep breath and a deeper drink. He clinks goblets with Laertes.

'Now your conscience must acquit me,' he concludes, 'since you have heard how he who slew *your* noble father pursued *my* life as well.'

Laertes nods.

'So it seems,' he allows. 'But why did you not proceed against these treasonous deeds?'

'Two special reasons. First, the Queen, his mother, thinks the world of him. Second, the great love the masses have for him. They, dipping all his faults in their affection, would praise his chains as virtues and hail him as a martyr.' Claudius sighs.

Laertes scowls.

'And so have I a noble father lost,' he infers bitterly. 'And a sister driven beyond her wits!' He clenches and unclenches his fist. Slaps his leathered thigh. To emphasize his grievance:

His *sister* has been made less perfect, therefore *he* has been outrageously wronged.

'But my revenge will come,' he promises darkly.

Claudius grimaces confidingly. He hasn't told Laertes of his plan to have Hamlet executed in England, but:

'Lose no sleep on that account,' he counsels. 'We are not one to let our beard be shook with danger and take it lying down.' For a moment the King is cheered by a lavish red image of Hamlet's head lying severed in a puddle of blood some yards from his twitching gushing body. 'You shortly will hear more,' he promises Laertes. 'I loved your father, and we love ourself. And that . . .'

On the brink of a heavy hint that Hamlet's desert has been ordered, Claudius is halted by an arriving Urgent Messenger: a nervous house-mouse in a cage of rats.

The King spots sealed packets in the mouse's paw.

'How now!' he roars. 'What news?'

'Letters, my lord,' the mouse squeaks. 'From Prince Hamlet. This to your majesty. This to the Queen.' He offers two letters.

Claudius recoils, aghast.

'From *Hamlet*!' he squawks. 'Who brought them?'

'Sailors, my lord, they say. I did not see them. They were given to me by Claudio. He received them of him that brought them.' The mouse fidgets anxiously. Alarmed by the awesome effect his tidings have on his King Rat master.

(Why is Claudio unable to bring Hamlet's letters himself? Because he is en route to execute a priority mission for Gertrude. As . . .)

Claudius is staggered.

Letters from *Hamlet*?

Fearfully he eyes the packets in his hand. But Hamlet should be severed! What can this mean? Are the Hamlet letters linked to the reported strange elusive vessels at sea? His mental tumbrils gallop and clatter drunkenly.

'Laertes, you shall hear them,' he swallows thickly. '*Leave us*,' he screams vindictively at the Messenger.

The mouse scutters thankfully out.

Claudius unseals Hamlet's letter, and reads with ginger loathing:

High and Mighty.
   I am set naked on your kingdom.
   Tomorrow I shall beg to see your kingly eyes.
   Then I shall, after asking pardon thereunto, explain
   my sudden strange return.

                                         Hamlet.

The King pores painfully through the letter. His eyes look stunned and desperate.

Laertes keeps silent. He smells a rat in the King's excessive reaction, but he can't see its whiskers.

'What can this *mean*?' Claudius whines to himself. 'Are all the rest come back? Or is it some scheming imposture?'

'Do you recognize the hand?' Laertes senses a possible prime-ministerial opening.

'It is Hamlet's writing,' mutters Claudius. 'He says "naked". And, in a postscript here, he says "alone". Can you advise me?'

Laertes is rapidly acquiring a value for Claudius.

'I'm lost in it, my lord,' the budding premier admits. 'But let him come! It warms the sickness in my heart, that I shall tell him to his teeth:

'"*You did this.*"'

Claudius appraises the younger man purply.

'If this is what it seems, Laertes: if Hamlet really has returned, will you be ruled by me?'

'In any course but peace with him.'

'I will rule only your own peace. If he has returned, has defected from his voyage, then I will ... manoeuvre an exploit where he shall not choose but fall. And for his death no blame shall breathe.

Even his mother will discount plotting, and call it accident.'

Laertes sharply sucks his teeth.

'My lord,' he hisses compliantly. 'I will be ruled. Especially if . . . *I* be the organ of his fall.'

'It shall be so.' Claudius smarms. 'You have been much praised in your absence, not least in Hamlet's hearing, for a quality wherein, they say, you shine. All your other attributes together could not pluck from him such envy as that one did, which in *my* opinion, is of the *least* importance.'

'What quality was that, my lord?' Laertes gobbles the bait.

Claudius pays out some slack. To cement Laertes' illusion of equality in complicity:

'A brilliant ribbon round the cap of youth,' the King denigrates approvingly. 'Yet needful too. For youth no less becomes its careless uniform than settled age becomes his sable robes, denoting worldly wealth and grave responsibility.' Claudius smiles thinly to himself, a fleeting mask of whimsical nostalgia.

Laertes itches for the King to get to the point.

'Two months ago,' Claudius continues in his own cunning time, 'we had a visitor from Normandy. I've served against the French myself, and know their expertise on horseback. But this young gallant had witchcraft in it. He *grew* out of his seat, like a Centaur.'

'A Norman, you say?'

'A Norman.'

'Lamord?'

'The same.'

'I know him well. He is the jewel of all his nation.' Laertes licks his lush lips. The mention of Lamord has kennelled him with qualms. Lamord is a fearless dashing young buck whose many qualities, natural and cultivated, put Laertes to shame. He is taller and slimmer, yet also more powerful and agile. He is younger, but still more expert in the arts of war. Worst of all, he writes lovelier songs and enjoys sexual success with more willing ladies. Lamord, in a nutshell, is a Hamlet without doubts – a born philosopher-king, lacking only the philosophy. He is a graceful natural, such as Laertes can only emulate, detest, secretly fear, and envy.

All of which is far from lost on Claudius.

'He spoke well of you,' he lubricates Laertes. 'And sang most grudging praises of your art in defence, especially your skill with a rapier. The fencers of France, he swore, have none to compare with you.' Claudius clears some slimy marbles from his thick fat throat, as he reels in slack.

'Sir,' he lies to Laertes, man-to-man, 'this report of Lamord's envenomed Hamlet with such envy that he howled for your return, to play with you. Now, following this . . .'

'*What* following this, my lord?' Laertes is suddenly defensive. The prospect of a duel with Hamlet turns the corners of his courage yellow.

Claudius has anticipated this apprehension:

'Laertes,' he snaps testily, 'was your father dear to you? Or are you like the *painting* of a sorrow? A face without a heart?'

'Why ask me this?'

'Because Hamlet has come back. So? Will you prove your father's son in *deeds*?'

'I would cut his throat in a church.'

'Certainly,' Claudius nods approvingly, 'no place should sanctify murder. Revenge should have no bounds. But, good Laertes, will you follow my instruction for the moment? Keep to yourself, within your chamber. When Hamlet returns we shall let him know that you are home.

'We shall organize courtiers to praise your excellence, and magnify the fame the Frenchman gave you. And thus, through Hamlet's envy, we shall bring you together for a contest, and wager on your heads. He, being careless, generous, and free from all contriving, will not inspect the foils. So, with ease, or a little shuffling, you may choose an unbuttoned sword – and, in a sudden thrust, *requite him for your father*.' Claudius grins maliciously, to sell his foolproof plan.

Laertes takes his time about replying. His podgy brain is sweating. He had thought Claudius wanted a straightforward duel between himself and Hamlet. The present prospect *seems* less fraught with certain ignominious death. And yet:

If Hamlet were to spot the untipped sword? And do for Laertes with that fearsome longbladed dagger?

He muses laboriously.

'I'll do it,' he announces at length. 'And, for safety's sake . . . I have a potion. So deadly that, where it but draws blood, no miracle can nullify its sting. I shall touch my sword with this contagion. Then, if I scratch him only slightly, he must still die.'

Hamlet die!

Claudius fizzles with delight. Laertes' poisonous acquiescence surpasses his rosiest expectation.

'Let's think further,' the King proposes cheerfully. 'For lest our project fail, shine guiltily through a bad performance, we need a second stage . . .

'Now. Let me see.' He claps his brow. Frowns. Ponders murderously. 'We'll lay a solemn wager on your contest,' he murmurs dreamily. Then startles Laertes with a jubilant:

'I have it! When your exertions heat you dry – make your bouts more violent to that end – and when he calls for drink, I'll have for him a chalice specially poisoned. So, if by chance he escape your venomed thrust, he need only sip some wine to set our minds at rest.'

The rotten egg thus hatches.

The plotters exchange wary smiles. Then:

Sinister rustling; faint footsteps without.

A door-handle turns.

'Hush!' commands Claudius. 'What noise?'

Gertrude enters. Hair primly bunned. Face set in determined composure. Suggesting expenditure of great effort and courage.

'How now, sweet queen!' Claudius greets his wife with gralloching sarcasm. Furious at the inconvenience of her intrusion.

Gertrude ignores him. The regal stiffness of her long-skirted bearing proclaims her moral superiority. She looks like a bringer of dreadful news.

And so she is.

Painfully to Laertes:

'One woe crowds another's heel,' she announces sadly. 'Your sister's drowned, Laertes.'

25
SUGARY SPIEL

'Drowned! Oh, where?' Laertes blinks stupidly at the Queen. It is hardly the season for bathing, and Ophelia was never an outdoor enthusiast. How, then, could she possibly drown?

Claudius glowers suspiciously at his wife.

She fiddles tremulously with the diamond brooch at the collar of her high-necked dress. Sighs. Explains in a tragic fairy-tale voice:

'There is a willow, which grows across a brook and shows its grey-white leaves in the glassy stream. There she did go. With fantastic garlands, of buttercups, nettles, and daisies. And long purple orchids . . .

'There she did go. To drape her robes of flowers on the hanging boughs. And there, beneath her beauteous weight, a thankless branch broke off, letting fall her weedy trophies and herself into the weeping brook.

'Her clothes spread wide. And, mermaid-like, for a while they bore her up. And all this time she chanted hymns to God. As if she did not heed her own distress.

'But this sad picture could not live. Soon her garments, heavy with their drink, pulled the poor wretch from her melodious lay, to muddy death.' Gertrude falters. Fingers a reddening eye.

Laertes gapes at her.

Is he struck speechless by the rampant implausibility of Gertrude's story?

In the dead of darkest Danish winter, isn't the Queen's talk of summery brooks and gorgeous garlands a little farfetched?

And if Gertrude *knows* these details, why wasn't some eyewitness able to save poor Ophelia from her muddy watery decease?

But these are not the reasons why Laertes goggles.

For Danish court etiquette demands that distressing news,

especially concerning kin of the recipient, must be shrouded in face-saving euphemism, particularly where the literal truth would cast religious aspersion.

Consequently? Laertes realizes instantly that Gertrude means to cushion for him the status-shattering tragedy of Ophelia's suicide.

So what *does* cause him to gape?

It is the boggling notion that his ambitious sister might wittingly give up the ghost of her worldliness.

And *did* she, in fact?

Earlier:

Claudio, though not tall, has enormous strength in his massive shoulders, chunky arms, and rootlike hands. A giant with short legs. His facial skin is thick and pocked. Framing the pale swarthy turnip of his round peasant face, a puddingbowl style of greasy black hair hangs lank to his shoulders. His features frown in concentration, but his devotion to Gertrude shines through.

Gertrude develops her harangue.

Claudio's not unkind eyes scowl in dark amazement.

Gertrude does not notice. She pads about her closet like a lioness as she talks.

Suddenly the prowling stops. The Queen eyeballs Claudio. Demands whether he has understood.

Yes. He bows adoringly, and departs.

Soon the Switzer is wandering bemusedly along an ancient-busted spider-crawling corridor. The spring is missing from his stoutly booted step, as his Queen's harsh pleasure weighs heavily on his singleminded soul.

Round a blind corner.

Claudio collides with Horatio.

Hamlet's doting chum is stepping out urgently. His two sailor messengers follow. He looks like a brambled schoolmistress. As he recognizes Claudio, Horatio's face lights up like a Roman candle against a starless sky.

With gushy mouthings and ostensive gestures Horatio petitions Claudio.

Such is hierarchy, not to mention the secrecy of Claudio's

mission, that he must defer to Horatio. But his knuckles tighten white in displeasure, as he nods dour assent.

Horatio claps his hands to say:

How splendid!

Then he bumbles away, eyes shining, to prepare his thoughts and chattels for reunion with Hamlet.

Viewing Horatio's departure with irate contempt, Claudio beckons sourly to the sailors. Leads them off in the opposite direction.

Forward . . .

To the Castle kitchens. Activity is minimal in these most warmest of the Castle's ruptures. It is late. All the globby guzzles of the day are over. Only the pastry boys are still at work, beating tomorrow's bread into doughy shape and yeasty texture, under the tetchy direction of a bulge-bellied chef. The latter snarls occasional orders at the floury striplings as himself he stirs and frequently samples a bath-size cauldron of steaming beef broth, with a wooden spoon the size of a gravedigger's spade.

Enter Claudio with the sailors.

He and the bloat chef greet each other warily, with the unwilling prudent respect of equals in different leagues.

Claudio points to the sailors.

The chef nods grumpily. Fills two bucket bowls with bubbling broth.

Claudio barks a curt command at the sailors. Relieves them of their letters. Thuds away.

Forward again . . .

To a servant dormitory in the Castle's lower colon. The snoring gloom is thick with drunken grunts. Scattered sleeping figures huddle beneath musty blankets, insulated against the bare brick floor by rough mattresses of bound straw.

Here lie the tousled heads and wheezing noses of the younger unmarried males in the Castle staff. In one seamy corner an oasis of rhythmic movement resembles two rats copulating beneath a blanket. The furtive onanism of a raw recruit. Barely into pubes, this youth has waited an hour for privacy of consciousness to massage his juicy tension into spurts of sweet release. His climax approaches. The syncopations grow more urgent. Lush yielding buttocks he throes to protesting ecstasy on the endless . . .

Bang. Crash. Shout.

The midnight joyous drains away like the arrogant puff from a cock pheasant's chest when he niffos Mr Fox, hey ho.

The door is open.

A walking torch appears. Its ghostly gargoyle head belongs to Claudio.

Bark, bark. Roar. He raps a terse injunction.

Dopily two unkempt heads awaken. In moments the suasive Switzer has their hairy white legs out of grey nightshirts and into sumptuous livery.

Call these suited servants House Mice One and Two.

House Mouse One drags a filthy perfumed comb across his head.

Claudio instructs him. To deliver Hamlet's letters to the King.

Mouse One takes the envelopes and disappears, blinking.

Claudio wraps a bone-crushing arm around the squirming skinny shoulders of House Mouse Two. Whispers deep in the young lad's ear. A puzzled frown evolves between this organ and its grimy enantiomorph. Mouse Two nods doubtfully before gangling away into the black-toothed corridor mouth.

Claudio waits. Darkly his sensual lips purse. Then he vanishes opposite.

Forward again . . .

To pretty Ophelia's bedroom. Tracted disarray. Mounds of crumpled ballgowns and priceless furs litter the floor. The bed is an unmade mess. Ophelia sits stiffly at her woodwormed virginal. Striking long-unpractised chords. Trilling fragments of outré chanson. She is still in her translucent chemise, but warmly draped around her shoulders is an enormous white fur, as if a polar bear had fallen from the sky to envelop her.

Now comes an unexpected knock on her door.

Deftly she shrugs off the polar bear, which falls folding to the floor with a gentle rustling growl.

More knocks.

Ophelia ignores them. Continues her broken rendition.

In agonizedly slow, creaking trepidation, Ophelia's bedroom door opens inward to admit the tasselled skinny frame of House Mouse Two. As per Claudio's instruction, he enters without permission, but this deplorable departure from House Mouse discipline terrifies him. To ease his confused embarrassment he bows several times. Locks his eyes to the floor tiles. Delivers his intelligence in a swallowing monotone. Retreats, twitching furiously.

His message?

That Lord Laertes wishes to speak to Lady Ophelia, utmost urgency, *soon as possible*, in the Original Sculleries.

Ophelia butchers a further verse of rent rhapsody. Swirling with suspicions:

Why the Original Sculleries? These funereal cells in the Castle's slimy entrails have been unused since the structural alterations made by Hamlet I. Their only notable features are a long-stagnant water well with horrific chimerae of Viking myth carved round the rim, and the fact that no one goes there any more. Why should Laertes want to meet her *there*?

Why not *here*? In her own room?

Could the House Mouse message presage villainy?

Ophelia shivers in lonely paranoia.

But her will is strong. Her greed is great. She persists in her ruminations; sure she has erected her derangement façade success-fully. So ... why should anyone lure her to secret murderous mischief?

Even if a malefactor *were* thus inclined, why bother with the uninviting squalor of the Sculleries?

Why not simply snuff her in the solitude of her normal haunts?

Moreover:

Is Laertes possibly plotting to depose Claudius and seize the crown for himself? In which case, Ophelia feels, the molten ore of his rashness must be tempered in the cool bath of her own intelligence.

Wife to King Claudius (an image fraught with sordid flabby bedroom appendages)?

Or sister to King Laertes?

The second option would not abolish the problem of her

pregnancy, but it would, she considers, give her power to select some virile young noble for a husband. Not that constant intercourse is all she demands of a man, but it isn't to be sneezed at either, is it?

So Ophelia's quandaries are to be, or not:

Queen to King Claudius?

Or sister and chief counsellor to King Laertes?

With these ambition-sodden prospects wobbling restlessly in the scales of her intellect, Ophelia impulsively snuggles back inside her polar-bear wrap.

Forward faster . . .

To a darkdark dankdark scene.

The invisibility pales to a green slimy squalor.

A walking torch approaches.

Into the funereal Sculleries. Large rat droppings cake the floor, like mud from dwarvish boots.

The walking torch is Ophelia. Shapeless in her bearskin. Peering anxiously beyond the dancing flicker of the torch her right hand carries. Past the wall of the ancient well. She gasps with horror at a ghastly sculpted gargoyle on the well's rim. The head is half man, half dog, with the tongue of a snake, the fangs of a sabre-tooth tiger, and a nose like an onager phallus. The howling agony in its blind grey eyes conjures up like a mushroom nightmare the unbelievable pain of roasting for ever in the merciless white-hot fires of hell.

Ophelia feels her way hesitantly round the well. Its diameter is twice her height. An ell below floor level the surface of the lifeless water has frozen into a germless skin three fingers thick. Hereon, curiously, more rodent faeces are deposited.

Parting and licking her fast-chapping fearful lips, Ophelia quietly calls out:

Laertes? Laertes!

Silence mocks her.

Laertes? *Laertes!*

Suddenly:

Wham. Out of the slimy gloom and into the huddled heart of Ophelia's bearskin shoots Claudio's massive open fist, striking like a cobra's head. Round her terrified throat his fatal fingers wrap, and squeeze, and choke.

The torch falls sputtering from her hand. Her agonized frame jerks rigid. Her nails claw frenziedly at Claudio's wrist.

In vain.

So monstrous are the Switzer's murderous muscles that one casual hand does the deed with ease. In his Latin eyes? No welling floods of papal compassion. Perhaps a hint of whimsical pity. Certainly no crazed gleam of evangelical conviction. For Claudio, extinguishing Ophelia is simply a distasteful incident in a comfortable career. So nonchalantly he throttles the weightless spirit from her swooning body.

Her eyes goggle hideous, like a deathmask of terminal dropsy. Her tongue hangs red and tumescent. Her futile resistance fades only with her dying breath. Her body slumps in the stiff relaxation of death.

With one balletic movement Claudio lifts the newly-dead aloft with his strangling hand, catches it under the knees with his left forearm, swings it round, shedding the weighty bearskin, and drops the late Ophelia down the throat of the ancient well.

The skin of stagnant ice cracks sharply as an old maidenhead before the penile battering of a looting soldier.

Claudio regards with satisfaction his task well executed. He stoops to retrieve the guttering torch. Its wild protesting flame throws yellow shadows in his facial craters. As he steals shamelessly hence to report to Gertrude, he takes from a leather pouch at his hip a fat turkey drumstick. Bites greedily. Chews thoughtfully.

Half floating, half sinking, Ophelia's tragic remains revolve slowly – a freezing crucifix in the morbid mandala mouth of the well. Her shift turns transparent in saturation. Her former charms peep palely through. Rigid nipples point proudly to heaven, provocative even in their cold sad irony of death. And her gorgeous fleece spreads out around her head like a blackening gold halo.

Soon . . .

The halo must succumb to the insistent sucking water. The shapely belly will bloat and drown all trace of Hamlet's seedling child. The water will freeze an ugly skin around the corpse, like soup fat congealing round a lonely bone.

But first:

The ghastly gargoyle heaves a subliminal groan. Something is wrong with its blind grey eyes. Small bubbles of heat appear, like fizz in a tankard of shaken ale. The bubbles explode in rose froth and red foam. The gargoyle mutates. Now it is a leering swine with tiger teeth. Now the head of Claudius, severed from his pouchy torso and hoist high on a bloody pike of endless pain. Now a fearsome fusion of leering Claudius and bleeding swine. The phallus nose, scarlet with lust, engorges obscenely. The bubbling eyes goggle. They are Ophelia's eyes in death. The phallus discharges in a continuous spurt of simmering blood. The goggling eyes slither out of their sockets as the rearing heads of wriggling serpents. The reptiles writhe away in shame. The bubbles blow out. The gory hues pale. The eruption fades. The gargoyle's indignant energy is spent, and Ophelia is forever dead.

So that now:

Gertrude sops her conscience with mitigations. First, murder as a political expedient is a contemporary commonplace. Second, her disposing of Ophelia is not cold-blooded, since she fervently believes that Ophelia's 'mad' wantonness imperilled her own safety. Thirdly, were the situations reversed, Ophelia would murder Gertrude with fewer qualms than Gertrude has shed over Ophelia.

Wouldn't she?

Having concluded her parabolic description of Ophelia's demise, Gertrude stops fiddling with her collar brooch. Looks down. Projects an aura of sad silent mourning.

Laertes, having blinked and mouthed incredulously throughout Gertrude's story, clears his throat with a choked splutter. How *could* his lusty busty sister have taken her own life?

Why?

The suspicion of foul-play knocks incessantly. With coffers of political capital brimming yellow in his cunning, Laertes stares at Claudius in bereaved accusation.

The King averts his clouded gaze. Partly to imply infinite condolence. Partly to mask his confusion. Gertrude's news of

Ophelia's death has come at the worst possible time for Claudius, weakening his hard-won hold on Laertes.

A pregnant silence comes to term.

Pine logs cremate.

In long-forgotten crevices the ancient cobwebs whisper. Do spiders hibernate? How do they feed in winter, when there are no flies?

Laertes shatters the brittle discomfiture, by adding to it.

'ALAS!' he hollers. 'Then she's drowned?' His face contorts grievously.

'Drowned, drowned,' Gertrude murmurs desolately.

Laertes falls heavily to his leathered knees. Rubs dry eyes with forceful fingers.

'Poor Ophelia,' he sobs. Flat hands conceal his eyes. 'When these tears are gone no drop of womanish tenderness will remain in me.' He sniffs for a wordless moment, then leaps loudly to his feet:

'Adieu, my lord!' He shakes a defiant fist at the King. 'I have a speech of fire that fain would blaze, were it not for my welling tears.' And Laertes rushes hotly from the room. Doubly wronged. Stashing ingots of political advantage in the vaults of his hellbent ambition.

Claudius stirs.

'Let's follow, Gertrude,' he instructs, tight-lipped. 'What work I had to calm his rage! Now I fear this will revive it. Therefore let's follow.' He scowls like a thwarted tomcat. The last thing the King wants, now, is an inquest into Ophelia's mysterious decease. But, being a political realist, he has his sooty suspicions.

Gertrude exits in silent mortified dignity, though in her heart two sparrows fall.

Claudius follows like a grotesque fat shadow.

In his heart more darkness falls.

Of course:

The King never intended sticking to his bargain with Laertes. Certainly he hoped to engineer a 'friendly' duel between Laertes and Hamlet, assuming the Prince's return to be the humble solitary affair suggested by his letter. But Claudius is too shrewd to suppose

Laertes has much chance of mortally skewering Hamlet.

So what was the King's original idea?

That Laertes might, with luck, *scratch* Hamlet in the contest. Then it would be publicly evident that Laertes had tried to *murder* Hamlet – his motives would be obvious. Thereafter, Laertes, would-be assassin of the heir to the throne, could be imprisoned and quickly executed. Hence Laertes would cease to pose a political threat, and Claudius could concentrate on Hamlet.

However, by suggesting that he tip his sword with deadly poison, Laertes unwittingly played more aces into Claudius' hand. The poison would give Laertes a fair chance of *actually* killing Hamlet, and then? Laertes could be summarily executed as Hamlet's murderer. Grand-slam to the King!

Also:

Once Laertes had mooted poison, why not hedge all bets with a lethal libation for Hamlet, in case Laertes should fail to draw blood at all? Either way, the villainy could easily be attributed to Laertes, and only formalities need precede the lopping of his hateful head.

Small wonder, then, that Claudius is furious with Gertrude. Having devised this elegant plan, whereby heads he wastes both Laertes and Hamlet, and tails at least he gets Laertes, Claudius is now worried that Laertes will use Ophelia's fishy death as an excuse to boycott the duel.

26

TOMBSTONE BLUES

The afternoon following Ophelia's murder.

A mile inland from the city wall of Aarhus, behind a fringe of evergreens, there nestles a modest graveyard. Appended not to any denomination, but maintained equally by all the church authorities in the city. In it those who have sinned greatly and without repentance (but are too important to inter entirely without ecclesiastical blessing) can be buried in sanctified ground, but without the ceremony reserved for the holy immaculate.

Fresh snow has fallen. Like fluffy mink it carpets the hard ground and hangs, gently swaying, on the fir-trees.

Through the pines that band the cemetery come sounds of physical toil. Beefy grunts riffed with working-man's expletive accompany the bone-shaking ring of a spadeblade biting clod.

Two yokels (like large cockroaches eating through a cool clean sheet and throwing up the murky offal of the mattress below) are digging Ophelia's grave.

'Is she to be buried in *Christian* burial that *wilfully* seeks her *own* salvation?' Digger One rests on his spade and goads his fellow.

Digger One is a racy wit, Digger Two a plodding foil.

'I tell you she is,' Digger Two wheezes, shovelling splinters of rock-hard earth upon the virgin snow. 'Therefore make her grave straight. The coroner has sat on her, and finds it Christian burial.' He wipes his brow. The temperature is below zero, but there is no wind, and the Diggers are sweating freely. They are clad in leather boots and breeches, with their coarse cotton sleeves rolled up.

'How can that be,' persists Digger One, eyes needling, 'unless she drowned in her own defence?'

'Why, it is found so.' Digger Two has faith in Authority. Also a two-tooth gap in his front lower jaw, which colours his pronouncements with the thlightly thibilant lithp of the earnetht thimpleton.

'It *must* be self-abuse,' retorts Digger One, with a blistering kindly smile. 'It *cannot* be anything else. For here is the point:' He clambers out of the shallow grave to demonstrate. 'If I drown myself wittingly, I do perform an *action*. For any action has three parts. It is to *act*, to *do*, and to *perform*. Therefore, she drowned herself wittingly.' He gloats at his shovelling fellow.

'No. Listen to me . . .' Digger Two's crude features prolapse in dismay. He has an aggressive wart beside his nose, but his eyes are soft brown and kind, like Horatio's.

'*You* listen to *me*,' his senior interrupts impatiently. 'Here lies the water, yes?' He hops one-legged round the grave, his other foot tracing an imaginary water margin in the snow. 'If the man goes to this water and drowns himself, then, however you look at it, he goes. Yes? But if the water comes to him and drowns him, he drowns not himself. *Therefore*,' he concludes jovially, 'he that is not guilty of his own death shortens not his own life!'

Digger Two pauses for breath. Exhibits a worried frown.

'But is this *law*?' he asks.

'Coroner's inquest law!'

'Will you have the truth of the matter?' Digger Two glances fearfully round the fir-trees that might be crawling with secret police. 'If this had not been a *gentlewoman*, she should have been buried *out of Christian burial*!' He gasps at the subversive audacity of his suggestion. Takes penitent refuge in redoubled digging.

Ring, ring. Ring, shovel.

Digger One grins tolerantly: 'And what a pity that great folk should have more freedom to drown and hang themselves than their fellow Christians!' He spits with gusto. Regards the sky. Frowns at the clouds of darker grey which threaten from the east. 'Come. My spade.' He retrieves his tool and jumps back into the grave to relieve Digger Two. Perceiving rougher weather on the way, Digger One is concerned to get everything ready for the funeral.

'The only real gentlemen,' he tells Digger Two as he bundles him out of the hole, 'are gardeners, ditchers, and gravemakers. They hold up Adam's profession.'

'Was *he* a gentleman?' Digger Two sounds doubtful.

'The first that ever bore arms!'

'Why, he had none!' Digger Two exclaims, thinking of weapons.

'What! Are you a heathen?' Digger One scoffs in short breathy bursts, between trimming hacks. 'How do you understand the Scripture? The Scripture says Adam digged. Could he dig without arms? I'll put you another question,' he grunts before Digger Two can respond. 'If you can't answer, confess yourself . . .'

'Yes, yes. Go on.'

'Who builds stronger than the mason, the shipwright, or the carpenter?'

Digger Two puzzles. Tired of the older man's ribbing, he is anxious to answer correctly.

'The gallows-maker,' he suggests at length. 'For his frame outlives a thousand tenants.'

'I like your wit well,' comes the pitiless rejoinder. 'The gallows does well. But how? To those that does ill. Now, *you* does ill. To say the gallows is built stronger than the Church. Therefore, the gallows may does well to you! Try again.'

'Who builds stronger than a mason . . . a shipwright . . . or a carpenter?'

'Tell me that,' grunt. 'Then be off.'

'I have it!'

'Yes?'

'No. I have lost it.' Digger Two's abjection doubles.

While:

An arrow flight inland from the graveyard copse, two figures tramp along a bridleway obscured by snow. Only spiky tips of dead long grass delineate their path, which leads, eventually, to a gate in the city wall.

The newcomers are talking intently.

One is Horatio. Labouring to satisfy his inquisitive companion is turning his brown affability a flustered bullfinch pink. The tails of his coat flap impedingly against the trudging ankles of his thick felt boots.

And Horatio's tall companion?

Cloaked in a long patchwork sheepskin, his aspect is wild and scruffy. His hair dark, streaked with grey, cut level with his ear lobes. He is wearing a black fur hat. Under it, the bald crown of his head is revealed when in irritation he scratches a sudden tickle. Less monkish is the beard which sprawls like an untended garden from ear to ear, concealing the stranger's mouth and jaw.

Stranger?

Not entirely. For this is indeed Hamlet, but . . .

The altered Prince shushes Horatio. Stops to listen. Hears the babbling from the graveyard, and Digger One's vibrant spade.

Hamlet looks inquiringly at Horatio.

Horatio shrugs.

Hamlet glances back to the pine-tree enclave, then heads his nose towards it.

Horatio follows.

Digger One has lost patience with Digger Two.

'Cudgel your brains no more about it,' he acidly consoles his colleague. 'For your tardy ass will never trot from beating. And when you are asked this question next, say, "A grave-maker!" The houses he makes last till doomsday.' He looks up at the curdling sky. 'Go,' he orders. 'To Yaughan. Fetch me a flagon of liquor.' Not surprisingly, he is thirsty. He also prefers the solitary exercise of his craft.

Digger Two regards him unhappily. Sees he is serious. Reluctantly departs towards the city.

Hamlet and Horatio move to a silent vantage behind a cluster of firs. Circumscribing the copse, a hip-high dry-stone dyke surmounts the snow. On this the newcomers sit as they spy through the trees.

Thigh-deep in his grave, Digger One views the obedient departure of Digger Two with mixed feelings and a wry smile. He is not a cruel man. Yet, curse-blessed with more intelligence than his occupation demands, he has a low tolerance for suffering fools.

Now alone, so he thinks, he hops out of the grave and addresses his coat, which drapes a nearby gravestone. From one pocket he fishes hunks of bread and cheese, which quickly diminish. From another pocket he tugs a hip-flask. As he drains it, a robin flits down from a pine-tree branch and perches demandingly on the collar of Digger One's coat.

The little bird's chest puffs redly. His candidly cruel greedy eyes proclaim:

I am hungry. Hungry, hungry . . .

Digger One grins. Flicks his feathered friend a crumb of bread and a morsel of Danish Blue.

There but for Fortune.

Refreshed by his aliments, and the relish of his compassion, Digger One jumps back into his hole and attacks its floor once more. He hasn't yet unearthed old bones from previous graves, and it is a rule with him that until such earlier remains emerge he hasn't dug deep enough. This reflection, plus knowledge that the King and Queen will attend the funeral, eggs him to lower with zest the bottom of Ophelia's last resting-place. As he hacks, and picks, and shovels, he sings in a breathy tenor:

> In youth, when I did love and woo,
> I thought it beyond compare
> To pizzle my prettiest sweetheart true
> Till the night fell from the air.
> But age with his cold creeping hand
> And wheedling spiteful tongue
> Now ploughs me back into the land
> As if I had never been young.

'Has this fellow no feeling for his business, that he sings at grave-making?' Hamlet murmurs quizzically.

Horatio doesn't see humour in the macabre.

'Custom breeds indifference,' he theorizes earnestly.

'Quite so,' mutters Hamlet. 'Daintier sensibilities are saved for idler hands.' He shakes his whiskers at the profundity of Horatio's sincerity.

Digger One has finally scraped old graves. He throws up a spadeful of bone fragments, which land on the snow like a spatter of vomit on a spotless lawn handkerchief, all dirty brown. Cheered by his find, he choruses:

> *Oh, Denmark is a pitiful place,*
> *The King's a fulsome fellow:*
> *Pig's vagina for his face*
> *With teeth all green and yellow.*

Yes, here we are
Without our star:
Lord Hamlet's sailed away.
Alack! Alack!
Bring Hamlet back:
Let's change our King today!

He kneels. Rummages. Throws up a skull. It lands on the adjacent mound of excavated clay, bounces, and rolls over the snow like a desiccated turnip.

Hamlet watches with jumbled feelings. Intimations of the murder of his father, his own killing of Polonius, and the eternal closeness of death to life, are stirred by the rolling skull.

'That head had a tongue in it, and could sing once,' the Prince whimsies gently. 'How the knave hurls it to the ground, as if it were Cain's jawbone, that did the first murder! That might be the pate of a politician, which this ass now abuses.'

'It might, my lord.' Horatio finds Hamlet's sombre musings depressing. He also feels several degrees colder than ever before. Even through his padded boots, fingers of ice grip his toes with the malice of nascent gangrene. Is the Prince indeed deranged, Horatio dares wonder, to dally in such a temperature?

Hamlet ponders on:

'Or of a courtier, who could say, "Good morrow, sweet lord! How are you, good lord?" Or all that remains of Lord Such, who praised Lord So-and-So's horse, prior to begging it off him. Hmn?'

'Yes, my lord . . .'

Whisper, whoosh. Scrunch.

A caked white sleeve falls from an overhanging bough, touches Horatio's shoulders with a plosive caress, and disintegrates in a fine soft spray.

Horatio startles.

Hamlet chuckles. Spurs on the hobby-horse of Digger One's skull:

'Just so. And now he belongs to My Lady Worm. Jawless, and bonced with a sexton's spade! Here is true democracy, if only we could live to see it. Did these bones cost no more than the breeding, to be played skittles with? Mine ache to think of it.' He shivers.

As Digger One cheerily sings:

Now I grow old, thank God it's cold!
It dulls the awful smell:
Galleons of gleet, and the King's fat feet,
And the Queen's back teeth as well.
A pickaxe and a spade, I say,
Fresh horses for the plough,
And tons of mud, to cover the crud,
Is what Denmark needs right now!

Yes, Denmark is a pitiful place,
The King's a fulsome fellow . . .

He lobs up another skull, It falls between the grave and Hamlet, sinking to its worm-burrowed eyes in the yielding young snow.

'There's another!' Hamlet warms to his chilly theme. 'Perhaps a lawyer! Then where are his sophistries now? Why does he suffer this rude knave to bonk his bonce with a dirty shovel? Not threatening prosecution for assault? Hum!' He glances sideways. Registers how miserably cold Horatio is.

The poor fellow's arms fold tightly across his chest. He is jittering like a frightened girl.

'This individual', Hamlet goads, 'might have been a great buyer of land. Is this then the redemption of his mortgages? The repossession of his repossessions? His pate full of dirt? Will his guarantors guarantee him no more than this? The breadth of a pair of dentures?' Hamlet flashes his own sturdy white teeth in a black smile (for contemporary false teeth are no joke). Pointing accusingly at Digger One's grave, the Prince adds:

'His great title deeds will hardly fit in this box! And must the inheritor himself have no more, ha?' He pokes Horatio's muffled ribs.

'No more, my lord,' Horatio chatters.

Hamlet pauses. Ponders the comic gravity of Digger One's occupation. Thinks back to his own educational visits to the Copenhagen lunatic asylum:

'Is not parchment made of sheepskins?'

'Yes, my lord.'

'Yet they are sheep which look to parchment for wisdom!' Hamlet riddles with schizoid logic. Glances again at Horatio's wriggling discomfort. Has mercy. 'I will speak to this fellow,' the Prince announces, rising.

He picks his way through the thin screen of pines and tramples the virgin snow to the grave.

Horatio scrambles after him, gratefully, flapping his arms like a big brown penguin in a panic.

Digger One observes their approach with surprise, but affects no notice. Unlike Digger Two, he fears no lurkers. For where would the secret police be, without master gravediggers?

'Whose grave is this, sir?' Hamlet asks politely.

Digger One looks up. Critically eyes the enormous shaggy man addressing him.

'Mine, sir,' he replies laconically. And choruses:

> *Alack! Alack!*
> *Bring Hamlet back:*
> *Let's change our King today!*

'I think it yours indeed! For you lie in it,' Hamlet quips with acerbity. He likes the man's wit, but his own royalty is offended.

'You lie out of it, sir,' Digger One returns. 'And therefore it is not yours. For my part, I do not lie in it, and yet it is mine!'

'You *do* lie in it. To *be* in it, and say it is yours. It is for the dead, not the living. Therefore, you lie.'

'It is a living lie, sir. It will fly again. From me to you.'

Hamlet smothers a grin of admiration for the grave-digger's self-assured cheek. He stamps round the grave, to keep warm.

Horatio follows.

'What man do you dig it for?' the Prince would know.

'For no man, sir.'

'What woman, then?'

'No woman!'

'Who *is* to be buried in it?' Hinting Impatience.

'One that *was* a woman, sir. But, rest her soul, she's *dead*!'

'How insolent the knave is!' Hamlet sticks mitted thumbs to his ears. Wags mitted fingers. Blows a raspberry at Digger One. Stops dead to exclaim.

Horatio cannons into him.

'I have noticed it these three years past. The peasant's toe bumps the courtier's bunion!' Hamlet tours the grave again.

Horatio totters after.

'How long have you dug graves?' the Prince inquires.

'I began the very day Old Hamlet buggered Fortinbras.' Digger One shovels out some old broken finger bones, which land like fox droppings near Hamlet's hugely booted feet.

Hamlet ignores this affront.

'How long ago is that?' he persists. Testing his disguise. To see if Digger One will overestimate his age.

Digger One obliges.

'Don't you know that?' he scoffs. 'Any fool could tell you that. The day young Hamlet was born! He that is mad, and sent into England.' He chuckles derisively.

Hamlet grins beneath his beard:

'*Why* was he sent to England?'

'Because he was *maaaaaad*. He shall recover his wits there. If not, it will not matter.'

'Why so?'

'It will not be seen in him there. The men are as mad as he!' Digger One snorts contemptuously.

'How came he mad?' Hamlet asks more seriously.

'Very strangely, they say.'

'*How* strangely?'

'Faith, even with *losing his wits*!' Digger One explodes in hoots of pleonastic mirth.

'Upon what ground?' Warningly.

'Why, here in Denmark,' the humorous worker gurgles. 'I been sexton here, man and boy, for thirty years.'

Hamlet lapses into silence for a few paces.

A feathery snowflake flurry falls.

'How long will a man lie in the earth before he rot?' the Prince explores a fresh tangent.

'Well!' Digger One heaves his hilarity behind a professional frown. 'We get poxy corpses nowadays that scarce hold out a week. But if a man ain't rotted before he dies, he will last eight years. A tanner will last you nine.' His frown fractures as a snowflake lands like apple blossom on his left eyebrow.

'Why should a tanner outlast ourselves?'

'His hide is so tanned with his trade! It keeps out water longer. And your water is a sore decayer of your whoreson dead body.' Digger One reaches into the hole behind him. Picks up a skull he is saving for his collection at home. 'Here's a fellow has lain in the earth some three and twenty years.' He turns it round. Appraises it sagaciously. The back of this skull is mashed flat, as if pulverized by a sledgehammer.

'Whose was it?' Hamlet is sceptical. How could a gravedigger identify a skull after twenty-three years?

'A whoreson mad fellow!' Digger One prevaricates provocatively. 'Who do you think?'

'I know not.'

'A pestilence on the mad rogue! Once he poured a flagon of Rhenish on my head.' The sexton's grin sours at this mortifying memory. 'This same skull, sir, was, sir, Yorick's skull. The King's jester.' His tongue insults the yellow-grey impassivity of the death-mask in his hand.

'This!' cries Hamlet, astonished. For Yorick was his childhood hero.

'The same.' Digger One regards with smug satisfaction the mute remains of his perished tormentor.

'Let me see.' Hamlet takes the skull, and scrutinizes with suspicion the mashed dorsal cranium.

27
POOR YORICK

Hamlet sadly cons the stark remains of his former playmate.

Snow falls faster now, like debris from a pillow-fight in heaven.

'Alas! Poor Yorick.' Hamlet brushes his whitening whiskers. 'A fellow of infinite jest. He must have borne me on his back a thousand times. Abhorrent thought!' He dabs at the broken toothless jaws:

'Here hung those lips that oft I kissed.'

The Prince looks up to the drooping sky. Then back at Yorick:

'Where be your gibes now? Your gambols? Songs? Cat got your tongue? Eh? *Now* get you to my lady's chamber. And let her paint lips thick as she may; in the end she will grin like you. Make her laugh at *that*.' On this note Hamlet retreats into a tragical reverie on the ultimate vanity of all human conceit, pretence, honest endeavour, and existence generally.

Yorick, of course, was Old Hamlet's clown. And none of the old King's courtiers gave him better entertainment than this maniacal humpback jester. With his great beaky nose and devilish bed-bright eyes, the crippled dwarf was a giant in wit, a rich landowner in privilege.

Not that Old Hamlet treated Yorick as a person. More like a pet chimpanzee. Yet this very fact was the source of Yorick's impunity. For how could a powerful King be shamed by the japes of a simian?

Thus was Yorick free to roam the Castle with absolute licence. Great nobles and privy councillors would find their clandestine intrigues and sexual assignations suddenly subject to cackling exposure. Haughty ladies with bristling bustles would shriek to find their cleavages overfoaming with upturned ale. Even Old Hamlet himself would occasionally fall victim to Yorick's endless apple-pies.

Such was the King's faith in Yorick's harmless tonic value that whenever he went crusading against the Norwegians, or the hapless Poles, he would leave the jester briefed to keep young Gertrude amused and out of the mischief that boredom and sexual frustration so easily can spawn.

So Yorick would tell the young Queen exciting stories, true and fairy. Drawing on his extensive knowledge of Nordic folklore and mythology. When history let him down, his imagination never did. In any case, Gertrude still lived hazily between fact and fantasy. Not infrequently Yorick would feed her natural appetite for scandal by recounting (in flowery euphemism where necessary) the amorous extravaganzas of her ladies-in-waiting.

Even late at night:

Gertrude would insist on a soothing bedside story from the sadly shaped yet sharp and vibrant little man. His rough but warm hypnotic voice had the power to charm away the loveless desolation she felt whenever her lord and master and lover and King was absent for long months (once even years) at a time, on utmost plundering missions.

Soon the entertainments embraced physical teasing.

Yorick might burst into the royal bedchamber when young Gertrude was listlessly brushing her lovely hair, snatch her brush and gambol round the chamber with it, forcing Gertrude to chase him. If he judged her mood propitious, he would creep up silently behind her and, through her curve-caressing night attire, give the shimmering royal buttocks a playful spank – or tender the royal nipples a friendly fondle.

These corporal diversions were not included in Old Hamlet's instructions to Yorick, and the King could hardly have viewed them with much favour.

But Gertrude kept them secret.

She enjoyed Yorick's impertinent molestations. They took her back to girlhood; before responsible Queenhood sat heavy on her buoyant spirit.

One day, after such a personal impudence from Yorick, when Old Hamlet had been away for many moons on a campaign of

215

imperial expansion, Gertrude noticed an ugly bulge below the clown's left knee. It showed through the gaudy stripes of his pantaloons like a large potato in a flour sack.

Gertrude's smile of delight froze into a troubled frown. She had come to accept Yorick's unfortunate deformities, even to love the grotesque tubercular hump on the midget's back. But the prospect of some further abnormality lumped her breast with shameful disgust.

What is *that*, Yorick? She pointed demandingly at the bulge.

Nothing, my lady. The little man stood back, the humour polluted in his yew-green eyes.

It is *not* nothing, Yorick, she said sternly. Tell me what it is.

He sighed heavily:

Nothing worth the name, my lady. Only the awful insult that the Good Lord's infinite mercy and wisdom adds to the injury of my terrible mis-shapenness.

Show me, Yorick. Let me see.

My lady, I cannot.

Gertrude resorted to spoilt-little-girl megalomania:

Show me, Yorick. That is an *order*.

Very well, my lady. Smiling bravely, but sadly, having just heard his death sentence pronounced, the rumbled clown turned his back on the curious Queen and fiddled with his pantaloons.

Quickly, Yorick!

Then, ever so slowly, he turned to face her again.

Gertrude gasped.

Oh, Yorick! she gulped.

For there, protruding aggressively upward from the jester's cod like a primed cannon from a gun emplacement, reared a human male genital organ more enormous than any the Queen had ever imagined. Longer and stouter than her forearms. With thick ropes of blood pumping along the straining carrot skin like the veins on a warhorse leg.

Oh, *Yorick*, Gertrude gulped again, pulse racing. I had no idea.

You see, my lady, he apologized gently. This is my wound. Which the *Good* Lord, in his *infinite* mercy, has added to my terrible shape.

Poor Yorick, she sympathized. Let me touch it. Torn between

216

fascinated disgust and disgusted fascination, she tentatively stroked his unforeshadowed phallus.

Bowing to his doom like an enlightened lamb to impending slaughter, Yorick wearily angled his charger forward.

Kneeling to inspect it closely, thus tantalizing Yorick further with her bosom, Gertrude felt a thrill of molten horror. Yorick's member mushroombulb she could not span, not even with both hands, fingers outstretched. The image of the agonizing havoc it might wreak on her internal organs mused her kneeling thighs with a delicious sensation of warm watery weakness.

Slowly, rhythmically, Gertrude rocked on her hams as though hypnotized. Heaving the head of Yorick's virility between her cupped palms, as if to kindle fire by friction.

Aaaaaaaargh. Yorick shuddered like a blasted willow in an earthquake. A tiny pellet of congealed sperm shot out of him and splatted flat on Gertrude's dressing-table mirror.

Looking back from maturity, the Queen would marvel at the clown's paltry ejaculate, compared with his ponderous penility. For Yorick never revealed to her his ultimate shame, his meta-insult. Deep in the folds of his tufty-cod? There hid one shrivelled testicle, the left being undescended.

However, once this secret sexual alliance between Queen and clown had begun, what could stop it? Not that it ever escalated into intercourse. Heaven forbid. Quite apart from her womb-knotting image of that outlandish human battering-ram pulverizing her innards, Gertrude could not bear the prospect of an illegitimate child in the unkingly mould of Yorick.

So:

Show me your wound, Yorick, the Queen would say. Or: is your wound hurting you today, Yorick? Let me see.

Yes, my lady, he would reply. And comply. With his pachyderm cocker yearning.

And Gertrude would succour him with hand-relief. This they ritualized into a game of Aim And Fire, at nominated targets in the bedchamber, with giggling points for distance, force, and accuracy. On a jackpot night young Gertrude might bestow a kneeling kiss on Yorick's artillery, in homage to the phoric penilification of all he meant to her. But never was there coitus. Heaven forbid.

And Yorick?

His part in the gonad games was played in a spirit of self-destructive fatalism. He would bare his totem and ejaculate in the sick delight of certainty that his supererogatory indiscretions with the belle Queen could only end in tragedy for him.

And so they did:

Polonius' agent in the Castle kitchens overhears two wide-beamed scrubbers bitch acidly about the time and (especially) energy spent by Yorick in the royal bedchamber late at night.

Polonius investigates personally. The following evening he penetrates the royal boudoir while Gertrude is still weaving with her ladies, after supper. Secretes himself beneath the royal four-poster.

Two cold hours later Gertrude reappears. Undresses. Redresses for bed. Soon she is brushing her waist-length hair.

Knock, knock.

Yes!

Yorick bounds in.

Ooooh, my lady, he moans. Performs a dislocated somersault. Lands on his feet in the middle of the royal mattress, causing Polonius, beneath, to gasp in silent pain and displeasure.

What is it, Yorick? Gertrude kindly inquires.

My wound, my lady. My wound is troubling me. I am in great *pain*.

Poor Yorick, coos the Queen. Let me see.

Out the monster comes. Huge and angry. Wagging and salivating like a hungry hound.

Craning on the cold-paved floor, Polonius almost ruptures. He had no idea.

From here on, the Premier can but jigger.

The gonad game runs its normal course. Gertrude's mastery of penile ballistics lands the skimpy salvo of Yorick's jissom dead-centre on her dressing-table mirror. Exclaimant with glee, she rushes to wipe the glass with a yellowing scrap of used parchment.

Yorick, disconsolate behind her back, stuffs away his melting gun.

Polonius battles to muzzle his enraged incredulity. That this should take place, and obviously not for the first time, while all the Castle and especially the Queen are entrusted to his care!

218

Glower, fume.

Target practice over, Gertrude retires to bed.

Yorick tucks her in. Lulls her to sleep with a fairy story about a Dog with eyes like millponds.

Gertrude's pretty eyelids droop. Her breathing lengthens.

The errant but strangely faithful clown snuffs the candles. Limptoes from the chamber. Heads for the coarse consolation of trysting with a kitchenmaid in the Original Sculleries.

Long minutes pass in silence broken only by ghostly rustling.

Then four-poster creaking as the unloved Queen is mounted tenderly in dreams.

At last . . . the beautiful body above him sounds sonorous in slumber. Polonius' aching bones unbend from their hiding-place and creep wrathfully from the scene.

Next morning:

Yorick's body was found before breakfast by a passing stable-boy. At first the lad thought the jester a victim of stolen kitchen wine. But a closer look, at the body and the battlements above, suggested death due to falling from a height.

Actually Yorick's murder was effected by the crushing of his head with a muffled mace, but how could pathological Polonius discover this?

So the story was circulated that Poor Yorick, no longer able to bear the cruel indignity of his physique, had taken his own life in dead-of-night despair. Since there was no *proof* that the unfortunate had not fallen from the battlements accidentally, and since he was a favourite with the absent King, it was prudently decided to bury his remains in the little limbo graveyard Ophelia soon will share.

Where his splintered skull enables Digger One to identify him twenty-three years later.

Thick snow settles like leaves in a windy autumn. As if God's Poems were emptying from his Wastepaper Basket upturned over all the world.

Digger One blinks anxiously skyward, but Hamlet ignores the weather. His thoughts are still of Yorick:

'Tell me, Horatio!'

'What, my lord?'

'Do you think Alexander looked like this in the earth?'

'Just the same.'

'And smelt so?!' Hamlet offers the empty head to Horatio's nostrils.

Horatio shrinks back, hurt.

'Pah!' Hamlet apologizes for his tease. Lobs the skull far over the hedging pine-trees.

Digger One glares in silence, having earmarked Yorick for his home museum.

'Just so, my lord,' Horatio mumbles sniffily.

Hamlet claps his shoulder warmly.

'To what lowly states we return, Horatio! Cannot our imagination trace the noble Alexander, till he plugs a kitchen sink?'

Horatio grimaces primly.

'Thus! Alexander died. Was buried. Returned into dust. The dust is earth. Of earth we make clay. And of clay we make plugs. Hence? Part of noble Alexander may this very day be stopping a beer barrel!' The Prince chuckles.

Horatio nods wearily. Then his eyes narrow in a listening frown.

Sounds of a funeral procession approach:

The high-pitched keening of hired mourners;

Frosty snorting of champing horses;

Brassy jingle of carriage-drawing harness;

Scuffing squeak of snow-kicking boots.

Hamlet cautiously propels Horatio away from the grave. Towards the border of trees. Opposite the entrance through which the procession must enter. As he withdraws, the Prince sings quietly to a nursery tune:

> Imperious Caesar, dead and turned to clay,
> Might stop a hole to keep the wind away.
> How strange to think that such all-powerful dust
> Should patch a wall to thwart the winter's gust!

The funeral procession alligates gravely through the narrow entrance.

Everyone is, of necessity, on foot.

First comes the coffin, shoulder-borne by six grudging men-at-arms. Then straggle the hired mourners, keening repulsively. And a priest, layered in dark sackcloth, with fat felt boots in place of monastic sandals.

After the priest:

Laertes. Stomping in muted fury. Swathed in martial black leather. Even sporting his sword, despite the solemnity of the occasion. Like a muscular starling on the warpath.

Following Laertes, sombre in sables, plod Claudius and Gertrude. Duty bound to pay their last respects, but impatient to return to the comparative warm comfort of the Castle.

Finally, a motley tailfeather of lords, ladies, courtiers, and attendant lackeys.

'But hush!' breathes Hamlet in surprise. 'Aside. Here comes the King!' He bows backwards in feigned awe, blocking the procession's view of Horatio. The Prince has no fear of being recognized directly, but he doesn't want to be seen with Horatio.

Horatio backs obediently.

'The Queen. The courtiers,' Hamlet continues, puzzled. 'Who is that they follow? And with such lack of ceremony? This bodes some suicide. And a corpse of rank,' he adds, remembering the graveyard's ecclesiastical function. 'Let us stand apart awhile, to watch.' He retreats himself and Horatio into the fringe of trees.

The funeral procession pays the strangers no notice.

28
OUTFACINGS

Digger One leaps out of the grave. Bows proudly. Waves to indicate that Ophelia's grave is fully dug.

The wizened priest signals to the bier-bearers.

They lower the coffin into the ground.

Mumble, mumble. The priest mutters a prayer in perfunctory Latin. Crosses himself hurriedly. Motions Digger One to fill the hole.

Digger One moves alertly to comply. But . . .

'What ceremony else?' Laertes rushes forward, eyes blazing bloodshot. The loss of family status implicit in his sister's death and limbo burial is intolerable.

The priest attempts to maintain his dignity. Ignores the interruption. Motions again to Digger One.

'That is Laertes. A *very* noble youth. Watch.' Hamlet's chuckling sarcasm is heard only by Horatio.

'What ceremony *else*?' Laertes yells, crowding the craven cleric. Menacingly clasping his sword hilt.

Claudius and Gertrude avert their frozen embarrassment. They are too cold and rutted in religious convention to intervene. Gertrude, moreover, is anxious lest the falling snow freeze on her skin and crack her make-up.

The churlish priest faces Laertes with borrowed courage:

'We have already extended our mourning as far as we may,' he announces sternly. 'Her death was doubtful. But for the sway of royalty, she would be buried in unsanctified ground. And there should she lodge *until the last trumpet*!' he stresses with sanctimony:

'For shards, flints, pebbles, and the cold prayers of charity *should* be thrown upon her. Yet here she is, allowed her virgin's wreaths, her maiden flowers, and the dignity of bell and burial.'

'Must no more be done?' insists Laertes, furiously.

'No more be done,' God's minister pronounces. 'We would profane the service of the dead, to sing solemn requiem, and grant such rest to her as is the right of peaceful souls, who pass on naturally.'

Will Laertes run the priest through his churlish heart?

No. Instead, to Digger One he howls:

'Lay her in the earth. And from her fair and unpolluted flesh may violets spring!' He glowers round the assembled company.

Will anyone take issue?

No.

Feeling that if family status *must* be lost, he'll lubricate the irritation with the last possible dribble of political advantage, Laertēs screams:

'I tell you, churlish priest, a ministering *angel* shall my sister be, when you lie howling in hell.'

'*What!*' exclaims Hamlet. 'The fair Ophelia?' He is astounded (not by the fact of her death, but) by the implication that such a worldly wanton would ever voluntarily terminate her own appetites and satisfactions.

Why?

The Prince stares searchingly at Horatio.

The poor good friend can only shrug dumbly. He was too busy preparing for his reunion with Hamlet to hear the sad saga of Ophelia's death.

Hamlet returns his rat-sniffing gaze to the grave.

Laertes stands back from the cleric in ill-tempered disgust.

Digger One moves forward again at the priest's bidding. Shovels frozen earth into the grave.

Bonk, thud. Snowy clods land on Ophelia's coffin.

Gertrude steps to the lip of the pit. Scatters in some perfumed petals from last summer's pot-pourri.

'Sweets to the sweet,' she blesses, in a small tight voice. 'Farewell! I hoped you would be my Hamlet's wife. I thought to deck your bridal bed, sweet maid. And not to strew your grave.' She crosses herself. Stands back.

The mention of Hamlet elicits from Laertes a gargle of rage like a whale breaking wind.

'Oh!' he bellows. 'Treble woe upon that cursed head whose wicked deed destroyed your wits and very breath.' He rushes back to the teeth of the grave. 'Hold off the earth awhile, till I have caught her once more in my arms.' Hogging the limelight to the nipple of his false emotion, Laertes drops into the grave. Kneels. Opens his arms to the cloddy coffin lid.

He looks up at the others. Most are staring at their boots in impatient embarrassment.

'*Now* pile your dust upon us,' Laertes challenges. 'Till of this molehill a *mountain* you have made!'

Now comes Hamlet, charging from the trees. Exasperated by Laertes' performance, and unable to resist such a purple re-entry, the Prince penetrates the gathering. Huge, wild, and bushy. Like a mad monk in sheep's clothing.

The attendant lords, ladies, courtiers and lackeys recoil, as do the royal couple.

Men-at-arms take a hesitant step forward, fingering their weapons in case this lunatic intends mischief to the King.

But Hamlet addresses the grave. Stands on its edge. Looks down at Laertes.

'Who is this, with grief so great?' the towering Prince cries. 'Whose sorry clichés blush the stars?' He pulls off his hat. 'This is *I*,' he roars, '*Hamlet the Dane.*' Growling like a Russian bear, and pulling off his balding wig, he drops into the grave and makes monkey faces at Laertes. His brown shoulder-length hair hangs loosely, as before, over his sheepskin collar.

The gathering gasps in exultation and dismay at the errant Prince's strange return.

Claudius' fearful pallor is concealed by the blowing snow. He glares spitefully at Horatio as the latter steps hesitantly forward from the trees.

'The devil take your soul!' Laertes troats, and goes for Hamlet's throat.

Hamlet slaps aside the shorter man's groping paws, grips his leather collar and hoists his body into the air.

'You do not pray well,' he sneers into Laertes' popping eyes. '*I* pray *you*,' he mocks, 'take your fingers from my throat. For, though I am neither spiteful nor rash, yet I have in me something dangerous, which your infinite wisdom would do well to fear.' And he hurls Laertes backwards against the pit wall.

Laertes hisses savagely and bounces forward, hand on sword.

'Away your hand!' cries Hamlet, scything a crippling chop on the upper muscles of Laertes' sword arm.

Laertes groans.

Hamlet proceeds to knock the stuffing out of him. In swordsmanship alone Laertes might stand a slender chance against the Prince. But in unarmed combat? At close range? He is hopeless as a banana in a barrel of monkeys.

'Pluck them asunder,' booms Claudius. He is anxious lest Laertes receive an injury which might hinder the projected rapier duel.

'Hamlet! Hamlet!' Gertrude exclaims, but mildly. She has never liked the adult Laertes, and besides:

May not the fracas distract wandering minds from the riddle of Ophelia's decease?

'Gentlemen . . .' the courtiers moo.

'Good my lord,' Horatio urges, 'be quiet.'

Claudius motions the men-at-arms. They separate the tussling combatants.

Laertes has had much the worst of it. He wheezes for breath in mortified sobs. Staggers to rest against the gravestone where Digger One's coat is draped.

Though the crumbling red robin has long since flown.

Hamlet now switches emotions. He rushes to Gertrude. Kneels in the snow before her.

'Why,' he exclaims plaintively, 'I will fight with him upon this theme until my eyelids no longer wag.'

'Oh, my son!' Gertrude cradles his shaggy-show-of-penitence head in her fur-muffled arms. 'What theme?'

'*I* loved Ophelia,' Hamlet wails. 'Forty thousand brothers could not equal that love.' He jumps to his feet. Shakes a petulant fist at panting Laertes. 'What will *you* do for her?' Hamlet shouts.

Laertes wheezes. Stares poisoned daggers.

'Oh! He is mad, Laertes.' Claudius seizes this opportunity to further the fiction.

'For love of God,' Gertrude echoes, 'forgive him.'

'Great Heavens!' Hamlet breaks free of Gertrude and berates Laertes.

The gathering's attention follows the Prince.

'Show what *you* would do,' he challenges. 'Would you weep? Fight? Fast? Castrate yourself? Drink vinegar? Eat a crocodile? *I*'ll do it.' Exposing the histrionic hypocrisy of Laertes' laboured grief:

'Do you come here to whine?' Hamlet asks kindly. 'To asperse me, by leaping in her grave?' Suddenly he switches again. Jumping dramatically back into the pit:

'Be buried living with her,' he screams, 'and so will I. And if you prate of mountains, let them throw millions upon us.' He gestures an expansive caricature of millions of mountains. Then, having finished on a tumultuous crescendo, Hamlet climbs calmly out of the grave and bows to Laertes. 'So you see,' he says, even more kindly, 'if *you* rant and babble, *I*'ll rant just as well.'

Several lords and ladies snigger invisibly at Laertes' apoplectic discomfiture.

Hamlet makes their sniggers visible by falling back on the snow, kicking his legs in the air as if juggling with his feet, and pounding his breast and screaming like a tantric baby.

Murder ferments in Laertes' eyes.

Gertrude intuits that the preservation of Laertes' lumpy dignity may keep the peace of the realm, so she intercedes to save his face:

'This is mere madness,' she pleads, deprecating Hamlet's caper. 'Thus, for a while, the fit flaps him. But soon his silence will sit drooping.'

Hamlet rolls to his feet. Brushes the snow from his elbows. Bows to Gertrude, to the gathering, and finally to Laertes:

'Hear you, sir. Why use me thus? I have always loved you. But . . . no matter. Let Hercules do what men must do . . . the cat will mew, and the pig will snuffle truffles.' On this insulting note, the Prince departs in a hairy flurry of matted sheepskin and scuffled snow.

'Good Horatio,' Claudius points authoritatively, 'look after him.'

Horatio obediently follows Hamlet through the graveyard's narrow entrance.

Claudius claps his mitts.

The attendant lords, ladies, courtiers and lackeys stir and disperse.

Claudius crosses confidentially to where Laertes is recovering puff.

'Have patience,' the King counsels in a throaty undertone. 'And remember the play we planned last night. We'll act it presently.' Then, to his Queen, in a fruity public voice:

'Good Gertrude,' he exhorts, 'set some watch over your son.' And to the tail of the assembly:

'This grave will have a lasting memorial: the times of peace and prosperity which we shall shortly see. Till then, let us proceed patiently.'

So begins the cavalcade back to the Castle.

Only Digger One stays on, to stop the gaping cavity with earth and stone, before it fills with snow.

While over the trees the yawning nosehole and cavernous eye-sockets of Yorick's skull stare ghoulishly into the disintegrating sky, patiently wondering if God will ever write Poetry again.

29
WICKED MESSENGERS

Uncertainty glows in the vaulted Castle gloom today.

Also a paradoxical air of freshness and warmth. Almost spring-like. Although, outside, the snow lies heavy still, bulging splinters of cold clean sunlight penetrate the Castle's fusty nooks.

This weather amelioration is matched, at least in the kitchens and servant quarters (if not the dungeons), by a curious ambience of levity and holiday bonhomie. Pleasantries are exchanged without venom. Trills of workaday warbling whistle are not infrequent.

Even Hamlet is well groomed and smartly clad. His beard has been trimmed from the sprawling tangle of yesterday to an elegantly pointed triangle.

Last night the Prince luxuriated for an hour in his first bath for weeks, having hot water added five times, and dreamily splashing in a delicious decadence of soft scented soapfoam. This balneal balm took him back to the days of his surveillance on Ophelia, and especially her après-bathing pursuits.

The intersecting images of her healthy buxom body in life and the squalid brown coffin of yesterday trapped Hamlet for a while in a circular groove of morbid conscience-searching. He never felt for Ophelia the eternal transcendence of conjugal love, of course. But she was extremely alive, and now she is absolutely dead. And Hamlet realizes that, in a strange way, he will miss her mightily.

Death, he reflects, makes the heart grow fondest.

After his bath the Prince slipped back into his extramural spy network to scan for useful intelligence. Round and up and down he prowled, as before, in dark anonymity, peeking through the inummerable and formerly invaluable chinks in the brickwork and observing at his leisure the whole spectrum of Castle life, from the quick-bang technique of a junior courtier and one of Gertrude's ladies to the sickening depravity of a pageboy tormenting a kitten in the kitchen. But the only flash of potential value showed Claudius and Osric in close confabulation. Hamlet strained hard to hear the vileness being spawned, but their muttering was overly subdued.

In any case, the Prince no longer feels at home in these crawling corridors of espionage and intrigue. Like a pilgrim to his childhood home, he finds the Castle and its inmates smaller, greyer, drabber, and of greatly less significance than their fossils in his memory. Accordingly, last night, he left his peekaboo grapevine for the last time, through his conjunctive bedroom fireplace, and lay down for a celebration slumber.

But even then, peace eluded him.

Because, for the first time in his life, Hamlet suffered the snowballing stabs of dental decay. Pain like a hot pulsing needle inflamed his offending molar throughout tossing hours of sweaty guilt-sewage reflections, before a short dawn sleep of sheer exhaustion.

This morning, Hamlet looks pale, drawn, nervy. His toothache, however, has subsided. Assuaged, perhaps, by the less cold weather.

The Prince is walking with Horatio along a huge echoing hall.

Flanking fires merrily crackling.

Thick sunlight beams like the arms of brawny giants punch cheerfully through dusty window cobwebs to highlight Horatio's balding brown and Hamlet's gaunt sallow.

The Prince is pacing tautly in a colourful bell-sleeved chemise and skin-tight knee breeches.

Horatio gazes benignly out of a passing window. Smiles hopefully into the sunshine. He has just finished telling Hamlet for the second time (in cross-examined detail) all that happened in his absence.

'Now, sir,' says Hamlet, satisfied at last. '*You* shall hear *my* story. You remember the circumstances?'

'Remember them, my lord?'

Hamlet recounts his adventures at sea. His attention dissolves to the freezing bilgy innards of the ship bearing him to doom in treacherous England. There:

He writhes sleepless under a mound of blankets on a narrow bunk in a tiny cabin. Penduluminous rocking of a hanging lamp reflects the vessel's anxious ploughing through high unfriendly seas.

'In my heart,' the Prince narrates, 'a mutinous fighting kept sleep at bay.'

He sits up suddenly. Peers about, rubbing his eyes.

'Praise be to rashness!' he exclaims impulsively. 'And to the divinity which shapes our destinies?'

'Amen!' Horatio assents religiously.

Hamlet chuckles.

He clambers out of his restless berth. Creeps next door, where the heads of Rosencrantz and Guildenstern lie addled amid the emetic stench of lurid vomit.

'Rashly,' Hamlet continues, 'my sea-gown scarfed about me, I groped in the dark to find them out. Their dispatch-box I located and quickly withdrew to my cabin. And made so bold – my fears forgetting manners! – to unseal their grand commission.'

With patient stealth he prises open the little box.

'And there, Horatio? Oh, royal knavery! I found, importing Denmark's health and England's too, and larded with divers spuries, an urgent request. That, my life being such a cess of crawling bugs and goblins, as soon as the letter was read my head should be struck off!'

'Is it possible?' Horatio gasps.

'Here's the commission.' Hamlet hands him a dog-eared scroll. 'Read it at your leisure. But will you not hear how I proceeded?'

Horatio frowns.

'I beseech you.'

Hamlet grins. 'I sat my brains down and devised a new commission.'

In the rolling squalor of his cabin on the barque. Poring over the offensive document. Screwing his eyes to scan by the scattered light of the rocking lamp.

'Then wrote it in my best fair hand.'

'Yes, good my lord?'

'An earnest entreaty from the King! Saying that, as England was his faithful friend, she would put the bearers to sudden death, no shriving time allowed.'

Horatio looks shocked.

'How was it sealed?' he asks at length.

'Even on this the gods were smiling. I had my father's signet in my purse. The original from which the Danish seal was taken. I boxed the parchment like the other, signed and sealed, and replaced it safely. The changeling was never known. Next day we had our sea-fight, and the rest you know already.'

'So Rosencrantz and Guildenstern go to die,' Horatio murmurs faintly. He finds the prospect hard to stomach.

Hamlet scorns:

'They are far from my conscience. Their execution is ensured by their own meddling choice.'

'What a King is this!' Horatio applauds uneasily.

'Now,' Hamlet's voice drops low, 'think of the man who has killed my father. Whored my mother. Pooped my hopes. Plotted my own death! Is not my *duty*, in perfect conscience, to slay him with this arm? And would I not deserve *Damnation*, if I let this canker live?'

Horatio cringes. Distressed by Hamlet's atheistic cynicism. Takes refuge in seriousness:

'He must shortly hear from England,' he warns.

'True. But the interim is mine. And ending a man's life takes only "*One*"!' Hamlet startles Horatio by lunging as if delivering a fatal sword thrust.

Horatio is not amused.

Hamlet tries a lighter-hearted angle:

'But I am *very* sorry,' he wails, parodying Laertes in the grave, 'that to Laertes I forgot myself. For, by the image of my own grievances, I see the portraiture of his. From now on I'll court hith favourth.' Here he lisps like Osric. 'Though the bravado of his grief did put me in a passion.'

Horatio's unease hears footsteps.

'Peace!' he urges. 'Who comes?'

Osric.

Sumptuous in silks and velvets of mandarin orange, hubris purple, and rich bile green. When he sees Hamlet he bows to his knees. Doffs his flop cap. Feint dabs of make-up pink his cheeks and flatten the hagbags beneath his eyes.

'Your lordship is right welcome back to Denmark.' He smiles winningly at Hamlet.

'I humbly thank you, sir,' Hamlet leers cloyingly back. Then, to Horatio:

'Do you *know* this waterfly?' he asks in a thundering whisper.

'No, my good lord.'

'Then your state is the more gracious. It is a vice to know him. Though but a chattering starling, he is spacious in the possession of dirt.' Hamlet underlines the homosexual pun by forefingering his anus.

'Sweet lord,' Osric perseveres subjunctively, 'if your lordship were at leisure, I should impart a thing to you from his majesty.'

'I will receive it, sir, with all diligence of spirit. Put your bonnet to its right use. It is for the head.'

'I thank your lordship,' Osric simpers. But he is reluctant to violate the conventions. 'It is very hot,' he suggests, keeping his shapeless headgear in his hand.

'No; very cold. The wind is northerly.'

'It is indifferent cold, my lord.'

'But yet, methinks, very *sultry*.'

'*Exceedingly* sultry.' Osric does his wheedling best to accommodate Hamlet's acrobatic opinions without appearing ludicrous. 'But, my lord,' he rushes on, 'his majesty has laid a great wager on your head –'

'I beseech you, remember!' Hamlet grabs at Osric's hat.

The wicked messenger dodges diplomatically sideways.

'Good my lord,' he begs. 'Let me hold it. For my peace of mind.'

Hamlet sniggers.

'Sir,' Osric battles on, 'here is newly come to court Laertes. An absolute gentleman. Indeed, the *paradigm* of gentry –'

'Thir,' Hamlet mimics, 'to enumerate his excellences would dizzy the memory and yet lag sadly behind the speed of his explosion to perfection.'

Osric astutely misses the point:

'Your lordship speaks most infallibly of him,' he greases.

'The point, sir!' raps Hamlet. 'Why waste our breath on the gentleman?'

'Sir?' Osric seems taken aback.

'Is it not possible to converse in *plain language*?' Horatio chips in. He dislikes Osric intensely.

'*Why* do you talk of this gentleman?' Hamlet hounds.

'Of Laertes?' flusters Osric.

Horatio jumps on the fop's disarray:

'His purse is empty already!' the gentle soul jeers. 'All his golden words are spent.'

'Of him, sir.' Hamlet.

Osric takes a harassed breath.

'I know you are not ignorant . . .' he tries.

'I would you did, sir,' Hamlet counters. 'And yet I should take your knowledge as no great compliment. Well, sir?'

'You are not ignorant of what excellence Laertes is – '

'I dare not confess that,' Hamlet feigns terror, 'lest I seem to compare with his excellence. In any case, to know a man well one must know oneself well. And no man knows himself well. Well?'

'I mean, sir, for his weapon. His followers say he is unbeatable.'

'What's *his* weapon?' Hamlet reaches to tweak Osric's ambivalent cod.

Osric dances aside.

'Rapier and dagger,' he answers.

'That's *two* of his weapons. But? Well?'

'The King, sir, has wagered six Barbary horses. Against this, Laertes has staked six French rapiers and daggers. Together with their trappings. Belts, scabbards, and . . .'

Hamlet sighs the heavy sigh of one who suffers fools and homosexual pedants with short-lived reluctance:

'Why is this "staked"?'

'The King, sir, has bet, sir, that in a fencing bout of twelve rounds between yourself and Laertes, he shall not beat you by more than three hits. And the matter would be tested shortly, if your lordship answer.' Osric bows mechanically, relieved to have delivered his message at last.

'What if I answer No?'

'I mean, my lord, if you would answer Laertes, by opposing him.'

Hamlet's frayed blue gaze rakes the pink-rouged moon of Osric's inscrutable fat countenance. On a careless impulse born of sleep starvation he claps his hands:

'Sir,' to be rid of Osric, 'I will walk here in the hall. It is time I took some exercise. If Laertes is willing,' he grimaces threateningly, 'let the foils be brought. I will win for the King if I can. If not, I gain nothing but my shame and a few odd hits.'

'Shall I answer for you thus?' Osric asks eagerly.

'With whatever embellishments you cannot resist.'

'I commend my duty to your lordship,' Osric effuses, and departs through a window beam of merciless sunlight, which accentuates the fissures in his make-up.

Hamlet sneers after him. 'At your service.' Then, to Horatio:

'He does well to commend it himself. No one else will.'

'The lapwing runs away with the shell on his head,' chortles Horatio, noting that Osric, as he leaves the hall, restores his hat to his head, like the top of a boiled egg in a bad dream.

'He paid due homage to his tit before he sucked it,' says Hamlet more seriously. 'Like so many of the same breed, which these shallow times dote on. They float along on a frothy scum of diverse opinions, until the bubbles burst, and then they sink and drown . . .'

For forty minutes Hamlet buzzes like an irate wasp around the torrid syrup of Metaphysical Freedom, the jammy joke of Personal Afterlife, and other sickly status-quo confections.

Horatio bears the Prince's stinging in good spirit, until a polished courtier walks in:

'My lord,' he drones, 'his majesty sends to know if it is still your pleasure to play with Laertes.'

'I am constant to my purposes,' snaps Hamlet. 'They follow the King's pleasure. If Laertes is ready, *I* am ready.'

'The King, and Queen, and all are coming down.'

Hamlet stares at the courtier in affected puzzlement. Then makes a great show of looking up at the ceiling, as if searching for the falling King and Queen.

'About time!' he observes.

The courtier coughs and nervously relates:

'The Queen desires you to make up with Laertes before you fall to play.'

'She well instructs me.' Hamlet waves in impatient disgust.

The polished courtier exits.

Horatio registers friendly embarrassment:

'You will lose this wager, my lord.'

'I do not think so. Since he went into France I have been in continual practice. I shall win at the odds.' But Hamlet's confidence is qualified. He smells more rats. Paces tigerishly about the hall.

Sunbeams redden the threadlike veins that contour his blue-white eyeballs.

'But you would not believe', he murmurs, patting his breast, 'how ill all is. Here about my heart. But it does not matter.' He dismisses the gnawing intuition with a contemptuous clap.

'*No!*' Horatio protests maternally. 'Good my lord . . .'

'It is but foolery,' Hamlet waves airily. 'The kind of misgiving that would perhaps trouble a woman.'

'If your mind dislike something, obey it.' Horatio echoes a sentiment he has heard Hamlet express often. 'I will say you are not fit.'

'No.' Hamlet grins gashly. 'We defy augury. If death is now, it is not to come. If not now, yet it *will* come. Readiness is all. To live well is to learn how to die well. Since no man can take the cake he leaves, what does it matter when he leaves his cake? Let it be.'

Brazen trumpets snort and rattling kettledrums roll in the shortening distance.

The last grotesque carnival approaches.

Hearing the swelling imminence of his confrontation, Hamlet sniffs derisively and executes a few quick martial-arts muscle looseners. He is confident that his own strength, speed and charisma will ensure victory, but he also respects Laertes' swordsmanship. Moreover, having sniffed the rats, he wants to be sharp enough to cleave them when they break cover.

Horatio looks on miserably. His impressionable eyes hot with apprehension.

30
SHAMBLES

Up front come Claudius and Gertrude. Hand in regal hand, and outwardly best of friends.

Then Laertes, glowering.

In the rear follow sundry lords, ladies, attendants and winebearers.

Osric carries on a red velvet cushion the weapons with which Hamlet and Laertes will duel.

Claudius is in good spirits. He is, he thinks, on the verge of being rid for ever of Laertes, Hamlet, or both. Moreover, today it is clear for miles out to sea, and there have been no further reports of strange shadowy vessels lurking ominously under cover of night and fog.

Gertrude, beneath her rigid coiffure and façade, looks dire. Months of strain show in thickening spider lines round her eyes and mouth.

As the body of the court stiffly enters, Hamlet is prone on the tiled floor, at the bottom of a press-up. He looks at the newcomers with interest, but without stirring.

Claudius appoints himself master of ceremonies. Pompfully he beckons to Laertes, who comes forward smouldering in black leather.

'Come, Hamlet,' booms King Genial. 'Take this hand from me.'

Hamlet springs to his feet. Bounds forward as in boyish enthusiasm.

Claudius takes the right hand of each younger man. Joins them in a conciliatory shake.

Hamlet beams sweetly into Laertes' eyes.

'Sir,' he trills. 'I have done you wrong. But pardon it, as you are a gentleman. Whatever I have done which offended your honour, I hereby proclaim was *madness*.' He shakes his head regretfully, like a physician presenting a gloomy diagnosis:

'Was it Hamlet that wronged Laertes?' he cries rhetorically. 'Never! If Hamlet when he's not himself does wrong Laertes, then Hamlet does it not! Hamlet denies it. Who does it, then? His madness! If this be so, then Hamlet too is wronged. Hamlet's madness is poor Hamlet's own enemy.' Here the Prince flashes a quick knowing wink round all present who have harnessed the myth of his mental illness to their own nefarious purposes.

'Sir,' he continues his barbed wooing of Laertes, 'before this audience, treat me . . . as if I had shot my arrow over the house, and hurt my own brother.'

Laertes' teeth grind. If he were a horse his hooves would pound the floor.

'I am satisfied in my *feelings*,' he hisses vindictively. 'But my *honour* is not. Nor will it be until my family's name is cleared. Till then', he almost spits the falsehood, 'I do receive your offered love *like* love, and will not wrong it.'

Hamlet laps this up:

'I embrace it freely,' he enthuses. 'And play this brother's wager without rancour. Give us the foils.' He snaps fingers at Osric. 'Come on.'

'One for me!' Laertes cries sharply.

Osric stirs in apparent embarrassment, not sure whether to serve Hamlet or Laertes first. He tentatively proffers in both directions the velvet cushion bearing the blades.

Hamlet waves him carelessly at Laertes.

'*I'll* be your foil, Laertes,' the Prince drawls. 'In my ignorance your skill shall shine like a star in the darkest night.'

'You mock me, sir,' Laertes growls.

'No, by this hand.' Hamlet hoists his left fingers in an unmistakable gesture.

Osric is still doddering, evidently unsure about the procedural correctness of offering the foils to Laertes first.

'Give them the foils, young Osric.' Claudius jolts him into decision. 'Cousin Hamlet, you know the wager?'

'Your grace has laid the odds on the weaker side.'

'I do not fear it. But since he has improved, we have therefore odds.' The King's fleshy mouth performs a benevolent-grin facsimile.

Osric, meanwhile, gives Laertes first choice of rapier.

Laertes tests one. Swishes it through the air with a sound like breath sucked through buck teeth.

'Too heavy,' he decides. 'Let me see another.'

While Laertes selects his sword, a pageboy, gibbering with hero worship, tenders Hamlet a padded waistcoat, to protect his torso on a par with Laertes' leathers.

Hamlet waves away the prophylactic garment. This too is gamesmanship – to create the impression of not expecting to be hit. But there is also a serious purpose – he values freedom of movement more than the waistcoat padding.

He rolls to the elbows the flowing sleeves of his chemise. Bends and unbends his surprisingly brawny forearms. Observant courtiers notice that one brawny arm is markedly more brawny than the other. It is the right. His fighting arm.

Osric now offers Hamlet the remaining foils.

The Prince scans them fleetingly, not obviously suspicious.

'This one suits me,' he supposes. 'They are all the same length?'

'Yes, my good lord.' Osric looks shocked that Hamlet could imagine otherwise.

The combatants now dance and feint for a few moments, limbering at opposite ends of the hall.

The body of the court gathers on the far side from the windows, to couple the warmth from the log fires with the last fast-dissolving spills of wintry sunlight without.

Claudius rasps:

'Set the wine upon that table.' Indicating that a long narrow trestle be brought from the wall and placed before Gertrude and himself.

Two liveried lackeys comply.

'If Hamlet scores the first or second hit,' Claudius continues, 'let all the battlements fire off their cannon. The King shall drink to Hamlet's better breath. And in the cup a magnificent pearl shall he throw, richer than four successive kings have worn in Denmark's crown.' He displays between thumb and forefinger a glint of white. Then:

'Give me the cups.' Claudius reaches for his own glistering goblet. 'And let the trumpet cry to the cannoneer outside. Let the cannons roar to the heavens, and the heavens back to the earth:

'"Now the King drinks to Hamlet!"' He takes a long swallow. 'Begin. And you, the judges, bear a wary eye.'

Osric and three lesser lords stir wary feet.

'Come on, sir.' Hamlet snaps his fingers at Laertes, as at a procrastinating coward.

'Come, my lord!' Laertes snouts back. And rushes forward, proclaiming his valour in thrusting poking. As if bent on a walkover.

Hamlet dances nimbly aside, deflects Laertes' sword arm into the air with his own left fist, and lightly prods the smaller man's right nipple.

'One!' claims Hamlet.

'No!' Laertes protests.

'*Judgement!*' Hamlet demands arbitration.

'A hit!' trills Osric. 'A very palpable hit.'

Hamlet grins triumphantly at Laertes.

'Come again!' Laertes screams in rage, and prepares to renew his onslaught.

Claudius intervenes.

'Wait!' he insists. 'Give me drink.' He holds his goblet to be refilled. 'Hamlet,' he cries proudly, 'this pearl is yours!' He plops the nacreous prodigy into the goblet. 'Here's health. Give him the cup.'

A close attendant transports the drinking vessel.

Kettledrums roll.

Trumpets blare.

A fusillade of cannon goes bang on the battlements.

Hamlet impatiently refuses the goblet.

'I'll play this bout first,' he insists. 'Set it by awhile.'

The close attendant returns the goblet to the table in front of the royals.

Claudius sits. His thick lips purse.

'Come!' Hamlet thumbs his nose at Laertes. They set to once more.

Thrust, parry. Parry, thrust.
Swish, clash.

Hamlet suddenly falls on all fours, like a bulldog.

Laertes, caught unawares, lunges savagely above the Prince's head.

Hamlet rises like a jack-from-the-box and knocks Laertes' guard asunder with his shoulder. Then, with all the time in a second, and with perfect cheek, he pokes his opponent's black-leathered belly-button.

'Another hit!' whoops the Prince. 'What say you?'

'A touch, I do confess.' Laertes can hardly deny this one without seeming ridiculous.

'Our son shall win,' grunts Claudius speculatively. Hamlet is making rather easier mincemeat of Laertes than the King had bargained for. Accordingly, the tumbrils of death-dealing contingency clatter louder along the squalid cobbles of the monarchial mental pathways.

Gertrude ignores her husband. Her maternal pride is stirred. She looks glowingly at Hamlet, then scathingly at Laertes.

'*He's* fat, and scant of breath,' she observes with distaste. 'Here, Hamlet. Take my napkin. Rub your brows.'

Hamlet gestures that his mother should restrain herself until the bout is over.

But Gertrude's blood is up. She is not to be silenced. Taking temporary leave of her dignity, she seizes the King's goblet. Raises it to her lips.

'The Queen carouses to your fortune, Hamlet!' she cheers.

'Good madam!' Hamlet admonishes her sternly, embarrassed by her skittish behaviour.

'Gertrude, do not drink,' urges Claudius, but mildly. A whole new spate of possibilities floods across the path of his tumbrils like a newborn river of blood.

'I will, my lord,' she disregards him. 'I pray you, pardon me.' She swigs copiously from the goblet.

'It is the poisoned cup!' the King marvels silently. 'Too late!' Unforeseen rosy-rank images of radiant young princesses loom ripe in his projections, bursting with the eggs of heirs and nubile promise of tumescent lust recovered. What a shame if Gertrude gulps the poison down! Another atrocity to lay at Laertes' treasonous door.

Gertrude takes a second sip. Returns the goblet to the table. She beckons Hamlet to share her proud maternal toast.

'I dare not drink yet, madam,' Hamlet declines stiffly. 'By and by.' Here peeps the iceberg ascetic.

'Come,' croons Gertrude, hot with alcoholic doting. 'Let me wipe your face.'

Hamlet shrugs aside her overtures. His fingers tell Laertes that their contest should continue.

Laertes has taken advantage of Hamlet's exchange with Gertrude, to remove the false blunt button from the poisoned tip of his rapier.

'My lord,' bleats Laertes to the King, 'I'll hit him now.'

'I do not think so,' remarks Claudius, unconcerned. Events seem even more in his favour than he had hoped. He squints blandly at Gertrude, to see if the poison is working.

But the Queen's roused faculties are still intent upon the duel, apparently unimpaired.

'And yet it is almost against my conscience,' Laertes mutters.

'Come for the third, Laertes,' Hamlet drawls insultingly. 'You do but dally. I pray you, thrust with your best violence. I'm afraid you are but trifling me.'

'You think so?' hisses Laertes. 'Come on!' Bolstered by wielding a doubly deadly weapon against the Prince's blunted foil, he charges forward.

Thrust, parry. Swish, clash.

Hamlet knocks his enemy's sword arm into the air and rolls into a somersault which brings him to his feet again behind Laertes.

Laertes whirls to face him.

Hamlet deals him a lightning poke in the solar plexus.

Next, beaming benevolently and affecting shy embarrassment at his winning streak, the Prince turns to Osric for judgement.

Osric pretends not to have seen the hit.

'Nothing,' he smarms. 'Neither way.'

Hamlet draws indignant breath to protest.

'Have at you NOW!' Laertes rushes and lunges while Hamlet's guard is down.

Instinctively Hamlet weaves sideways to dodge the foul play, but not quickly enough. The fatal tip of Laertes' weapon slashes through his upper left sleeve and slices a strip of ragged flesh from his arm.

Instantly the Prince realizes.

The first rat has broken cover.

He glances quickly at his wound.

Rich blood flows red all over his white chemise.

His mouth contracts in a tight cold fury. And he blasts Laertes with the full weight of his martial artistry, as if the rules of fencing had never been invented. He swipes and jabs Laertes backwards until the villain's posterior is roasted by the leaping fire behind him.

Then the Prince feints to the left.

Laertes is wrongfooted.

Hamlet kicks him hard in his codpiece.

Laertes doubles up in genital agony.

Hamlet dances forward and delivers a numbing straight-finger chop to Laertes' sword elbow.

Laertes' arm folds helplessly in a jack-knife reflex. His fingers shock open and his bloody blade clatters on the floor.

Hamlet scoops up the fallen weapon. Brandishes both swords at the dumbstruck audience. Hurls his own buttoned foil at Laertes.

Laertes struggles painfully to his feet, clutching the pointless toy which Hamlet has forced on him. Half-paralysed by scrotal pain, he yet realizes he is fighting for his life.

Hamlet colours the chilling air with a blood-bubbling whoop and presses home his fatal onslaught.

Thrust, thrust. Clash, clash.

Laertes makes one last desperate effort. Rushes forward raining windmill blows on Hamlet's defence.

Hamlet makes light of it. He wards off Laertes' raining steel with his own weapon. Leaps in underneath and punches Laertes on the inside of his sword wrist.

Laertes' blade flies futile into the air.

Hamlet steps back for a split-second to savour his victory before skewering Laertes through the breadth of his burly torso.

Laertes staggers back, croaking wetly. Blood pumps obscenely through the vaginal slit in his black leather jerkin. Heavy crimson with darker blotches it gushes, flecked with terminal flakes of gralloched gut.

This explosion of ostensibly friendly contest into foully fatal combat has been so rapid that none of the onlookers has had time or wit to intervene.

Claudius makes an insincere effort:

'Part them!' he orders belatedly. 'They are incensed.'

'No!' jeers Hamlet. 'Come again!' He brandishes his sword invitingly.

But Laertes will never attack anyone again. He is tottering in crazy bleeding circles.

Hamlet dabs his own bleeding arm.

Laertes, his face a soiled cream-white, cradles his spilling belly with both hands, vainly trying to staunch the flowing crimson sand of the life coursing through his fingers.

Now Gertrude:

Suddenly bottle-green, she rears to her feet, like an ancient whale harpooned. Purple blood seeps sluggishly over the cracked spider lines round the ticking left corner of her mouth. A harsh choking rattle scrapes from her vocal cords to the unbelieving ears of most of the gathering. Her eyes ejaculate. She collapses over the trestle table in front of her.

'Look to the Queen there, ho!' Osric issues this command with surprising conviction.

Several lackeys rush to conform.

Hamlet pays scant attention to his mother's lurchings. He assumes she has merely been drinking his toast to indecorous excess.

Horatio, meanwhile, buttonholes Osric:

'They bleed on both sides.' The good friend expresses belligerent concern, unable to conceal his revulsion for Osric. 'How is it, my lord?'

'How is it, Laertes?' Osric adroitly passes the buck to Laertes, who, weakly swaying, and spewing out his life's precious fluids, is in no state to refuse it.

Laertes, in fact, is overcome by a mawkish confessional spasm:

'Why,' he gurgles, 'as a rat in my own rat-trap, Osric, I am justly killed, by my own treachery.' He discharges a string of blood and mucus, which hangs from his lips like a surge of vomit caught on a flypaper.

Hamlet turns away in disgust.

'How is the Queen?' he inquires.

'She swoons to see them bleed,' Claudius lies hastily.

But Gertrude is in no mood to co-operate. She screams a nightmare scream of frenzied slaughterhouse fear. Kicks her legs akimbo like a strumpet begging for grotesque satisfactions. Rolls helplessly off the trestle table. To the floor. Landing at Hamlet's feet with a rib-cracking thud.

'No, no!' she moans in a dying wheeze. 'The drink! The drink . . . oh, my dear Hamlet! The drink! I . . . am . . . *poisoned*!' She shudders, feebly flutters, and dies.

Hamlet kneels beside her incredulously. How could so many rats break cover simultaneously? His brows ripple like thunder-clouds. With a tardy filial forefinger he dabs the purple mess in the corner of Gertrude's mouth.

Then the Prince quivers to his feet. Blazing, his eyes scorch the souls of the frightened onlookers.

'Oh, VILLAINY!' he roars.

Even the cobwebs shiver.

'Ho! Let the door be locked. TREACHERY! Seek it out!' Hamlet stalks vengefully round the gathering, sword in hand, staring and sniffing for tremulous guilt and stench of sweating complicity.

But it is Laertes, weakly wallowing in his futile repentance, who spills the King's filthy beans. From his half-kneeling terminal agony, he keels over on the floor with a wet-leather splat.

'It is *here*, Hamlet!' he croaks, securing all attention.

Hamlet stands over his dying assailant. Stares down sternly into his closing puffed eyes.

'Hamlet,' Laertes splutters through the stringy fluid on his lips, 'you are . . . *slain*. No medicine in the world can save you. There is not half an hour of life left in you. The treacherous instrument is in your hand, unbuttoned and poisoned. The foul plot has turned itself on me.' He sobs pitifully:

'Lo! Here I lie, never to rise again. Your mother's . . . *poisoned*.' Suddenly he contorts into rigidity, supported only by spasmic head and heels. 'I can do no more,' he wails. 'The King! The King's to blame!'

Like outraged lighthouses all eyeballs swivel and finger Claudius as he sidles behind two muscled men-at-arms, his complexion like an untended lawn after winter.

'The point poisoned too!' exclaims Hamlet, examining the blade in his hand. 'Then, venom, do your work!' He leaps on to the trestle table, bounces forward like a human cannonball, scatters the bunched muscles of the startled men-at-arms, and plunges the murder weapon through Claudius' throat. Drives the blade in to the hilt and leaves it wagging in his uncle's gorge.

Tainted blue blood spurts round Claudius' Adam's apple like wine from a fractured cask.

'Treason! Treason!' A horrified mumble round the court. Yet no one dares hinder the tempestuous Prince.

'Oh!' squelches Claudius, from the pulsing puncture in his throat. 'Yet defend me, friendsh!' he slobbers hysterically. 'I am but hurt!'

Nobody believes him.

'Here, you incestuous, murderous, *damnèd* Dane!' Hamlet snatches up the fateful goblet and tips it against the dying King's lips. 'Drink of this potion . . . is your pearl here?' Hamlet pours. The poisoned red wine mingles down Claudius' jowls with the cough of his life's blood ebbing.

The King slumps to his knees. Collapses squintly on his padded fat hams. Heaving and barking in treacly gut asthmatics.

Hamlet's left boot squashes Claudius' nose. He seizes the sword in his uncle's throat, pushes with his foot, pulls with his hand, then the bloody blade re-emerges from the King's gullet with the sucking sound of a sewer unblocking.

'Follow my mother!' Hamlet snarls.

Claudius' head jerks back. He falls supine. A final belch of blood erupts from his death wound, and he dies, unloved and undefended.

After the tremendous effort of this double vengeance killing, Hamlet sags. His face pales. His eyelids droop. Laertes' poison is at work. The Prince's brow is fevered, his mouth dry. His tongue is like a pumice stone. Weakly he smiles. Soon comes the final trial of his beliefs.

To die well?

Unlike the mendacious indignity of Laertes' final moments, in which he assigns Claudius sole blame for the whole poisonous plot:

'Serves him right!' screams the fat boy's last energy. 'It is a poison concocted by himself.' Muscles all over Laertes' body contract as if his leather attire were a pouch of ravenous rats, all fighting to escape.

'Exchange forgiveness with me, noble Hamlet,' he begs fearfully. 'May you be forgiven my father's death and my own, and I . . . yours.' His last words tail into a soggy rattle. He dies before Hamlet can reply.

'Heaven make you free of it,' murmurs the Prince, sardonic to the last. 'I follow you.' Next, with his dwindling powers he stages a performance for the numbstruck onlookers. 'I am dead, Horatio,' he announces, sad but calm. 'Wretched Queen, adieu!' he salutes his departed mother.

Then to the terrified gathering he declaims:

'You that look pale and tremble at these events, who are but silent audience to this act, had I but time . . . were this cruel policeman, death, less strict in his arrest . . . Oh! . . . I could tell you . . . But let it be.'

The Prince's body is now a ladder for death to scale. His dying breaths he saves for:

'Horatio!' he grips his friend's gentle shoulder. 'I am dead. You live. Report my actions fairly to the inquisitive world.' He stumbles. Bumps against Horatio. Peers mistily up into the soft brown depths of the shorter man's eyes.

Shameless tears line Horatio's cheeks.

'Never believe it!' he sobs. Snatches up the havoc goblet. 'I am more a Roman than a Dane!' he shouts bravely. 'There's still some liquor left.' He makes as if to drink the last of the poison, to accompany Hamlet into the whateverafter.

Then hesitates.

Hamlet claws the goblet from Horatio's weakly resisting fingers:

'Give me the cup. Let go. By heaven, I'll . . . *have* it!' The Prince upturns the goblet, and the last dribble of doctored wine falls innocently to the floor in tiny bloodlike tears – mere drops, compared with the ocean of gore in which Claudius and Laertes like punctured islands lie.

Hamlet drops the goblet. Steps forward to hug Horatio in the last warm embrace of true friendship. But he overestimates his strength. Trips, and falls heavily to the floor. Moans quietly, more in sadness at the loss of his powers than at the imminence of his demise. Thousands of tiny heartless hands, he feels, are stripping the muscles off his bones.

'Oh God, Horatio!' he groans.

Horatio kneels. Pillows the Prince's fading head on his comforting knee.

A ruby-red bubble of oxydized blood forms across Hamlet's left nostril, and bursts into droplets as he exhales with great effort.

'What a wounded name shall live behind me,' he reflects softly, 'things standing thus unknown.' In his dying moments, Hamlet appreciates that his kingdom may suffer if it is thought he died in dishonour. So, for his people, Hamlet asks Horatio to recount and justify his actions, by denouncing what he takes to be the root of Denmark's strife – wicked Uncle Claudius:

'If ever you held me in your heart,' the fleeting King breathes faintly, 'forget your humble station for a while, and in this harsh world draw your breath in pain, to tell my story.'

Horatio wipes tears from his trickling nose.

His sniffing is counterpointed by faint military marching in the distance.

Drums rattle and roll briskly.

A bugle blares jauntily.

Disciplined boots thud.

Somewhere behind them, a cannon salute:

Boom, boom . . .

'What warlike noise . . . is this?' Even in the arms of death, Hamlet's whispering curiosity is insatiable.

'Young Fortinbras,' answers Osric glibly. 'With conquest come from Poland. To the ambassadors of England he pays this warlike tribute.'

31
EPITAPH

Hamlet is too weak to fully comprehend Osric's reply. Otherwise? He would inquire where Osric came by his surprising information.

But . . .

The new dying King forces his sinking eyes open for the last time.

'Oh!' his throat whispers, for his mouth is already immobile. 'I *die*, Horatio. The poison overpowers my spirit. I cannot live . . . to hear the news from England. But pass my crown to Fortinbras. He has my dying voice.'

Horatio nods dumbly.

'Tell him . . .' Hamlet's throaty whisper breaks in pain. 'The rest is silence,' he concludes.

His eyes flicker. His rattle fades. He is . . . dead.

Horatio takes from a waiting page the red velvet cushion on which the duelling foils reposed. He places it under Hamlet's head. Gently smooths shut the lifeless lids of Hamlet's staring eyes.

'Now cracks a noble heart,' Horatio sobs. 'Good-night, sweet Prince. And flights of *angels* sing you to your rest.' He crosses himself.

With his return to the womb of the Church, Horatio takes on a new authority.

'Why comes the drum hither?' he inquires aggressively, clambering to his feet.

Before the shuffling stricken lords can reply, Horatio's answer appears in person!

The rattling drums and jaunty bugle burst upon the scene, together with Fortinbras, and a platoon of tight-marching shocktroops.

248

Bringing up the rear, wearing resplendent costumes and puzzled frowns, are the two ambassadors from England.

'Where is this sight?' Fortinbras asks curtly.

His soldiers stamp to attention.

Horatio glares at the unfeeling intruder with eyes that are dry, having been wiped, yet hot, having wept.

'What do you wish to see?' he shouts defiantly. 'If sights of woe are to your taste, then cease your search.'

Fortinbras nods shortly. Takes his medium-height, heavily-built, short-haired, clean-shaven person on a tour of the hall. Notes with satisfaction the ashen faces of the speechless onlookers. Scrutinizes each dead body in turn. Laertes he rolls over with the toe of his seasoned boot, better to inspect the corpse's features.

As he proceeds, Fortinbras smacks the gauntleted palm of his left hand with the gauntleted first two fingers of his right. A comfort habit, or a casual count of deaths?

He turns back to Horatio.

'What havoc!' he remarks unconcernedly. 'So many princes at one stroke?' He glances quizzically at Osric.

Who is studiously investigating his fingernails.

Here the English ambassadors step forward, their robes rustling like indignant dried grass. The senior ambassador coughs insistently.

'This sight is dismal!' he pipes in reedy tones. 'And our news from England comes too late.' He looks with distaste at the bloody pulp which was Claudius. 'We come to tell him that his commandment is fulfilled. That Rosencrantz and Guildenstern are dead. Where should we have our thanks?' He and his junior cast anxious eyes around the blood-soaked hall, like neurotic spaniels.

Horatio interprets:

'Not from his mouth,' he points at Claudius. '*He* gave no commandment for their death.'

The ambassadors gape in horror at the diplomatic implications.

Horatio ignores them. Addresses Fortinbras, whom his submissive temperament recognizes as the remaining dominant male:

'But since, hard on this tragedy, you from the Polish wars, and you from England, are here arrived, let's show these bodies to the people. And let me tell the world how these things came about. So shall you hear of carnal, bloody and unnatural acts.' Now the limelight is all his, Horatio waxes purple:

'Of fateful judgements and casual slaughters. Of deaths brought about by cunning and intrigue. And, concerning this final scene,' he indicates the corpses on the floor, 'of how most evil purposes fell back upon themselves. All this can I relate.'

Fortinbras accepts Horatio's submissions. Smiles the warm smile of a powerful man who knows how to win allegiance. Wraps a strong arm round Horatio's grieving shoulders. Gives him an encouraging squeeze.

'Let us haste to hear it,' he agrees. 'And call the noblest to the audience.' He rubs his nose thoughtfully. 'For me, with sorrow I embrace my fortune.' He sighs. 'I have some ancient rights in this kingdom, which my fortune now claims!' He shakes his head sadly.

Horatio takes the bait eagerly:

'Of that also must I speak! As Hamlet's dying voice was all for you. But first, let the bodies and the facts be shown. Lest, while men's minds are still wild, more tragedy should flow.'

Fortinbras grins broadly at Horatio's old-womanish good sense. He claps his gauntlets.

'Let four captains bear Hamlet, like a soldier, to the market-place,' he commands. 'For he was likely to have proved an excellent king. And let the soldiers' music and the rites of war speak loud.'

Four muscled captains peel from Fortinbras' bodyguard and gingerly place Hamlet's body on the trestle. Taking a corner each, the captains hoist the table shoulder high.

Fortinbras clicks his fingers.

The drums roll slow.

The bugle blows a harrowing funeral march.

'Take up the bodies.' Fortinbras waves at the other three cadavers. 'Such a sight becomes the battlefield, not the court. Go, bid the soldiers shoot.'

Three more captains jump to obey.

One lifts Gertrude's body respectfully, as if she were his newly-dead bride.

The other two shoulder Claudius and Laertes like sacks of meat.

Out on the battlements:

A new salute fires. The guns boom solemnly, at fifteen-second intervals.

Fortinbras points to the door. Blank eyes unblinking.

The soldiers bearing Hamlet lead the exit in a foot-dragging march.

Horatio walks deferentially behind Fortinbras.

The others follow in order of rank.

Thence through the deadening chill of Danish dusk to the market place.

To offer the dead bodies for inspection.

Horatio, getting his first real taste of public life, will relay his knowledge of the fortuitous and conspiratorial intricacies underlying these tragic results.

Thus, by telling most of the truth, and nothing but most of the truth, Fortinbras, with Horatio his unwitting mouthpiece, will restore Denmark's ruffled fortunes to a smoother keel.

And what a magnificent PR job Horatio does. Explaining to the summoned sleepy market-place congregation:

How Claudius was the moving villain; who murdered Old Hamlet as he lay in defenceless slumber; who connived to have Hamlet executed in England; who later conspired with Laertes to murder the Prince with treachery and poison; and so on.

What Horatio doesn't explain, of course, is what he doesn't know, which is what Fortinbras doesn't tell him.

For example:

Horatio has no idea that the murder of Old Hamlet was suggested by Fortinbras. Or that Fortinbras had total tabs on Claudius and his schemings all along, through having nobbled not only chubby Osric but also the pallid ambassadors, Voltimand and Cornelius.

How did Fortinbras inspire such fealty?

Work for me and prosper, he advised them, if you don't fancy feeding worms.

Consequently:

Neither Horatio nor the Danish public has any inkling that even loathsome Claudius himself was duped, and that his right hand did indeed know what his left was doing.

251

Naturally, then:

Horatio can't inform the populace that the Apparition on the clifftop *was* a phoney. Staged by the Player King and his mercenary troupe. Instigated by Osric, who had orders from Fortinbras to leak hints to Hamlet that his father had been burked by Wicked Uncle Claudius.

Nor can Horatio inform the citizens that:

Fortinbras, when he landed with his army, had no intention of going near Poland. Instead? After marching ostentatiously south for several miles, Fortinbras about-turned his troops in the night, and bivouacked in the deer forests of Silkeborg, where, so long ago, Ophelia surrendered her innocence to Laertes.

Or that:

The ominous nocturnal sightings of strangely warsome vessels at sea, which latterly so soured King Claudius' digestive joys, were but another diversion launched by Fortinbras.

Keep the old sot's aggression projected outward on phantoms of the waves, he reasoned, and we will be safe camped in Silkeborg.

The ghostly ships in the night, unbeknown to Horatio and almost everyone else, were also looking out for the furtive beacon fire which would alert Fortinbras' main invading force (meanwhile drifting in readiness some further miles out to sea) to land and attack if necessary.

Finally:

How could Fortinbras arrive so perfectly on cue? At the scene of the tragic fencing bout?

Horatio must surely be forgiven for not realizing that:

Osric had ridden through the night, much against his comfort-loving inclinations, to inform Fortinbras in the Silkeborg bivouac of the impending treachery and carnage in the Castle.

Fortinbras turns up with typically immaculate timing, and so evinces a degree of grim humour when he claims:

'For me, with sorrow I embrace my fortune.'

Yes, the metavillain, the superstrategist, is Fortinbras. By comparison, in retrospect, Claudius was a mere bumbling drunkard.

But what does it really matter?

Now the drama is over?

Old Norway soon dies of a heart attack.

Fortinbras is King of Norway and Denmark for forty years. And he rules with much greater political acuity and justice than could ever have been expected of the chimerical Hamlet.

Stability returns.

The economy recovers.

The arts flourish.

Scientific research, particularly into astronomy, receives lavish patronage.

Even the weather improves.

Agricultural productivity increases, and the epidemic of dire-omen discovering is cured.

Original Fiction in Paladin

Paper Thin   £2.95 ☐
Philip First
From the author of THE GREAT PERVADER: a wonderfully original
collection of stories about madness, love, passion, violence, sex and
humour.

Don Quixote   £2.95 ☐
Kathy Acker
From the author of BLOOD AND GUTS IN HIGH SCHOOL: a
visionary collage–novel in which Don Quixote is a woman on an
intractable quest; a late twentieth-century LEVIATHAN; a stingingly
powerful and definitely unique novel.

To order direct from the publisher just tick the titles you want
and fill in the order form.   **PF2**

All these books are available at your local bookshop or newsagent, or can be ordered direct from the publisher.

To order direct from the publishers just tick the titles you want and fill in the form below.

Name _____

Address _____

_____

Send to:
Paladin Cash Sales
PO Box 11, Falmouth, Cornwall TR10 9EN.

Please enclose remittance to the value of the cover price plus:

UK 60p for the first book, 25p for the second book plus 15p per copy for each additional book ordered to a maximum charge of £1.90.

BFPO 60p for the first book, 25p for the second book plus 15p per copy for the next 7 books, thereafter 9p per book.

Overseas including Eire £1.25 for the first book, 75p for second book and 28p for each additional book.

Paladin Books reserve the right to show new retail prices on covers, which may differ from those previously advertised in the text or elsewhere.